Cookie

JACQUELINE WILSON

Cookie

Illustrated by Nick Sharratt

SQUARE
FISH

Roaring Brook Press
New York

SQUARE
FISH

An Imprint of Macmillan

Square Fish and the Square Fish logo are trademarks of Macmillan and
are used by Roaring Brook Press under license from Macmillan.

Cataloging-in-Publication Data is on file at the Library of Congress
ISBN 978-0-312-64290-7

First published in Great Britain by Doubleday,
an imprint of Random House Children's Books
Originally published in the United States by Roaring Brook Press
Square Fish logo designed by Filomena Tuosto
First Square Fish Edition: October 2010
www.squarefishbooks.com

10 9 8 7 6 5 4 3 2

AR: 4.4 / F&P: X / LEXILE: 680L

To Martha Courtauld –
I love all your ideas

One

I turned on the television. I timed it perfectly. The music was just starting. I saw the cartoon picture of Sam and Lily spinning around, Sam waving, Lily delicately nibbling a carrot. They whirled faster and faster while a voice sang, *"Who do you want to see?"*

Little children piped up: *"Sam and Lily in the Rabbit Hutch!"*

I sang it too, but very quietly, just mouthing the words. There was only Mom at home and she was out in the kitchen. She wouldn't mind a bit if I wanted to watch a baby show like *Rabbit Hutch* but I still felt embarrassed about it. Imagine if some of the really mean, snooty girls at school, Skye Wortley or Emily Barrington or Arabella Clyde-Smith, came barging through our front door and caught me watching a TV show for five-year-olds. They teased me enough anyway. I could hear them screaming with laughter over Beauty and her little bunny-wunny friend in the Rabbit Hutch.

I shut my eyes tight.

"Hey there!" said a soft gentle voice from the television.

I opened my eyes. There was Sam smiling at me, the real man, not the funny cartoon picture of him. I smiled back at him. I couldn't help it. He had such a lovely funny grin. His brown eyes shone and he ducked his head a little so his soft shiny brown hair flopped across his forehead.

"How are you doing?" Sam asked.

"I'm fine," I whispered.

He nodded and then looked down at Lily. He was holding her close against his chest. He needed both hands because there was a lot of Lily. Her lop ears brushed the collar of Sam's checked shirt, while her back paws dangled past the belt of his jeans. Sam held her firmly so she felt safe. She relaxed against him, slowly blinking her blue eyes. She knew he would never ever drop her.

"I wonder what you've been doing today?" said Sam, looking at me.

"School," I muttered.

"Which one?" Sam asked.

"Lady Mary Mountbank. I started there last year," I said, sighing.

"Is it that bad?" said Sam sympathetically.

I considered. It wasn't *all* bad. Rhona Marshall had asked me to her birthday party. She'd given my arm a special squeeze as she gave me the pink invitation card and said, "I do hope you can come."

2

I liked Rhona a lot, even though she was best friends with Skye. Rhona never ever joined in the horrible Beauty routine. She just looked embarrassed and raised her eyebrows at me and once she whispered, "Take no notice." This was sweet of her, but how could I *help* noticing when they were chanting stuff right in my face.

Miss Woodhead had been kind to me too. She especially liked my Roman project. I know this sounds as if I'm showing off, but she said I was a joy to teach. She said it quietly just to me and I went bright pink I was so pleased. But one of the others heard her and by break time half the class were muttering it and then making vomit noises. Skye made such loud vomit noises she nearly made herself really sick all down her school skirt. That would have been great.

I didn't have time to babble all this to Sam so I just shrugged my shoulders. He'd understand.

"Lily likes *her* school," he said. "But her lessons are easy-peasy. One lettuce plus one carrot plus one cabbage equals one big bunny snack! Just so she doesn't get *too* fat I've made her a new rabbit run in the garden. Do you want to go and do your exercises, Lily?"

She nodded.

"Shall we go and watch her?" Sam asked.

I nodded.

3

Sam carried Lily outside into the garden and gently lowered her into her new run. He'd put carrots and cabbages and lettuces at the very end of the run. Lily spotted them straight away and took off like a greyhound, her ears flapping.

"Would you run like that if your mom put your dinner at the end of the garden?" Sam joked.

Mom and I often did eat in the garden, special picnics. Sometimes we even put our coats and scarves on and wrapped blankets around us and had *winter* picnics.

"You bet, Sam," I said.

Mom always made us magic picnics. She didn't *cook* anything, she didn't ever really cook, but she made each picnic special. She sometimes chose a color theme, so we'd have bananas and pineapple and cheese pasties and custard tarts and lemonade, or tomato quiche and apples and plums and KitKats and raspberry juice. Sometimes she'd choose a letter of the alphabet and we'd have sausages and sandwiches and strawberries and shop-bought sponge cake carefully cut by Mom into an S shape.

When I was little she'd lay places at the picnics for my dolls and teddy bears, or she'd let me dress up in my Disney princess dress and she'd serve everything on the best china and curtsy every time she spoke to me.

4

I loved loved loved my mom. Sam understood. He said the word *mom* softly, knowing it was a special word.

"I wonder if you miss your mom, Lily?" said Sam, squatting down beside her.

Lily nibbled a lettuce leaf, not really listening.

"Remember when you were really little, Lily, just a weeny newborn-baby rabbit?" said Sam.

He looked at me. "Do you know, she was only *this* big," Sam said, cupping his hands and holding them only a little way apart.

I cupped my hands too, imagining a little fluffy baby Lily quivering under my embrace.

"Do you remember when *you* were just a weeny newborn-baby person?" said Sam. "I bet you weren't much bigger. Do you have a photo of you when you were a little baby?"

I nodded. Mom still had that photo inside her wallet, though it had got creased and crumpled. Dad had the same picture in a silver photo frame on his big desk at work. It was so embarrassing. I was big and bald and I didn't even have a diaper on. My belly button was all taped up and you could see my bottom.

"I bet you looked cute then," said Sam, chuckling.

I didn't smile back at him. I nibbled my lip miserably. I didn't look remotely cute when I was a baby, but at least I was cuddly. Mom said she held me all day and half the night too, she was so happy to hold me. She said she cried because she was so thrilled she'd got a little girl.

Dad cried too.

Most dads don't cry, especially very very very tough dads like mine. My dad actually cries a lot. He cries at films on the television, even children's cartoon films like *The Lion King* and *Beauty and the Beast*. He cries at the news on television, when a little child is rescued in an earthquake or when a man with artificial legs runs in a race. He cries heaps whenever his favorite wins on *The X-Factor* or *Star Search*. He said I was his little star with that special X-factor the day I was born. He scooped the newborn-baby me out of Mom's arms and cradled me close.

"Just what I wanted! A little girl at last," he crooned. "And such a beautiful little girl too, with those chubby cheeks and big blue eyes. Just wait till your hair grows, my darling. I bet you'll be a little blonde like your mom. You're going to turn into a perfect beauty."

Then he let out such a yelp I started crying.

"I'll take her, Gerry," Mom said anxiously.

"Beauty! Don't you get it? That's her name, our little sweetheart's name! We'll call her Beauty," said Dad. "Isn't that a great name for her, Dilly?"

Mom promised me she thought it was an *awful* name, but you didn't dare argue with Dad, even in those days.

I was christened Beauty. It's a ridiculous name. It would be a silly show-off shallow name even if I just magically happened to be beautiful. But I am so *not* beautiful. I don't take after Mom, I take after Dad. I am small and squat, with a big tummy. My blue eyes turned green as gooseberries when I was still a baby, and you can't really see them anyway because I have to wear glasses. My hair's mousy brown, long and lank. Mom tries to tie it up with clips and ribbons but they always fall out. You can see why Emily and Arabella and Skye tease me so. I am a laughingstock because of my name.

I wasn't laughing. I had silly baby tears in my eyes now, safe with Sam and Lily.

"Hey, don't cry," said Sam.

I sniffed, ashamed. "Not crying," I mumbled.

It seemed to be raining inside my glasses. I poked my finger up and tried to make it work like a windshield wiper.

"Why don't you clean them on the corner of your T-shirt? Your glasses will get all smeary wiping them like that," Sam said softly. "So what are you *not* crying about?"

"My silly name," I sniffed. "Beauty!"

"I think Beauty's the most special name in all the world."

"No it's not. And it doesn't suit me," I said tearfully. "Skye Wortley at school says I should be renamed Plug Ugly."

"Silly old Skye," said Sam. "I expect she's so mean because she's jealous of you."

"Oh, Sam, that's the first time I've ever heard you say something stupid," I said. "As if someone like Skye would ever be jealous of *me*. Skye's got lovely long, wavy, fair hair and big blue eyes—*sky* blue—and she's clever and she's great at dancing and she's got Rhona as a best friend and—and—"

"Well, you've got sand-colored hair and great green eyes and you're even cleverer than Skye and who cares about dancing and you've got Lily and me for your best friends," said Sam.

"Truly? You and Lily are really my best friends?

"Absolutely definitely, aren't we, Lily?" said Sam, bending down and scratching her head. She stopped nibbling the cabbage, looked up, and nodded her head so vigorously her ears flapped forward.

"Well, you're my best friends for ever ever ever," I whispered rapturously.

We smiled at each other, the three of us.

"See you tomorrow, Beauty," Sam whispered.

Then he raised his voice.

"Nearly time to go now. Time we were getting back to the hutch, Lily. You've had enough dinner now. Maybe it's time for *your* dinner? I wonder what you're having? Lily's favorite dinner is raw cabbage, as you can see, but somehow I don't think raw cabbage is *your* favorite best-ever food. Still, maybe your pet likes it. Why don't you send me a painting or drawing of *your* pet's favorite food? Send it to Sam at the Rabbit Hutch, OK? Bye then." He waved, then picked up Lily and helped her waggle her paw.

"Lily's waving good-bye too," said Sam.

"Bye, Sam! Bye, Lily!" I said.

Rabbit Hutch faded, and the cartoon Sam and Lily whirled around and around and the voice said, "Who have we just seen?"

"*Sam and Lily in the Rabbit Hutch*," I sang.

"*Sam and Lily in the Rabbit Hutch*," Mom sang too, coming in from the kitchen. "Do you want a little snack, sweetheart? I've bought a couple of those little pink iced buns, the ones with jam inside."

"But Dad said I wasn't to eat them anymore," I said.

I'd had a pink iced bun when we were all walking around the Flowerfields shopping center. I'd bitten into it and jam spurted all down the front of my best blue frilly top. Dad had knocked my hand hard so that the bun flew out onto the floor.

"Don't you ever buy her that pink jammy muck again," he'd hissed at Mom. "Look, she's ruined her best little blouse. She shouldn't be stuffing her face anyway, she's getting ginormous."

Mom had meekly promised not to buy me any more buns and had pulled me into the ladies' room to sponge all the jam off. I'd cried a little bit and she'd given me a hug but begged me to cheer up because I'd make Dad worse if he saw me with a long face. I'd done my best, though I'd felt particularly mournful as the pink buns were my favorites.

"Dad won't know if you gobble it up now," said Mom. "Hang on half a tick."

She disappeared into the kitchen and came back with two pink buns on her best little green-leaf cake plates.

"Here, I'll keep you company," said Mom.

We both sat cross-legged on the furry white hearth rug, eating our buns.

"Yum, yum," I said.

"Yep, yummy yummy," said Mom.

"I'd better not spill jam all down me again," I said.

"Me too!" said Mom, licking the icing on her bun as if it was a lollipop.

We munched companionably.

"M-o-m?"

"Yes?"

"Mom, why do you think Dad gets so . . ." I couldn't think of the right word.

"Angry?" Mom suggested.

Dad didn't just get angry. It was way way way more scary. He was like a volcano. You never quite knew when he'd erupt and explode and engulf you in molten lava.

Mom wriggled forward on her bottom until her knees nearly touched mine.

"I don't know why he's like that," she said. "I used to think it was just me. I know I can be a bit silly sometimes—Silly Dilly, OK? But you're not silly, Beauty, you're the smartest little kid ever. He's got no reason whatsoever to yell at you the way he does. I wish I could figure out a way to stop him. I've tried talking to him about it but that just makes him rant even more."

Mom looked so miserable I felt awful. I crammed the last bit of bun into my mouth and then put my arms around her.

"Don't worry about it, Mom. Dad's not angry *all* the time," I said. "Sometimes he can be the loveliest dad in the whole world."

Sometimes.

Very, very rarely.

Starter Happy Homes

Standard Happy Home

Deluxe Happy Home

Two

We always knew if Dad was going to be in a good mood because we could hear him whistling as he parked the car in the driveway and walked to the front door.

He was whistling now, his silly "Happy Homes" song. Mom breathed out slowly and smiled at me. I smiled back, licking my lips to make sure I hadn't left the tiniest trace of jam.

"Hello, hello, hello, my two best girls," Dad called, opening the front door.

"Hello, Gerry," Mom called quickly.

"Hello, Dad," I echoed.

We heard Dad taking his shoes off and putting them in the special rack by the doorstep. It was one of his many rules. All outdoor shoes must be left at the front door because we mustn't risk scratching the polished parquet floor. Then he cleared his throat and started singing as he slid up the hall in his socks.

"Happy Homes, Happy Homes
Where everyone smiles
And nobody moans—"

13

He skidded into the living room, grinning at us, his arms outstretched.

"There's a mommy"—pointing at Mom.
"And a daddy"—pointing at himself.
"And a gorgeous little girl"—pointing at me.
"So if we're Happy in our Home
Then give us a twirl!"

He twirled around foolishly, his toe pivoting on the thick pile of the living room carpet.
He paused.
"GIVE US A TWIRL!" he shouted, wafting his hands in the air.
Mom and I stood up immediately. Even if Dad was in a very good mood like today, the slightest thing could still upset him and make him turn.
Mom twirled around, holding up her skirt prettily, pointing her toes. I twirled too. I whizzed around too fast as I was in such a hurry to get it over. I managed to trip over my own slippered feet and nearly fell headlong.
"Whoopsie!" said Dad, catching me. "Dear goodness, Beauty! You're so clumsy! I think we'd better send you back to those dancing lessons."
My iced bun turned a somersault inside my tummy. Dad had sent me to ballet lessons when

I was six. I was the oldest in the baby class. There were some tiny girls who were only three or four. They were all much better at dancing than I was. I couldn't do bunny hops—I simply landed with a bump on my bottom. I couldn't skip—my arms and legs got all wobbly. I couldn't point my toes properly—they wanted to point in, not out. And I couldn't twirl gracefully to save my life.

I stuck it out for a year, until Miss June the dancing teacher tactfully told Mom that I didn't seem to be *enjoying* my dancing classes so perhaps it might be better if I tried another hobby.

"Please don't make me do ballet again, Dad!" I said.

"Don't you want to learn to dance like a little fairy?" said Dad.

"Fairy elephant, more like," I said.

Dad chuckled and ruffled my hair. He sat down in his big leather armchair and then pulled me onto his knee. He pulled Mom onto his other knee, as if we were both his little girls.

"Hey, Gerry darling, did you get the planning permission for the Water Meadows project?" Mom asked.

"I'm still working on it, but it looks very likely," said Dad. "That's what we need, two hundred spanking new, top-of-the-range Happy Homes with river views. They'll make our fortune, Dilly. You wait and see."

"You've already made our fortune," said Mom.

"I've worked hard for my girls, my wife, my daughter." Dad paused. "And my *ex*-wives and my lazy sons."

Mom gave me a little frown. That meant, *Don't say a word!*

I was fascinated by the first Mrs. Cookson and the second Mrs. Cookson and my three half brothers, Gerry Junior, Mark, and Ryan. When we'd all met at Gerry Junior's wedding and Grandma's funeral I'd loved feeling part of a great big family. But Dad didn't seem to like any of them anymore. He especially didn't like giving them any money, even though there seemed like plenty to go around. The first two Mrs. Cooksons had their own Happy Homes and now Gerry Junior and his new wife Julie had their own Happy Home too.

"So that makes them blooming lucky," Dad said. "*I* didn't have that kind of start in life. I had to make my own way."

Dad had started off working on a building site at sixteen. He worked his way up, until he ended up buying the building firm. Then he branched out, becoming a property developer, building lots and lots of Happy Homes. There were starter Happy Homes for young couples, standard three-bedroom Happy Homes for ordinary families, and deluxe five-bedroom, two-bathroom Happy Homes for rich families.

We used to live in a deluxe Happy Home, but now we'd moved to an even bigger, fancier home especially built for us. We had *six* bedrooms, three bathrooms, a sauna, *and* a hot tub outside. I even had my own en suite bathroom, dusty rose to match my pink bedroom, with silver dolphin taps.

Dad said I was the luckiest little girl in the world. He didn't know of another child anywhere who had her own en suite bathroom. He kept asking me why I didn't want to invite any of my friends from Lady Mary Mountbank for a sleepover. They could sleep in one of the twin beds with the dusty rose silk coverlets patterned with sprigs of violets, sprawl on the pink and violet velvet cushions, comb their hair at my Venetian-glass dressing table, and admire every inch of my en suite bathroom.

I hadn't invited anyone so far. It made *me* turn dusty rose in the face to admit it, but I didn't really *have* any proper friends. I did wonder if I dared ask Rhona to tea, but that would annoy Skye and make her meaner to me than ever. Maybe Rhona wouldn't come anyway.

I wasn't even sure I wanted her to come myself. I'd probably feel dreadfully shy and not know what to say to her. What would we play for all those hours before bedtime? I liked reading when I was by myself but you couldn't really read together. I liked painting but I had to do it in the kitchen with newspaper spread everywhere, long before Dad came home. I wasn't supposed to do any painting whatsoever in case I spilled paint on the carpets.

Dad didn't even allow markers in case I got ink on the cream sofas. I was always very careful but Rhona was a giggly girl who never sat still. What if she flung her arm out when she was painting and accidentally splattered the wallpaper? If Dad saw he'd get into a rage whether Rhona was here or not.

I felt sick at the thought of Dad ranting in front of Rhona. I often cried because he scared me so. Perhaps he'd make Rhona cry too. Then she'd tell everyone at school. She'd definitely tell Skye because she was her best friend.

I kept pretending to Dad that I'd simply forgotten to ask anyone for a sleepover. He seemed to have forgotten himself for the last few weeks . . . forgotten until this very moment!

"You still haven't had any of your friends over, Beauty," said Dad, bouncing me on his knee as if I was a little baby.

My heart started thudding. I nibbled my lip anxiously.

"Don't *do* that," said Dad, lightly tapping my mouth. He frowned at my teeth. "They're sticking out *more*, Beauty. We're definitely going to have to get you braces."

"I don't want braces," I mumbled.

"You don't want to end up looking like Bugs Bunny, do you?" said Dad, making a silly rabbit face with his own teeth protruding.

"The dentist said to wait a year or so, darling," Mom said. "He's not even sure Beauty really needs braces."

"Nonsense! She needs perfect choppers. All girls do," said Dad. "*Anyway*, who's your best friend at school, Beauty?"

"I like Rhona, but she's Skye's friend, not really mine," I said.

"Can't you *all* be friends?" said Dad. "Invite them both over. What about this Saturday?"

I breathed out thankfully.

"I can't this Saturday, Dad. That's when Rhona's having her birthday party," I said.

"And you're going to this party?"

"Well, she's given me an invitation."

"Lovely. Well, we'd better get cracking organizing a party for *your* birthday!"

I started nibbling my lip again.

"*Stop* it!" said Dad. "Yes, we'll throw a really big bumper party for your birthday for every girl in your class, all your new Lady Mary Mountbank friends."

"Do I really have to have a party, Dad?" I said desperately.

"I'm not sure about a lot of overexcited children running around the house," Mom said quickly. She knew how Dad fussed so about the carpet and the cream sofas.

"We won't have them running riot *here*," said Dad. "We'll take them out somewhere fancy. Leave it to me, I'll work on it. I want my Beauty to have a really fantastic birthday."

"It's ever so kind of you, Dad," I babbled, though my heart was sinking.

I just had to hope he might somehow forget about it. I wasn't sure many of the girls in my class would come, especially not Skye or Emily or

Arabella. Or if they did, they'd all call me names the way they did in class.

"What does my best girl want for her birthday present, eh?" said Dad.

"I don't know," I said.

"Well, think!" said Dad. He tapped my forehead. "What's going on inside that little noodle of yours, eh? I bet you've got some idea of what you'd really, really like for a present."

"Well . . ."

"Ah! I thought so," said Dad. "Come on, what is it?"

Mom leaned forward, looking tense. Dad shifted his knee, tipping her off his lap.

"You go and make a start on dinner, Dilly, I'm starving. Whack a steak on the grill. Even you can manage that."

I tried to get up too but Dad hung on to me.

"No, no, you stay and keep your old dad company, little Beauty. I want to get to the bottom of your birthday wishes. What are you pondering? I can tell you've set your heart on something."

I wriggled, wondering whether I dared ask.

"Come on, sweetie. No need to be shy of your old dad. What is it, eh? Have you got your eye on some outrageously expensive outfit? It's OK, baby, I'm used to your mom. I'll happily fork out for the junior designer doodahs of your choice—with a dinky little handbag and maybe your first pair of shoes with tiny heels, yes?"

"Well, actually, Dad, I wasn't really thinking about clothes."

"Aye aye! Something more expensive, eh? It's OK, darling, the business is doing well. You heard me tell your mom I'm on the brink of the biggest deal yet. Do you fancy your very own little laptop? Or a personal flat-screen TV for your bedroom?"

"No, Dad. It's very kind of you but I truly don't want anything like that."

"Then what *is* it? Come on, spit it out. I'll get you anything you like, my lovely."

"Then please could I have a rabbit?" I whispered.

"What?" Dad cupped his ear.

"A rabbit," I repeated. "I'd really like a white one with floppy ears, but really any kind of rabbit would be . . ."

My voice tailed away when I saw the expression on Dad's face.

"Are you *thick*, Beauty?" he said.

"I—I don't know, Dad," I said, not sure whether he wanted me to say yes or not. It didn't look as if I could win whatever I said.

"You come on like Miss Smarty Pants but I SAY YOU'RE THICK," said Dad, jabbing me in the back at every word.

The last jab shoved me right off his lap onto the carpet. I tried to scuttle out of Dad's way but he caught hold of me by the wrist.

"Don't, Gerry!" Mom said, darting back into the room.

"I'm not hurting her," said Dad. He deliberately loosened his fingers so that they were just like a fleshy pink bangle on my arm. "*Am* I hurting you, Beauty?"

"No, Dad," I said.

"And *are* you thick?" he said.

"Yes, Dad," I said.

"*Yes, Dad, certainly, Dad, as thick as* three *short planks, Dad,*" said Dad, in a horrible high squeaky imitation of my voice.

"Please let her go, Gerry," said Mom. "What has she done to upset you?"

"She's only gone and ignored one of the very basic rules of this household—this particularly luxurious house, custom made by my own best craftsmen for our benefit. I don't think it's asking much to want us to take care of this lovely home. I'm not what anyone would call a finicky man, now am I?"

Mom and I didn't dare contradict him.

"I just like my house to be well looked after. No scratches on the parquet, no chips on the plaster, no dirty hairs or stains on the carpet. What *causes* scratches and chips and hairs and stains, mmm, Beauty? Do you really not know the answer?"

"Pets, Dad," I whispered.

"Yes. A-plus. And what has my view on pets always been?"

"I know I can't have a dog or a cat, but I did think a rabbit might just be OK, because it wouldn't be *in* the house, it would live in a little hutch outside."

"In a little hutch? Where, precisely? In the middle of my lawn? The rosebeds? The patio?"

"No, just by a wall somewhere."

"Yes, that would really add to the classy atmosphere, rabbits in smelly hutches. What else would you like, pigeons in cages, ferrets scrabbling in a run?"

"Not ferrets, Gerry. They'd eat the rabbits," said Mom, trying to turn it into a joke.

"You shut your face, Dilly," said Dad. "No one's asking you."

"Don't talk to me like that, Gerry, please," said Mom. She tried to say it firmly but I could see she was trembling.

"I'll talk how I please in my own house," said Dad. "Now listen to me, Beauty. I don't mind animals on a farm or in a field. I can get very fond of a winning horse at a racetrack. I just won't have animals in the house—or surroundings, OK? When we were peasants in mud huts back in the bad old days, folk shared their homes with a cow and a goat and a guard dog, but we're not peasants now and this isn't a mud hut, this is a luxury home. Get that?"

Dad stuck his face right up close to me so that his head seemed horribly big. I could see the vein throbbing in his forehead, the blood vessels in his eyes, the hairs up his nostrils, the flecks of spit on his lips.

He looked like a storybook ogre about to eat me up. I felt tears pricking my eyes. I knew I mustn't cry in front of him. I always looked so ugly when I cried. My eyes screwed up, my nose ran, and my mouth went square. It always made Dad madder than ever.

I mustn't cry, I mustn't cry, I mustn't cry, I said inside my head, but the tears were already spurting down my cheeks.

"Go to your room right this minute, Beauty," said Mom. "It's naughty of you to nag at your dad for a pet, you know the rules."

25

I knew Mom wasn't cross with me too. She was just trying to save me.

"Yes, get upstairs, now!" Dad thundered.

I was off like a shot. I was in such a hurry I tripped on the stairs and scraped my shins, making me cry harder. I flopped onto my rose-silk bed and hugged my old rag doll PJ. I had a shelf of big fancy china dolls in Victorian costume. They had ringlets and bonnets and parasols and long flounced dresses and tiny heeled boots. They were all collector's dolls and very beautiful but I couldn't play with them properly. They just stood on their shelves and stared straight through me with their spooky glass eyes.

I'd had PJ ever since I was a baby in a cradle. Mom made her for me. Her eyes were crossed and her mouth was crooked and her arms and legs were uneven. I'd given her a drastic haircut when I was little, which didn't help her appearance. PJ stood for Plain Jane but I didn't mind a bit that she wasn't very pretty. Her mouth still smiled and she felt soft and she had her own special sweet smell. When I was little I liked to suck my thumb and nuzzle my nose against her cloth cheek. It made me feel safe.

I tried sucking my thumb now, holding PJ close. I could hear Dad shouting downstairs. Poor Mom. She was getting the worst of it now.

I wanted to run downstairs, turning into Super-Beauty, my arms pumping, legs bounding a mile a minute. I'd floor Dad, seize Mom in my arms, and with one mighty bound we'd soar through the open window, up up up, away from our Happy Home.

Three

I curled up in my bedroom, clutching PJ like a big baby. I smelled steak grilling. I didn't like meat much—it always made me think of the poor dead animal, but my mouth watered even so.

It didn't look as if I was going to get any dinner. I sucked my thumb mournfully and then prowled around my bedroom looking for something—anything—to eat. I opened up my lunchbox. I'd finished my egg sandwiches and carrot sticks and chips and muesli bar and apple and orange juice. I put my head right inside the plastic box, licking the crumbs. I sucked the last drop of juice from the carton and crunched up the brown apple core.

I found half a Polo mint at the bottom of my school bag and gobbled that down in a flash. The only other remotely edible object in the room was the little chocolate chicken Mom had given me at Easter. I liked it so much I said I was never going to eat it; I was going to keep it as an ornament.

That was months ago. I'd not been the slightest bit tempted up till now. I reached out, undid the yellow ribbon, and pulled the little brown chicken out of its cellophane wrapping. I held it in my hand. I made it go *cluck cluck cluck* in an anxious fashion.

"It's OK, little chicken, no need to be scared," I whispered. "I'm not going to eat you. I just want to look at you. Well, maybe I'll have just one little weeny lick . . ."

I stuck out my tongue and ran it along the chicken's glossy back. Soft milky chocolate glided over my taste buds. My mouth watered so that I drooled all over the little chicken. Then my teeth bit. I beheaded it, chomping the chocolate and swallowing it in seconds.

The chicken looked awful now its hollow innards were exposed. I ate the rest of it as quickly as I could, until the only sign the chocolate chicken had existed was the empty cellophane wrapper and the brown smears on my fingers.

I wished I hadn't eaten it now. I'd chomped it down so rapidly I hadn't really tasted it. It had taken the edge off my hunger but now I felt sick.

I wondered what would happen if I *was* sick. I'd once not made it to the bathroom in time and thrown up on the carpet and Dad had been so angry. I needed to distract myself quickly. I got out my school books and did my math quickly, finishing all of it in twenty minutes, even though they were quite difficult problems. I started doodling in my notebook, making up my own problem.

Dad is a good man because
a) he loves us
b) he's given us a beautiful home
c) he works very hard for us

Dad is a bad man because
a) he gets so angry
b) he orders us around
c) he's a great big bully

So is Dad a good man or a bad man???

I had no idea how to find out the answer. I flipped over the page and started trying to draw the chocolate chicken from memory. I colored it in with my crayons, feeling guiltier than ever. I did it very carefully, not going over my lines, even leaving little white spaces in the brown to give the illusion of glossy chocolate sheen.

I printed: *Dear Sam and Lily, This is my pet chicken*, neatly at the top of the page. *I didn't give her some dinner. She was MY dinner!*

A little later Mom came into my room carrying a tray.

"Dinner is served, madam," she said, making a little curtsy, pretending to be a maid. She gave me a jaunty smile but her eyes were red.

"Oh, Mom," I said. "Have you been crying?"

"I'm fine, I'm fine," she said quickly. "Come on, pet, eat your supper."

She'd made me a tuna-and-sweet-corn sandwich with a few French fries and a little tomato salad. She'd cut the crusts off the sandwich and arranged the fries like a flower and cut the tomatoes into zigzag shapes, trying to make it all look special. I wanted to wolf it down appreciatively but I still felt a bit sick. Maybe it was eating all the chocolate chicken.

"I'm not sure I can eat it all, Mom," I said.

"Never mind. I'll have a little snack, shall I?" said Mom. "Oh fries, yummy yummy."

"In my tummy," I said automatically. "Mom . . . is Dad still mad?"

"He's OK now. He's just run out to the office to check on something." She paused. "This new Water Meadows deal means a lot to him, Beauty. Maybe that's why he's so . . . touchy at the moment." Mom's voice sounded odd, like she was reading aloud. She wasn't looking me in the eye.

"That's nonsense, Mom," I said. I nestled up close to her. "I'm sorry you got shouted at when it was my fault, getting him all worked up about the rabbit. He was so angry I thought he was going to whack me one!"

"Your dad would never ever hit you, sweetheart," said Mom. "You're his little Beauty."

She put her arms around me, knocking my glass of orange juice over. "Oh no! I'm so clumsy. We'll have to change the sheets, otherwise it'll look like you've wet the bed!" said Mom, trying to joke again. Her smile was stretched so tight it looked as if her face might split in two.

"I'm so sorry, Mom," I said, starting to cry.

"There now, pet," said Mom, rescuing my crayons and drawing pad from my damp bed. "Oh, what a lovely chicken!"

"I ate it, Mom," I confessed. "The real chocolate chicken. I ate it. It's all gone."

"Even its little chocolate beak and claws?" said Mom. "Well, good for you! You had to wait long enough for your dinner."

She shook her head at the picture.

"You're so good at art, love. Can I keep it? We could frame it and hang it up in the kitchen."

"Well, I did it for Sam. You're supposed to send your pictures in to the show and then they show the best ones on TV. But I think I'm a bit too old to send my picture in. It's supposed to be a show for very little kids. Don't ever tell anyone I watch it, Mom."

"As if I would. It's a lovely show. *I* like it. So maybe it's a show for little kids and little moms. I like that Sam."

"So do I. And Lily." I sighed.

"Oh, Beauty, I *wish* you could have your own rabbit. I'd give anything to change your dad's mind. But there's no way he'll let you have any kind of pet, darling."

I put my head on my knees.

"I hate him," I muttered.

"No you don't. He's your dad and—"

"And he loves me very much—*not*," I said. "If he really loved us he wouldn't get mad and he wouldn't shout at us and he'd let me have a rabbit."

"He doesn't *often* shout," said Mom. "It's just when he's really stressed out. He can't seem to help it. He doesn't always *mean* it. And I'm sure he feels sorry afterward."

"Yeah, like, *I'm sorry, Dilly, my mouth just opens and out come all these awful words and I swear and say dreadful things but I can't help it.* Has he *ever* said something like that, Mom? Has he ever even apologized?"

"Don't." Mom smoothed my straggly hair, tucking it behind my ears.

"Maybe I'll ask Dad to get me boxing gloves for my birthday and then I'll bash him one if he shouts at us," I said.

"Ha ha," said Mom. "How about eating one little triangle of tuna sandwich, eh? Just a little nibble."

I tried a tiny bite. Then another. And then

suddenly I was starving hungry and able to dig into my dinner. Mom had a triangle of tuna sandwich too, and we shared out the chips.

"Mom?"

"Yes, love."

"Sometimes I wish it was just you and me."

"Shh!" Mom looked anxiously over her shoulder even though we knew Dad was at the Happy Homes office on the other side of town.

When we'd finished our dinner and I'd got ready for bed, Mom stayed in my room and we read stories together. Mom's mom, my nana, never read her any stories at all, so it's fun for Mom reading them for the first time with me.

We used to read lots of stories about fairies and then another series about a princess. Mom had just bought me a new princess book.

"Oh dear, it's not the same series. I've made a mistake. Typical me! It looks a bit odd and old-fashioned. It's probably boring. We don't have to read it if you don't want to," said Mom.

"I think it looks good," I said. "Look, I'll start it off, OK?"

We put the tray on the floor and Mom squashed in beside me. I started reading about this little girl, Sara Crewe. I was interested that it said right in the first paragraph that she was odd-looking. Later on she said she was one of the ugliest children she'd ever seen. I especially liked that part.

Mom liked the bit where Sara's father buys her a whole new set of clothes, and then another elaborate set for Sara's new doll, Emily. Mom took her turn reading while I drew lots of velvet dresses and hats with feathers and fur coats and muffs and old-fashioned lace-trimmed underwear—a long row for Sara and a little row underneath for Emily.

We got so absorbed we jumped violently when we heard the car pull up outside.

"Oh, lordy, that's Dad back. Quick, chuck your crayons on the floor and settle down to sleep, pet, OK?"

Mom gave me a quick kiss, kicked my tray under the bed, switched off my light and rushed out of the room. I lay still. We'd forgotten to change my orange-juicy sheet and it felt uncomfortably damp and sticky.

I listened out for shouting. I could hear Dad talking but I couldn't make out what he was saying. Then I heard *pad pad pad* as he came up the stairs in his socks. My heart started thudding. I shut my eyes tight and tried to breathe deeply, as if I was asleep.

I heard my door creak open.

"Beauty?" Dad whispered.

I tried not to twitch. I breathed in and out, in and out, in and out . . .

"Beauty!" said Dad, very near me now. His head was so close I could feel his breath on me.

"I think you're awake," said Dad. "I'm sure I saw your light on when I drove up."

Eyes shut, keep breathing, don't flinch!

"Oh, well. Never mind. You're a very naughty girl, plaguing your old dad about pets, especially when I've got a lot on my mind at the moment. No wonder I get angry! But remember this, sweetheart. Your daddy loves you. You're his special Beauty." His voice thickened as if he was about to cry.

He gave me a kiss on my cheek. He stayed bent over me for a few seconds. I think he was hoping I'd put my arms around his neck. I kept them stiffly by my sides, my fists clenched. He sighed and then went out of my room, pulling the door shut behind him.

I still didn't dare move, just in case he poked his head back in and caught me fidgeting. I stayed in exactly the same position, cramped and uncomfortable, until I heard the television downstairs. Then I dared stretch out. My arms and legs throbbed. I breathed out so deeply my nostrils quivered. My insides still hurt though, as if someone had taken my long wiggly intestines and tied knots up and down them, like a string of sausages. I clasped PJ against my sore tummy and eventually went to sleep.

Four

D ad had usually left for work by the time I got up in the morning. However, when I went downstairs for breakfast he was sitting at the kitchen table drinking coffee and reading his newspaper. My tummy squeezed back into sausages even though Mom smiled at me reassuringly. She was looking extra pretty in her shiny peach satin nightie and bathrobe, her long blond hair falling past her shoulders, her neck and arms as smooth and white as ice cream.

"Hi, doll. Would you like an egg?" she said.

I shook my head, pouring myself a bowl of corn-flakes.

"I've got two flaky corns on my feet. Would you like to snack on them too?" asked Dad, looking up from his paper.

I made myself giggle, though he'd made that joke hundreds of times already. It came out like a little mouse snicker. Mom poured him another cup of coffee and gave him another round of toast. Dad flicked it with his fingers.

"For God's sake, Dilly, this isn't toasted properly. It's meant to be *toast*, right? Shove it back in the toaster." Dad raised his eyebrows at me. "Your mother, Beauty! *Not* what you'd call a cook. Maybe it's just as well you said no to that egg, because she hasn't got a clue how to boil it."

I smiled uncomfortably. "There's not time, anyway, Mom," I said, looking at the clock. "Shall I watch Dad's toast while you go and get dressed?"

"I'm taking you to school today, Beauty," said Dad. "I've got to pop into the Guildhall to see about this planning malarkey, so I'll drop you off on the way."

I sat chewing my cornflakes into mush. It was a small mouthful but it seemed to be swelling right up to the roof of my mouth, squishing in and out of my teeth, coating my tongue with orangey-gold slime. I tried swallowing but my throat wouldn't work. I didn't dare spit the cornflakes out into my bowl. I was doomed to keep them multiplying in my mouth until they spurted straight out of my ears.

"Beauty? What are you making that silly face for? Aren't you pleased I'm giving you a lift in the Benz? Make all your little friends envious, eh?"

I nodded, incapable of speech. My nod was the biggest fib ever. I didn't want Dad to take me to school. I especially didn't want him to take me in his shiny silver Mercedes. Mercedes was my middle name. It caused almost as much hilarity as my first name. Skye suggested I

40

should be called Ugly Station Wagon Cookson. This always made Skye and Emily and Arabella fall about laughing.

"*Say* something, then, don't just nod your head," said Dad.

I swallowed desperately. Some of the cornflake slurp slid down the back of my throat.

"Sorry, Dad," I mumbled, taking a long drink of juice.

The cornflakes were still such a soggy clump that I choked. I clamped my hand over my mouth while Mom patted me on the back. I leaned against her, rubbing my cheek against the soft silkiness of her nightie. I wished I was little enough for her to pick me up and hold me safe in her arms, still way too small for school.

I cleaned my teeth and went to the bathroom and stuck my arms into my brown blazer. Dad sighed when he saw me.

"I don't know! I fork out for the poshest girls' school in the whole county and they want you all to wear that ugly uniform the color of dog's muck."

"Gerry!" said Mom.

"Well, honestly, why can't it be pink or lilac or some pretty girly color? She looks like Little Orphan Annie." Dad tousled my hair in exasperation. "At least Little Orphan Annie had curls. Can't you do something with Beauty's hair, Dilly? What about a perm?"

"She's still a little girl! And I think Beauty's got lovely hair just as it is," said Mom.

"You'd like to be a little curlynob, wouldn't you, Beauty?" said Dad. "Couldn't you put it up in those roller things at night for her, Dilly?"

"People don't use rollers anymore!" said Mom. "Not since bouffant hairdos went out of fashion."

"Oh well, pardon me. I'm just a sad old guy who hasn't got a clue about fashion," said Dad.

There was an edge to his voice. I held my breath, wondering if he was going to start ranting all over again, but he just shook his head at Mom and slapped her lightly on the bottom.

"That's right, you put me in my place, Dilly," said Dad. "Come on, then, Beauty, let's get you to school."

There was no way I could get out of it. I slumped down low on the soft leather backseat as Dad tooted his horn and shouted and swore his way through the traffic.

"Idiot! Call yourself a driver! Come *on*, stop dawdling. I'm late already," Dad fumed, honking at the car in front of us.

"Tell you what, Dad, I could jump out here. It would only take me two minutes to walk up the road. Then you could go straight into town to the Guildhall."

"What? No, don't talk nonsense, darling. I'm delivering you right to the school gates," said Dad.

There was no point wasting breath trying to persuade him. He pulled up absolutely spit-spot in front of the school gates, even though there was an official notice on the gatepost warning parents not to park there. I didn't dare point this out to Dad, but lots of the mothers and fathers delivering their own girls to school were staring, some even raising their eyebrows and shaking their heads.

The Mercedes was always a noticeable car. Now it seemed as big as a double-decker bus. I undid my seat belt, struggled with the door handle and hurtled out of the car.

"Thanks for the lift, Dad," I gabbled.

"Hey, don't I get a kiss from my Beauty?" Dad called loudly from his open window.

Arabella and Emily were standing watching. They nudged each other, sniggering, as I kissed Dad's cheek.

"Bye bye, Beauty!" he called.

Arabella and Emily were practically wetting themselves.

"Hello hello, Ugly!" said Arabella. "So Big Daddy brought you to school today, eh?"

"Don't you know you're not supposed to park outside the gates? Does your dad think he's so special in that great big silver sardine tin that rules don't apply to him?" said Emily.

I tried to march past but they took an arm each, hanging on to me. I craned around and saw Dad waving at me cheerily, thinking I'd met up with my two best friends—instead of my two worst enemies. No, Skye was the worst enemy of all. There she was, singing and dancing in the playground, showing off some silly routine she'd learned from the television, tossing her long blond hair and wiggling her hips. She should have looked ridiculous but she didn't. She sounded like a *real* singer and strutted like a *real* dancer. You couldn't help watching her. It wasn't just me. We were all watching, everyone in the whole playground, and all the girls were wishing they were Skye, even me.

Skye finished with a flourish, arms up, as if expecting applause. Some of the girls started clapping as if it was a real show and Skye was the star. Rhona clapped too, begging Skye to show her how to do the little skippy strutty bit.

"Show us too, Skye!" said Arabella, dropping my arm. "You're so good, you ought to go on *Watchbox*!"

"Hey, Skye, did you see old Ugly coming to

school in her dad's silver rubbish car?" said Emily, giving me a little shove.

"Oh my, the Flashmobile," said Skye, shading her eyes, pretending to be dazzled. "Ooh, let's all act like we're impressed."

She pranced around, Arabella and Emily copying her. Rhona went on skipping and strutting, working her way over to me.

"I'm useless at this stuff," she said cheerily. She glanced at Skye and Emily and Arabella. "Take no notice, they're just being silly," she said.

"Yeah," I said shakily.

"You are coming to my birthday party, aren't you, Beauty?" she asked.

I nodded shyly.

"Ooh! You haven't *really* asked Ugly, have you?" said Skye, putting her hands on her hips. "You are a total ninny, Rhona. We don't want creepy old Ugly."

"Yes I do," said Rhona. She reached out and squeezed my hand. Her brown eyes looked into mine. Her cheeks were very pink, maybe from the dancing. "I'm so glad you're coming, Beauty."

She really sounded as if she meant it, as if she wanted us to be friends. Then the bell rang and Rhona made a face. "Oh, blow. Lesson time," she said.

I made a face and sighed too, though I was always relieved when the bell rang. I *liked* lessons. Miss Woodhead was kind but very strict, so we weren't allowed to mess around and chat in the classroom. We had to sit up straight at our desks and listen carefully and put our hands up if we wanted to say anything. I could cope with lessons easy-peasy. It was the playtimes that were the problem, before school and mid-morning break and the endless lunch hour.

We had to play outside unless it was pouring rain, but we were allowed in if we needed to go to the bathroom. The minute I'd finished lunch I rushed to the restrooms and locked myself in the end stall. I'd tucked my copy of *A Little Princess* inside my school blazer. I sat peacefully for more than half an hour, at Miss Minchin's Seminary with Sara. The eldest girl at the school, spiteful Lavinia, was *so* like Skye.

I wished I was more like Sara, who never seemed the slightest bit upset by Lavinia and all her catty remarks. Sara was loved by all the other girls, especially the little ones. They hung on her every word and called her a princess and begged her to tell them stories. I imagined myself sauntering next door, going into the kindergarten class, sitting on one of their squashy cushions and telling them one of *my* stories.

They'd think I'd gone mental. The little girls didn't seem to like me any more than the big girls.

Sudden tears prickled in my eyes and splashed the insides of my glasses. I gave a monumental sniff and wiped my glasses on my blouse.

"Don't you *dare* cry," I told myself fiercely. "Stop being so stupidly sorry for yourself. Lots of people like you. Rhona likes you. She's asked you to her birthday party. She wants to be friends."

I felt a lot better—until I heard two girls from our class, Louise and Poppy come into the bathroom. I knew it was them because they kept calling out their silly nicknames, Lulu and Poo-poo. I think I'd almost rather be called Ugly than Poo-poo, but Poppy didn't seem to mind at all. They kept up this long silly conversation, shouting to each other from their individual stalls.

"Hey, Lulu, what are you going to give Rhona for her birthday?"

"I thought I'd maybe give her one of those special stuffed bears with a recording inside its tummy, Poo-poo. I could make it sing *Happy Birthday*."

"*Great* idea, Lulu. Maybe we could give her *two* bears? I could give her a boy and you could give her a girl?"

"Yeah, OK, Poo-poo—though it *was* my idea first. Don't tell anyone else or Rhona will get *lots* of birthday bears."

"How many of us are going, Lulu?"

"She's invited everyone, Poo-poo, the whole *class*."

I tensed up like I had stomachache, bending forward so that *A Little Princess* dug into my chest uncomfortably. So Rhona hadn't singled me out. She hadn't invited me to her party because she particularly liked me. She'd invited *everyone*. Maybe she didn't like me at all, but she was kind and didn't want to invite every other girl in the class, leaving me out altogether.

I waited for Louise and Poppy to stop their silly twitterings in the toilets. When they went I let myself have a two-minute howl. I timed myself by my watch, clamping my hand over my mouth and pinching my nose to make myself stop. I mopped myself dry with toilet paper but it was the shiny scratchy sort and it made my eyes redder than ever.

"Look at Ugly-Wugly! She's been *crying*! Boo-hoo, boo-hoo, little baby," said Skye, as we went back into the classroom for afternoon school.

"Are you OK, Beauty?" said Rhona, looking concerned.

"Yes, I'm fine, thank you," I said. I tried to say it in an airy confident way but my voice was still a bit wobbly and I gave a loud hiccup at the end of my sentence.

"Oh dear, she's got the burps now," said Skye, spluttering. "Someone thump Baby Ugly on the back, quick."

"Watch out or I'll give *you* a thump," I said fiercely and I gave her a shove right in the chest.

It wasn't a particularly hard shove but she wasn't expecting it. She staggered, arms flailing, shrieking like a siren.

"For goodness' sake, Skye, stop making that dreadful noise!" said Miss Woodhead.

"I'm in *pain*, Miss Woodhead. Beauty Cookson punched me here and it *hurts*," said Skye, hands clutching her front dramatically.

"*Beauty* punched you?" said Miss Woodhead, raising her eyebrows.

"Yes, she did, Miss Woodhead. I was watching," said Arabella.

"I saw her too. Beauty just *attacked* poor Skye for no reason at all," said Emily.

"I expect she had reason enough, but that's still no excuse for fighting, Beauty! I'm not having my girls brawling like guttersnipes. I don't particularly care for tell-tales either. Now sit down and settle down, all of you, before I get really angry. I *was* thinking of having a special story time this afternoon but I'm not sure you're in the right mood. I think we'd better have a spelling test instead."

49

Everyone groaned and glared at me, as if it was all my fault. They groaned even louder when we marked our spellings at the end of the lesson and I got twenty out of twenty.

I hurtled out of school when the bell rang. Mom was waiting for me. She was wearing jeans and a pink T-shirt with a fairy on it. She'd tied her hair into two cute plaits secured with pink bobbles. She looked about fourteen, so much younger and prettier than any of the other moms.

"Hi, Mom," I said happily, linking arms with her.

Way back in the playground I heard Skye and Arabella and Emily calling after me. I didn't turn around. Mom did though.

"Is that you they're calling?" she asked.

I shrugged.

"What is it they're saying?"

"Just something stupid. *They're* stupid. Come on, Mom, let's get home quick. I don't want to miss my show."

"OK, OK. Sam is calling to you, is he?"

"You bet he is."

We made it home with tons of time. Mom gave me a glass of milk and a banana sandwich. I was starving as I'd had very little breakfast and I'd rushed my lunch. I sipped and munched as Sam waved at me and Lily nibbled her carrot.

"*Who do we want to see?*" sang the children.

"*Sam and Lily in the Rabbit Hutch,*" I sang, through a mouthful of milky banana.

"Hello there," said Sam, smiling straight at me. "How are you doing?"

"So so, Sam," I said.

He gave me an understanding nod.

"Lily here is getting very excited," he said, cuddling her.

Lily lolled sleepily against Sam's chest, her blue eyes dreamy.

"She doesn't *look* very excited, Sam," I said.

Sam gave me a little wink. We had to keep up the pretense for all the little kids watching the show.

"Guess how old Lily is," said Sam. "Go on, have a little think. How old are *you*?"

"I'm a bit embarrassed to tell you, Sam. I think I'm much older than most of your viewers," I said.

"Well, Lily's a bit younger than you," said Sam. "She's very nearly one year old. She's very mature for a nearly one-year-old, isn't she?" He tickled her gently under her chin. "You can toddle out into the garden and fix yourself a lovely veggie tea and you can tuck yourself in bed and get yourself up in the morning and give yourself a good wash. Could *you* do that when you were nearly one?"

"Maybe I had a shot at it," I said, giggling.

"I thought I'd throw a little birthday party for our Lily. Do you think she'd like that?"

"I think she might like a party," I said. "But not with tons and tons of people."

Sam nodded. "I don't think Lily wants a *big* party with lots and lots of friends. She's a bit shy sometimes. I think we'll give her a *little* party. Just Lily and me—and you too, of course. You can come, can't you?"

"Of course I can come! Oh, Sam, I wish *you* could come to my birthday party. Just you and me and Lily. And Mom. And *maybe* Rhona. She's asked me to *her* birthday party but I'm not sure I want to go. Skye will be there. She's Rhona's best friend and my worst-ever enemy. She's so horrible. I don't know why Rhona wants to be her friend."

"Maybe Rhona will get fed up with Skye and make friends with you?" said Sam.

"Oh, I wish! But it's never going to happen," I said, sighing.

"You never know," said Sam. "But remember, Lily and I are still your best friends."

"I'll always remember that," I said.

Sam gave me a special secret smile, and then he raised his voice, talking to everyone else.

"What do you think I should get Lily for a birthday present? Have you got any good ideas? How about painting me a picture of an ideal present for our birthday bunny? Send it to Sam at the Rabbit Hutch, OK? Bye then."

I waved good-bye and then I went upstairs and drew a very special picture of Lily with a little paper crown perched on her head and an I AM ONE TODAY badge tied around one floppy ear. I drew her a birthday carrot cake with real baby carrots decorating the icing on top. I drew one big candle in the middle.

Then I got a new piece of paper and drew my own birthday cake. I'd seen exactly the one I wanted, with white icing and pink rosebuds. I *loved* proper birthday cake. I loved the soft sponge and the jam and the buttercream and I especially loved the sweet icing.

I looked at my paper birthday cake and then pretended to blow out my candles and make a wish.

Five

I went to Lily's birthday party of course—along with a million other little kids, all of us singing "Happy Birthday to You" into our television sets. Lily looked up and blinked her big blue eyes especially at me. Sam was wearing a fantastic new T-shirt in her honor, dark green with little white Lily-type rabbits running across his chest. Lily seemed very appreciative, cheekily poking out her little pink tongue at Sam.

"She likes my green T-shirt, doesn't she? Maybe she thinks it's a great big cabbage!"

Sam gave Lily real cabbage leaves for her tea and, *guess what*, a carrot cake with a candle, almost exactly the same as the one I'd drawn!

"You gave me the idea, Beauty," Sam whispered. "Lily loves her cake, though I'm not sure she's up to blowing out her candle. Will you help her? One, two, three—*blow!*"

I blew, Sam blew, children all over Britain blew—and Lily's candle went out.

"There! Now Lily has to make her special birthday wish. She'd like to share her birthday wish with you, Beauty. Close your eyes and wish hard."

I closed my eyes and wished: *I wish I could really meet you and Lily, Sam!*

Sam gave Lily a cozy new bed for her birthday present, with a special green blanket and a straw pillow. She tried it out, looking very cute, though she lay in it the wrong way around, her head under the blanket and her big fluffy-tailed bottom on the pillow.

"Silly old Lily," Sam said fondly. "Out you come, sweetie. It's not bedtime yet. It's time for all your party games. We're going to play Blind Bunny Buff and Pass the Parsnip and Hunt the Carrot."

Lily took no notice.

"Do you know something? I think she's really gone to sleep!" Sam said. "Oh well! Maybe you'd like to invent a special party game for Lily? Would you like to paint it for me? Send your paintings to me at the Rabbit Hutch. I'm looking forward to seeing them. Bye for now—oh, just a minute!" he said, as the music started up to show it was the end of the show. "Beauty? I do hope you enjoy Rhona's party!"

"Thank you, Sam," I said.

I went upstairs and drew a picture of me with Lily on my lap. I'm quite small and Lily's very big so it looked as if I was giving a polar bear a cuddle. I had my arms outstretched to cope with Lily's width, one hand clamped around her haunch to keep her safely wedged on my lap, the other hand stroking her head.

This is a very simple but very special party game, I printed at the top of my picture. *It can be played at very small parties by one person and one pet. It's called Stroke the Rabbit.*

Then I sat cross-legged on my bed with my arms out as if I was holding an imaginary Lily. I stroked thin air until my arms ached.

I heard Dad's car pull up in the driveway. I listened hard as he came in the front door. He wasn't singing his silly Happy Homes song. He wasn't dancing down the hall in his socks. It looked like he was in a bad mood. I decided to stay in my room as long as possible. At least I couldn't hear any shouting.

After a long time Mom called up to me that supper was ready. I started down the stairs and went to go into the dining room, where Mom usually set the table.

"No, no, we're having supper on trays in the living room. Dad's a bit tired," said Mom, taking me gently by the shoulders and turning me round. She gave me a little reassuring pat as she did so.

Dad was slumped in his chair, his shirt buttons undone and his belt buckle loosened. He looked as if he needed to ease his head too. There were lines stretched tight across his forehead, pinching the top of his nose.

My tummy tensed but he gave me a surprisingly warm smile.

"Hello there, little Beauty. What have you been up to, eh?"

"I've just been doing my homework, Dad," I said.

"That's my clever girl," Dad said, sighing. "You come and cheer your old dad up now. I've spent the whole day arguing with sticklers who won't budge an inch and it's doing my head in. Tell me about *your* day, darling. What did you get up to with all your chums?"

I took a deep breath and launched into an utterly fictitious account of my day with my best friend Rhona. Mom served us Marks and Spencer's spaghetti bolognese while I nattered on about Rhona and me making up a dance routine together and everyone clapping. I was getting a little carried away as I couldn't dance to save my life but Dad seemed to believe me.

"That's my girly!" he said happily.

"Will Rhona be having dancing at her party tomorrow?" Mom said.

"I don't know. Maybe," I said cautiously. "It says wear casual clothes on the invitation. Oh, and we're supposed to take our bathing suits too."

"Have they got their own pool then?" said Dad. "Where does she live, in Groveland Park? Most of the houses there have pools, but they're all the size of postage stamps. I bet you'll just sit on the edge and swish your tootsies in the water."

"I wish they'd say exactly what they mean by 'casual,'" said Mom. "Does that mean you wear your jeans?"

"Beauty's not wearing jeans to a *party*," said Dad. "No, she'll wear her little pink number."

I stopped eating. Dad had taken me to one of his golf dinner and dances at Christmas. He'd insisted on buying me an elaborate bridesmaid-type satin dress with gauzy puff sleeves and gatherings and frills flouncing everywhere. I looked truly terrible in it, like I was wearing an old lady's quilt.

I imagined the remarks that Skye and Emily and Arabella would make.

"*Not* my pink dress!" I blurted.

Dad stopped eating too. And Mom.

"What's the matter with your pink dress?" said Dad. "It cost a small fortune from Harrods. Don't you like it?"

I forced a smile.

"Oh I love love love it, Dad," I said. My voice went high and squeaky I was trying so hard. "That's precisely the *problem*. It's so ultra-gorgeous and glamorous that I'm terrified of getting it spoiled at the party. I could easily spill juice all down it or tear one of the frills."

"Not if you're *careful*," said Dad, but he nodded approvingly all the same. "I'm glad you want to look after it. Still, no jeans, you don't want to look like a dirty scruffy tomboy at this party. How about your pretty blue blouse and your little white pleated skirt? You look sweet in that."

It was my second-most-hated outfit. They would still sneer and snigger at me—but it was marginally better than the pink quilt outfit.

"Yes, good idea, Dad," I said.

"Mom could maybe tie blue ribbons in your hair?" said Dad. He ran his fingers through my long limp hair, sighing. "Couldn't you *find* some rollers, Dilly, and give it a bit of a curl?"

"Beauty would hate having those uncomfy rollers prodding her head," said Mom.

Dad wound spaghetti round and round his fork.

"You girls have to suffer a bit for your looks," he said, chomping, his tongue and teeth coated with tomato sauce. "*I* know! Take her to the hairdresser's Saturday morning, get *them* to primp and fiddle with her hair, do it up fancy-like."

"Well . . ." Mom saw my desperate expression. "I don't think we'd be able to get her an appointment at the hairdresser's on such short notice."

"Oh, Dilly, why are you always so hopeless? Look, get Beauty there when they open and *insist* on an appointment. You could do with getting your hair done yourself, it's a bit"—he made wobbly gestures with his hands—"sort of *tired.*"

All of Mom looked tired nowadays. It was such hard work trying to keep Dad happy. She was very pale, with violet circles under her eyes. She still looked very pretty but like she hadn't had any sleep for a week.

She looked at me apologetically. "OK, I'll take Beauty tomorrow morning and we'll both get our hair done."

"That's the ticket," said Dad, breaking off a piece of bread and wiping it around his plate. "I want my girls to do me proud."

"We know that, Gerry," said Mom, with the tiniest edge to her voice.

Dad was up very early on Saturday to go to play golf. He crept around getting dressed and going to the bathroom, but tripped at the top of the stairs. His golf clubs made such a clatter that I shot out of bed and ran onto the landing, convinced the house was falling down.

Dad collected up his clubs, cursing furiously.

"Oops, pardon my French," he said, when he saw

me. "Back to bed, Beauty. I'm just off to my golf club. Got to keep in with the right guys. This is the way your dad sorts out all his little problems. Just call me Gerry the Fixer. Ta ta, baby. Enjoy your party."

I didn't go back to bed. I pattered into Mom's bedroom and slid in beside her. Mom put her arms around me and cuddled me close. Both our hearts were still thudding fast because of the noise. We were just drifting back to sleep when there was another crash from downstairs, and sounds of Dad swearing.

"Oh God, that sounded like a bottle of juice. He's jerked the fridge open so violently it'll have fallen out," Mom murmured.

"Can't you even arrange the fridge properly, Dilly? I've got cranberry juice all over my cream golf trousers!" Dad yelled up the stairs.

I couldn't help giggling—and Mom started spluttering too. She covered our faces with the comforter so he couldn't hear.

"Dilly!" Dad shouted furiously. "Get that lazy butt of yours downstairs and sort this fridge out before I get back!"

He slammed out of the house, banging the front door. We waited, listening for the thud of the car door, the hum of the engine. The gravel crunched as Dad drove off. Mom and I sighed and lay flat on our backs, limp with relief that he'd gone.

"I think he's woken all the neighbors, not just us," said Mom.

"Do you think he'll still be angry when he gets home?" I asked.

"Not if he wins at golf," said Mom, yawning.

"What time do you think he'll be back? Will he want to pick me up from Rhona's party?" I asked anxiously.

"Maybe," said Mom.

"So I've really got to wear my blue blouse and that pleated skirt?"

"You look lovely in it, really. And we'll get your hair all curly."

"Mom, they're all going to laugh at me."

"No, they won't," said Mom. "You'll look wonderful. They'll be envious."

"You're just saying that to make me feel better," I said, giving her a little shake.

"Well, OK. I wish I *could* make everything better for you, Beauty." Mom paused, gently stroking my neck and shoulders. "Are you unhappy, pet?"

I took a deep breath. "No, I'm fine," I said.

"Now *you're* just saying that to make me feel better. Oh, lovey, I don't know what to *do*. Your dad's getting worse, isn't he? But if I try to stop him he gets even angrier."

"I know."

"And at school—do they still tease you lots?"

"Yep."

"Does Rhona?"

"No. She's always kind to me."

"Well, that's great. Can't you be friends with her?"

"Mom! She's Skye's best friend. And Skye is my most deadly enemy. She hates me."

"Well, *we* hate *her*," said Mom. "And her horrible patronizing mother. When we got you into Lady Mary Mountbank she came up to me in the playground and welcomed me to the school like it was her own family house. And then she goes, 'So are you Beauty's big sister?' and then she gives this great shriek when I said I'm your mom. 'You must have had her so *young*,' like I'm a child bride. Well, OK, maybe I *was*—but it's none of her business, eh?"

"I liked it better at Jenner Street Primary, Mom."

"I know, love, but your dad set his heart on you going to Lady Mary Mountbank. It *is* a really good school. You'll go on to high school, swan off to college, get a brilliant degree, have a fantastic career, whatever. I don't want you to end up like me. I've never had a proper job. I was just a receptionist at Happy Homes—and I wasn't even a *good* receptionist. I was too shy to speak up properly and I kept getting muddled using the telephone switchboard. Your dad called me into his office all set to fire me only I was wearing some silly skimpy top and he got distracted and asked me out on a date instead."

"Maybe if you weren't so pretty you'd have simply got the sack. You'd have found some other job and some other man, someone the complete opposite of Dad." I tried to imagine him. I saw Sam, as if I had a tiny television set inside each eye. "Someone gentle, who listens and lets you do what you want. Someone who never ever shouts. Someone who's always always always in a good mood."

Mom lay still, holding her breath as if I was telling her a fairy story. Then she gave a long sigh.

"Yeah, right," she said sadly. Then she tickled me under the chin. "No, *wrong*. If I hadn't married your dad I wouldn't have had *you*, babe."

"But you'd have had *another* girl. You could have met a truly handsome guy and then I'd maybe be a *real* beauty."

"You're my Beauty now—and we're going to make you even more beautiful at the hairdresser's."

Mom was trying hard to sound positive. I hoped the hairdresser's would be totally booked up, maybe with a bride and her mom and six bridesmaids and a flower girl—but they were depressingly empty when we went in the door. They could fit us in with ease.

My hairdresser was named Becky. She was very blond and very slim and very pretty, almost as pretty as Skye. I was worried she'd act like Skye too, sniggering and making faces in the mirror to her colleagues as she shampooed my straggly hair and then twisted it into spiral curls, lock by lock. But she was really sweet to me, chatting away as if we were friends. She spent ages on my hair. When she'd finally finished dabbing at it with her styling comb she stood back, smiling.

"There! Don't you look lovely!" she said.

I didn't look lovely at all. My hair twizzled this way and that in odd thin ringlets. My ears stuck out comically in between the curls. I wanted to hide my head in her wastepaper basket and weep, but she'd tried so hard to please me I politely pretended to be delighted with my new-look corkscrew head.

Mom had a similar hairstyle but it really did look lovely on her. Her little, pale heart-shaped face was framed with a halo of pale gold curls. Skye's mother was actually right—she really did look like my big sister. When we went around the town shopping lots of men stared at her and a gang of boys all wolf-whistled.

"No one would laugh if *you* were called Beauty, Mom," I said. "Hey, let's swap names. You be Beauty and I'll be Dilly."

"Dilly's a silly name too. Dilys! I suppose my mom thought it was posh. Let's choose different names. I'll be . . . hmm, what shall I be called? Something dignified and grown up and sensible." Mom giggled. "All the things I'm not." She saw the sign on the front of a shop. "How about *Claire*?"

"OK. I'll be Sara, after Sara Crewe. Let's be best friends, Claire."

"Are we the same age then?" said Mom.

"No, I'm a couple of years older than you," I said firmly. "So I get to sort things out for both of us."

Mom laughed. "Yep, I think you'll be good at that," she said.

We played the Claire-and-Sara game as we went round the shopping center looking for a good birthday present for Rhona. She was our friend, but only our second-best friend. *We* were best friends, and now that we'd left college we shared an apartment together and we both had fabulous jobs. Claire was a television presenter and Sara was a children's book illustrator.

"Maybe you'll work in the same studio as the *Rabbit Hutch* show and you'll get to meet Sam and Lily, Claire," I said.

"Oh, I know Sam already," said Mom, acting Claire. "Don't tell, but we're actually dating." She looked at me a little anxiously. "Is that OK, Sara, or do *you* want Sam as your boyfriend?"

"Maybe," I said.

"Well, perhaps we'll have to share him," said Mom, giggling. "I'll go out with him one week and you can go out with him the next."

"And I'm going to draw Lily. Yeah, I'm going to make a picture book all about her."

"Do you think Rhona would like a book as a birthday present?" said Mom, swapping back to herself.

"I'm not sure what sort of books she likes," I said. I thought about it. "Do you think *she*'d like *A Little Princess*? It's my absolute favorite book."

"Then I'm sure she'd like it too."

So we bought her a copy in WH Smith's, and then we went into the actual Claire's shop and bought her three slim silver bangles and then we went to New Look and bought her a pink T-shirt with *Princess* written in silver lettering on the front.

"There, it all goes beautifully together," said Mom. "She'll love her presents, Beauty."

"Do you really think so? They're more interesting than a stuffed teddy bear, aren't they? That's what Lulu and Poo-poo are giving her."

"She'll like your presents best, Beauty," said Mom. "Just you wait and see."

Six

"There, you look lovely, Beauty," said Mom, giving me little strokes, as if I was Lily.

"No I don't," I said.

"Yes you *do*, darling, honestly," said Mom.

I dodged around her to get to the long mirror in her bedroom. I knew she was simply saying that to make me feel good—but I still wondered whether somehow she could be right. I looked in the mirror, hoping for a miracle.

It hadn't happened. I stared back, a pudgy, awkward girl with corkscrew curls, a frilly blue blouse, and a white skirt way too tight. I looked at myself until I blurred, because my eyes filled with tears.

"I look like a total fool, Mom," I said flatly. I stuck out my tongue at my image and waddled about in my black patent leather shoes, turning myself into a clown.

"Stop it, darling. You look great. Well, maybe the shoes aren't quite right. They do look a bit clumpy," said Mom. "We should have got you some lighter party shoes. White, or maybe silver?"

She suddenly darted to her wardrobe and

rummaged at the bottom among her own shoes. She produced a pair of silver dance shoes and waved them triumphantly in the air.

I stared at her as if she'd gone nuts.

"I can't wear *them*, Mom. They're yours! They'll be much too big."

But when I sat down and put them on they very nearly fitted me. I was alarmed at the thought I had feet as big as my mom's already. They'd be totally enormous by the time I was grown up. I'd have to wear real clown's boots, those long ones as big as baguettes.

"They look great on you!" said Mom.

"But they've got high heels!"

"They're not *that* high. Anyway, it'll make all the other girls jealous if you're wearing proper heels," said Mom.

I considered this. "OK. So how do you walk in them?" I said, wobbling to my feet. I took one uncertain step and nearly fell over. "The answer is, with great difficulty!" I said, clutching Mom.

"You'll be fine, Beauty. You just need to practice," said Mom.

I staggered around the bedroom and out onto the landing. I toured my own bedroom, my bathroom, Mom and Dad's bathroom, Mom's dressing room, and one of the spare bedrooms. I fell over once and twisted my ankle twice.

"Maybe the heels aren't such a good idea after all," said Mom.

I begged to keep them on, knowing that none of the other girls had proper high heels, not even Skye.

Wonderfully, Dad wasn't back from his golf game when it was time to leave for the party, so Mom drove me in her little purple VW Bug. Dad bought it for her on their tenth wedding anniversary. It had purple velvet cushions in the back and two fluffy purple teddies with their arms wrapped around each other and silly smiles sewn on their snouts to show they were in love with each other. I knew for a fact that one color Mom didn't care for at all was purple, but she squealed obediently when she discovered the car outside our house. It was tied up with an enormous purple satin ribbon so that it looked like a gigantic Easter egg.

I sat in the back with the canoodling teddies while Mom drove to Rhona's house. We set off in good time but we ended up arriving ten minutes late. Mom drives very slowly and cautiously. She takes ages edging out onto the main roads, not making a move until there's not another car in sight. She also got lost twice.

"I'm sorry, babes, I'm so useless," she said, drawing up outside Rhona's house at last.

There was a big bunch of pink and blue balloons

tied to the gate to show there was a party going on. The living room glowed rose with pink fairy lights. I saw hordes of girls rushing around, waving their arms and dancing. We could hear the music from inside the car. Skye bobbed into view, flinging back her long silky hair as she step-tapped sideways.

My tummy tightened.

"I don't think I really want to go to the party," I said.

"Oh, Beauty! Come on, darling, you'll be fine once you get inside," said Mom, squeezing my hand tightly. "You're going to have a lovely time."

When I teetered up the front path in my high heels and knocked on the front door, Rhona opened it immediately. She smiled as if she'd been waiting especially for me. She was wearing a red stripy top and a short black skirt. She had red lipstick on too, though it had gone a bit wobbly at the edges.

"Happy birthday, Rhona! You look lovely," I said.

Rhona was blinking at my new corkscrew hair.

"Wow, Beauty, you look so different," she said. She swallowed. "*You* look lovely too," she said.

Her eyes slid down my blue frills and white pleats. When she saw my shoes her mouth widened in genuine delight.

"Oh my goodness, look at your *shoes*! Mom won't let me wear even the weeniest heels, she says I've got to wait until I'm at least thirteen. Oh you're so *lucky*!"

I walked in proudly, keeping my legs rigid, willing myself not to wobble.

"Here's your present," I said, offering it shyly.

I'd spent ages wrapping it up. Rhona didn't snatch it carelessly or shove it in a corner. She held it carefully, stroking the silver paper and pink satin ribbon.

"Rhona! Come *on*, it's the 'Don't Feel Like Dancing' song!" Skye called from the party room.

"Just a minute," said Rhona.

She undid the ribbon, smoothing it out and then winding it in a little silky ball. She slid her finger under the wrapping paper and eased it off. She slipped the three silver bangles over her wrist and waved her arms so that they jangled. She held her pink *Princess* T-shirt against her, showing that it would fit her perfectly. She opened her book and peered at it politely.

"Thank you so much, Beauty," she said, giving me a big lipsticky grin. "They're wonderful presents."

"I'm so glad you like them," I said.

We smiled at each other. I wanted to freeze-frame us so we stayed in that magic moment in her hall, on the edge of her party, Rhona and me. But then Skye shouted again and Rhona rolled her eyes at me.

"Come on," she said. "Just wait till they all see your gorgeous silver shoes!"

They didn't notice my high heels at first. They were too busy gawking at my hair. Skye gave an exaggerated double take when she saw me, standing still, hands on hips. She was wearing an even shorter skirt than Rhona and a little black vest top that showed her totally flat tummy. She'd inked a blue star round her belly button that looked almost like a real tattoo.

"Oh my God, who's this? Hey, it's the Corkscrew Kid! Old Ugly Curlynob!" She got started on my blouse next, pulling the pussycat bow, saying her granny had exactly the same blouse, she'd bought it for ten pence at a jumble sale. Emily and Arabella hooted with laughter.

"Shut up, Skye," said Rhona, but no one could ever shut Skye up.

I turned my back on her and went over to the sofa. An entire *squadron* of teddy bears were squashed up together, jostling each other with their furry paws.

"Look at Beauty's fantastic shoes," said Rhona.

"She can't walk properly in them," said Skye. "Wiggle-waggle wobble-bum."

I plonked myself down in the midst of the teddies, blinking hard. The others started dancing— Rhona and Skye, Emily and Arabella, Lulu and

Poo-poo, everyone. Some girls danced in a little group together. I could have got up and danced with them, but I didn't. I picked two of the teddies and made them dance instead, up and down the arm of the sofa.

Then they had a singing contest. Skye had given Rhona a karaoke set for her birthday. She had first go to show us how to do it. Skye was brilliant at it of course, using the mic professionally and dancing along to the music. Rhona tried hard when it was her turn but she kept getting the giggles and losing her place. Arabella and Emily performed as a duo and were quite good, jumping up and down and shaking their hips in unison.

"Whose turn is it now?" Skye asked.

There was a general clamour of *Me! Me! Me!*

Skye ignored all of them. She was looking straight at me.

"You have a go, Ugly Corkscrew," she said.

"No thanks," I said.

"Come on, you've got to join in. Don't be a party pooper," said Skye. "It's your turn now. Choose your song."

I'd never even heard of most of the songs. Dad hated all modern pop music, calling it "that waily-thumpy rubbish." He listened to old rock bands from ages ago. I could sing those songs all right, but they weren't an option.

I fidgeted helplessly. Skye raised her eyebrows.

"Get *on* with it, Ugly. Come on, come on, come on!" She turned it into a chant. The others started joining in.

"We'll sing a duet, you and me, Beauty," said Rhona.

Skye frowned. "No, let her sing solo. You've had a turn anyway, Rhona."

"Yes, but it's my party, so I can sing as often as I want," said Rhona, smiling sweetly. She scanned the songs on offer. "We'll sing *Baby Boo.*"

She took hold of me and pulled me to the mic. I squeezed her hand.

"I don't know it!" I whispered.

"You don't need to. I'll sing the main bit and you just go *Baby Boo boo boo, boo boopy do* after each line. It's easy-peasy, Beauty."

She started the music and sang the line. I mumbled my way through the silly *Baby Boo* refrain. Rhona sang the next verse and then I went through the *Baby Boo* babble again. I realized Rhona was right. It *was* easy-peasy. She got the giggles again in the last verse because there was a whole lot of silly stuff about making you moan, obviously a reference to s-e-x. When Rhona collapsed *I* sang the lines because I knew the tune now. We sang the last line together and yelled the chorus: "*Baby Boo boo boo, boo boopy do,*" finishing with a twirl.

I wobbled wildly in Mom's heels and clutched Rhona. We both ended up on the floor, shrieking with laughter. The others laughed too, but they were laughing *with* us, not *at* us. Well, Skye wasn't laughing.

"I hope you realize what a fool you're making of yourself, Ugly," she hissed. "Don't think Rhona wants to be your friend. She's just being kind because she feels sorry for you."

I tried not to take any notice but I worried that she might be right.

I got to sit on one side of Rhona at her birthday tea. Skye sat the other side of course. It was wonderful food: giant turkey-and-bacon-and-salad club sandwiches held together with toothpicks; sausages dipped in tomato sauce; potato wedges with sour cream and salsa dips; four-cheese pizza with pineapple topping; mini burgers with relish and pickles; an enormous trifle with whipped cream and cherries; fairy cupcakes with pink and lilac and baby blue icing; chocolate ice cream cake and a huge birthday cake in the shape of an *R*, decorated with little silver hearts and crystallized roses.

"It looks so *beautiful*," I said in awe.

"Oh, my mom loves cooking," said Rhona. "Let's dig in!"

I picked up my plate and started munching.

Rhona's mom poured us all glasses of juice—cranberry, orange, or raspberry.

"Which juice would you like, dear?" she asked me.

"Cranberry, please," I said indistinctly, my mouth full. I swallowed. "Oh, Mrs. Marshall, this is absolutely delicious."

"Thank you, darling. I'm glad you're enjoying it," she said, smiling at me, and then moving on.

"Good grief! Look at the way Ugly's piled her plate high," Skye muttered. "She's such a greedy guts, no wonder she's got such a big belly. Look, it's sticking out all the pleats in her ridiculous skirt."

Rhona pretended not to hear but Arabella and Emily sniggered. I wanted to push Skye's head *plop* into the bowl of trifle. I tried to act as if I hadn't heard her. I ate my entire plateful—though the food tasted like cardboard now.

It was easier after tea because the grown-ups came into the living room with us and Skye was too sly to be blatantly mean to me in front of the Marshalls. Mr. Marshall stuck a false moustache under his nose, balanced a silly hat sideways on his head, and said he was Bumble the Conjuror. He did a lot of tricks that didn't work properly. I wasn't sure if this was deliberate or not. I tittered uncertainly when he picked the wrong card or tapped the wrong box. Rhona roared with laughter and kept yelling, "Oh, *Dad*, you are so so *stupid!*"

I held my breath the first time she said it, but Mr. Marshall didn't turn a hair. He just made a funny face, sticking one finger in his mouth, looking all droopy and woebegone. Rhona laughed all the more.

I wondered what my dad would do if I called him stupid.

Mr. Marshall's conjuring act went on a little too long and some of the girls started chatting among themselves.

"Can't we go swimming now?" Skye asked.

"You need to let your food go down properly first," said Mrs. Marshall. "Let's all give Mr. Bumble a clap and then we'll play a nice quiet party game."

She fetched a big tray full of twenty tiny objects and told us to look at them carefully. I stared hard, memorizing everything. There was a watch, nail polish, lipstick, a ring, a rubber spider, a Band-Aid, a pencil sharpener, a flower, matches, a bottle opener, a tape measure, a straw, a key, a nail, a postcard, a stamp, little scissors, a thermometer, perfume, and a very tiny teddy in striped pajamas. Everyone went "Aaah!" when they spotted the little teddy because he looked so cute.

Mrs. Marshall covered the tray with a big cloth and gave us each pens and paper.

"Write down as many things on the tray as you can remember," said Mrs. Marshall.

There was a great groan.

"That's not fair! I was just looking at that little teddy," said Skye. "Let me have another look at the tray."

She went to pull the cover off.

"Certainly not, Skye!" said Mrs. Marshall.

"But I don't know what else was on the wretched tray!"

"I'm afraid that's just your bad luck," said Mrs. Marshall.

She said it cheerily, but I started to wonder if *she* didn't like Skye either, even though she was Rhona's best friend.

I closed my eyes and saw a picture of the tray inside my head. I opened my eyes and started scribbling quickly on my piece of paper. Everyone else was moaning and sighing and conferring. I didn't need to. I wrote: watch, nail polish, lipstick, ring, spider, Band-Aid, pencil sharpener, flower, matches, bottle opener, tape measure, straw, key, nail, postcard, stamp, scissors, thermometer, perfume . . . and tiny teddy bear.

"Wow, look at Beauty! She's written a huge long list," said Rhona.

"Oh, that Ugly! It's just the sort of stupid nerdy

thing she *would* do. I think this is a boring game. Can't we play something else?" said Skye.

"No, let's carry on. I think this is a good game," said Emily, who was writing rapidly too.

She ended up with twenty answers and was sure she'd won—but when Mrs. Marshall checked she'd made up four items.

"Still, sixteen correct is positively brilliant," said Arabella. "I could only come up with five. Still, at least I'm not last." She glanced at Skye, who had only written one word—teddy.

"I wasn't playing," Skye said quickly. "So, well done, Emily, you've won."

"No, no," said Mrs Marshall, running her finger down my list. "*Beauty*'s won. She's got every single item right. That's brilliant, sweetheart!"

Skye groaned and made a face. "Trust Ugly," she said.

She said it loud enough for Mrs. Marshall to hear. She frowned at Skye and then turned to me.

"Well done, Beauty. You get the little teddy bear as your prize."

"Oh, *lucky* Beauty," they all said.

Rhona picked the tiny teddy off the tray and tucked him in the palm of my hand.

"I'm glad *you* won him, Beauty," she said.

There was a quiz game after that. I knew all the answers in the history and literature and geography sections. I started to worry that it wouldn't be polite to win this game too—but I could only answer one question in the television section and none at all in pop music and famous celebrities, so I didn't win anything. Emily *did* win this time, though she didn't get a tiny teddy, she just won a pen and notebook.

"*Now* can we go for a swim?" Skye whined.

"Yes, dear," said Mrs. Marshall brightly. "Change in Rhona's bedroom. The pool's outside. Take a running jump. Be my guest."

Some of the girls were wearing their bathing suits under their clothes so it was easy for them to get changed quickly and decently. I struggled to unbuckle Mom's shoes, wriggle out of my tights, and get my underpants off without anyone looking. I wished I was a lot smaller and my white skirt more voluminous.

"Look at old Ugly showing off her bum," said Skye. "Wibble wobble, wibble wobble."

She cast off her own tiny skirt and top in two shakes. She was wearing an emerald green bikini, high cut so that it made her slender legs look longer than ever. She twisted her long fair hair into a knot on top of her head and secured it with a green hair clasp.

Most of the girls had similar cool glamorous swimsuits. Arabella had a red halter-neck bikini and she looked very grown up in it, though she had to keep tugging at the top to keep it in place. I had a silly baby suit, pale blue patterned with ice-cream cones. It was last year's bathing suit, because I hardly ever went swimming. It clung to me, emphasizing my tummy. I sucked it in as far as I could. It felt as if they were all staring at me. I felt incredibly self-conscious padding across the carpet and out into the hall. I clutched the tiny teddy for comfort.

Mrs. Marshall smiled at me.

"I don't think that teddy is really into swimming," she said.

"I'm not sure *I* am either," I said.

I could swim the breast stroke, I'd had proper lessons, but I couldn't risk getting my new hairdo wet. I let the others jump wildly into the pool and caper about. I sat hunched on the edge, feet dangling in the water. I tried to keep my stomach sucked in, hanging on tight to Teeny Teddy.

Rhona came and sat beside me. She was wearing a tankini, a pink-and-white top with little shorts. Her tummy stuck out a little too but she didn't seem to care in the slightest.

"I'm so glad you got to win the little teddy, Beauty," she said. "I've got a twin one just like him, with those sweet little pajamas, only mine's got red stripes instead of blue."

"What do you call yours?"

"Teddy!"

"Oh, Rhona, he's got to have a proper name!"

"Well, I don't know. What are you going to call *your* teddy?"

I sat him in the palm of my hand, staring at his little furry face. He had a long snout and a serious expression. He might be tiny but he certainly wasn't a baby.

"I think he's quite elderly in teddy years. He's wearing the sort of pajamas that grandpas wear. I think I'll call him . . . Nicholas Navybear."

Rhona giggled. "That's a great name. OK, so what can mine be called?"

"You said your teddy's got red pajamas, so yours can be Reginald Redted."

"Perfect!" said Rhona, giggling.

"Rhona! Get in the pool!" Skye shouted.

Rhona laughed and kicked her legs, splashing. "In a minute," she said cheerily.

I wished I had Rhona's happy-go-lucky knack of being friends with everyone.

"You'd better name all my other birthday bears too, Beauty," said Rhona.

"Rhona, Rhona, Rhona! Get in the pool! We want to give you your birthday bumps," Skye shouted.

"I'm talking to Beauty just this second," said Rhona.

"Who wants to talk to boring old Ugly?" said Emily.

"Don't call her that," said Rhona.

"Come on, jump in the pool," said Arabella.

"*Rhona!* Come *here!*" Skye yelled imperiously.

Rhona raised her eyebrows. "Watch this!" she muttered to me.

She stood up, took a running jump, tucked her knees up and landed right beside Skye, totally capsizing her. I couldn't help laughing. Skye spluttered to the surface, shaking her head. She blinked—and saw me grinning.

"Oh, so you think it's funny, do you, Ugly?" said Skye. "Well, come and join in the fun with us then."

She swam three strokes toward me and tugged hard on my ankles. I shrieked as I shot into the water, right over my head. When I surfaced, gasping, Skye screamed with laughter.

"Look at Ugly! Her curls are all unraveling! She's getting unscrewed!"

I put my hands up to my hair. What would Dad say now? I tried winding one of the curls quickly around my fingers but it wouldn't go back into shape.

I had both hands free.

Oh no!

Nicholas Navybear had drowned.

Seven

I dived down looking for him. Rhona dived too. Everyone dived, even Arabella and Emily.

"You dive too, Skye," said Rhona. "You're the best at diving and it's your fault for yanking Beauty into the water like that."

"It was just a *joke*," said Skye sulkily, but she dived too.

I dived until my eyes streamed and my heart thumped. I was desperate to find little Nicholas. I'd only owned him for twenty minutes but I already loved him with all my heart.

I couldn't find him. Rhona couldn't find him. Arabella and Emily and all the others couldn't find him. Skye couldn't find him, though she swam a whole length underwater looking for him.

"I think we'd better call off the teddy search, girls. You're all getting a bit blue and goose-pimply. Out you all get!" said Mrs. Marshall, handing out warm towels.

I tried one last dive, holding my breath and keeping my eyes wide open, my hands scrabbling sideways across the pool tiles like pink crabs. There was no sign of Nicholas Navybear.

"Come along, Beauty, you must get out now," said Mrs. Marshall, hauling me out and wrapping a big towel around me.

Mr. Marshall was in charge of the hot chocolate to warm us all up.

"Don't look so upset, sweetheart," he said to me, popping two extra marshmallows into my mug. "I'm sure we'll be able to find you another little teddy."

He was so kind I felt tears pricking my eyes.

"Oh, lordy, look at old Ugly. She's blubbering just because she's lost her little teddy-weddy," Skye muttered.

"You can be so mean sometimes, Skye," said Rhona.

She ran off, towel wrapped around her like a toga. When Rhona came back she had something clutched in her hand. Something small and furry, in striped pajamas.

"Rhona's found him!" said Arabella.

"No, no, this is *my* teddy," said Rhona. She thrust him into my hand. "But he's yours now, Beauty."

"I can't take Reginald Redted!" I said.

"Yes, of course you can. I've just got tons of new birthday teddies. So you have Reginald Redted."

"Reginald Redted!" said Skye, rolling her eyes. "What kind of crazy name is that?"

"I think it's a brilliant name," said Rhona. "Beauty made it up."

"Oh, well, no wonder it's so weird," said Skye. She blew out her cheeks and stuck out her stomach, pretending to be me. "Weginald Wedted," she said. She was supposed to be imitating me, though I haven't got a lisp. It didn't matter so much that Skye was being horrible, not when Rhona was being so extra-specially lovely to me.

"I'll look after him so carefully, Rhona—but I won't keep him forever. I'll give him back to you at school on Monday," I suggested. "We'll share him, OK?"

"Yes, that's a great idea," said Rhona. "We'll be co-parents. Cool!"

"We'll have to have a little teddy bear's picnic for him, with very tiny honey sandwiches."

"Oh yes! You have such good ideas, Beauty," said Rhona.

I beamed at her.

"I'm so glad you've cheered up, Beauty," said Mrs. Marshall. "Now, you girls must all go and get changed out of your suits. Your moms and dads will be here to get you any minute now."

I prayed hard inside my head as I struggled back into my frilly blouse and pleated skirt: *Please let Mom fetch me, don't let it be Dad!*

Wonderfully, it *was* Mom, looking shy and anxious, nibbling her lip, not really joining in any of the conversations with the other moms. Most of them didn't realize she *was* a mom.

I thanked Mr. and Mrs. Marshall for having me and then I thanked Rhona all over again for Reginald Redted.

"He's *our* Reggie now. He's a very lucky bear to have two mothers," said Rhona, and she gave me a big hug.

"This is a bear hug," I said, and we both laughed.

"Bye, Beauty," said Rhona.

"Bye, Ugly-Wugly," Skye called. She was collected by her Polish au pair.

"What did that girl call you?" Mom asked, as we got in the car.

"Oh, just silly stuff," I said quickly.

"Did she call you *Ugly*?" said Mom. "How dare she! I've a good mind to go back and slap her!"

"It's just her stupid nickname for me."

"Do they all call you that?"

"Rhona doesn't."

"So all the others do?" Mom sounded as if she was going to burst into tears.

I clutched Reginald Redted for courage. I tried to smile at Mom reassuringly.

"It's no big deal, Mom, honestly. We've all got

nicknames. One of the girls is called Poo-poo. It's just their idea of fun."

"Mmm," said Mom. "I still think Ugly is a *horrid* nickname. Can't they call you something else?"

"They do sometimes," I said, but I knew Weirdo, Wobblybum, Brainbox, and the new Corkscrew weren't necessarily any kinder than Ugly.

"I think you'll have to invent a *nice* nickname for yourself," said Mom. "Let me think."

She drove slowly, humming along to the music on the car radio.

"They used to call me Dilly Daydream at school. And your dad used to be called Cookie because of his surname. *Your* surname. Can't your new nickname be Cookie?"

I thought about it. I quite liked the name Cookie. It sounded funny and bouncy and happy. Not really like me.

"I can't just get them to start calling me Cookie," I said. "It doesn't really work like that, Mom. *They* decide what they're going to call me."

"Mmm," said Mom again. "Well, we'll find a way of *encouraging* them along the Cookie route."

She took one hand off the steering wheel and patted my shoulder sympathetically. She very gently tugged a lock of my damp hair. "That was a bit of a waste of fifty quid," she said.

"Will Dad be mad, do you think?" I asked.

"Maybe," said Mom, sighing.

Dad *was* mad. He usually came home jolly after golf but we knew as soon as we heard the door slam and the *thump thump* as he threw his shoes in the rack that he was furious. He stamped into the living room in his socks and poured himself a large whisky, barely looking at us.

"Oh dear," said Mom, in her sweetest trying-to-please voice. "Didn't you have a good game, darling?" She made a little shooing motion to me so I started sidling out of the room.

"I won both games, as a matter of fact," said Dad, glaring at her. "My golf swing is pretty lethal at the moment—and I was playing with a bunch of blithering idiots. I just don't *get* it. I've given them every incentive. It would be so *simple* for them to fix things for me, but they all blabber on about their hands being tied. It's so frustrating sucking up to the lot of them all day long and getting nowhere, absolutely blooming nowhere."

I dithered in the doorway.

"Is this the Water Meadows deal?" said Mom. "I thought you said it was all sewn up."

"Some cowardly nincompoop unstitched it all. He says there's no way they'll ever grant planning permission."

"Oh dear," said Mom.

94

"Oh dear! That's a bit of a limp reaction. Is that all you'll say when the guys I owe start clamoring for their money and I haven't got the wherewithal to pay them? Will you just say 'Oh dear' when the entire business goes down the toilet and we're out of this lovely house, sitting in the gutter looking stupid?"

I crept into the hall, biting my nails.

"Gerry, don't. You know you'll sort things out, you always do. Come on, put your feet up, relax a little. Shall I run you a hot bath?"

"You can get me a hot *meal*; I'm starving. Shove any old muck in the microwave, as if I care. I didn't pick you for your culinary skills, I picked you for your looks."

I hated the way Dad talked to Mom as if she was some silly doll.

"Hot meal coming right up, darling," said Mom.

She *sounded* like a doll too, as if someone had pulled a tab in her back to make her parrot a few silly phrases. I knew she was simply trying to sweet-talk him out of his mood but it still made me squirm.

It seemed to be working though.

"You're certainly looking good tonight, babe," Dad said. "Like the hair! It's perked up a treat. So what about Beauty? Let's see *her* new hairdo."

"Oh, Beauty's upstairs," Mom said loudly. "She got tired out at her party."

I scooted up the stairs two at a time but I was still wearing Mom's high heels. I tripped over, bumping my knees.

"Beauty?" said Dad, going to the door. "Hey, Beauty, I'm talking to you. Come downstairs into the light. Let's have a proper look at you."

I walked down the stairs, holding my breath.

"Good God, you're a right sight!" said Dad. "You look uglier than ever!"

I felt the tears pricking my eyes. I pressed my lips together, trying hard not to cry.

"Gerry, shut up," said Mom.

"Don't you dare tell me to shut up in my own house!" Dad said. "What in God's name have they done to the kid? Her head is covered with rat's tails."

He took hold of me and tugged my hair in disgust.

"Stop it! Don't you dare hurt her!" said Mom.

"I'm barely touching her. So did you actually pay good money—*my* good money—for this terrible hairdo, Dilly?"

"It was a silly idea to start with. Beauty's just a little girl, she doesn't need fancy hairdos. It didn't really suit her, all those curls. Then it was a swimming party, so of course she got wet."

"I thought you were just going to dog paddle, Beauty? What's the matter with you? Whatever made you dunk yourself head-first in the pool and ruin your hair? Don't you *want* to look pretty? Don't make that silly face, nibble nibble at your lip like a blessed rabbit. Stand up *straight*, don't hunch like that, sticking out your stomach!"

"Don't say another word to our lovely daughter! Beauty, go upstairs, darling," said Mom.

I ran upstairs to my bedroom. I put my hands over my ears so I couldn't hear them arguing about me. I saw myself in my Venetian glass mirror. I tried brushing my hair. It stuck limply to my head. I looked at my big face and my fat tummy and my ridiculous clothes. Dad was right. I did look a sight.

No wonder Skye and Arabella and Emily and all the other girls called me Ugly. It wasn't just a play on words because of my silly name. I really was ugly ugly ugly. It was like staring into one of those distorting mirrors at the fairground. My hair drooped, my face twisted like a gargoyle, and my body blew up like a balloon. My clothes shrank smaller so that my blouse barely buttoned and my skirt showed my underpants.

I seized my hairbrush and threw it at my reflection in the mirror. There was a terrible bang and I saw myself crack in two. I gaped in horror. I'd smashed the mirror, the ornate Venetian glass mirror Dad had bought especially for my bedroom. A long crack zig-zagged from the top to the bottom of the glass.

I shut my eyes tight, praying that it was all a mistake, an optical illusion because I was so upset. I opened my eyes a fraction, peering through my lashes. Everything was blurry—but I could still see the ugly crack right across the mirror.

I kicked the hairbrush across the room. Then I sagged onto the carpet, down on my knees. I clenched my fists. I was still holding Reginald Redted in my left hand. Why hadn't I hurled *him*? He'd have bounced off the glass and somersaulted to the floor, no harm done. I held on to him. He looked back at me quizzically.

"I am in *such* trouble," I whispered. "Dad always goes totally berserk if I break anything, even if it's a total accident. When he sees the mirror he'll realize I threw the brush on purpose."

I rocked backward and forward. I could hear the angry buzz of his voice downstairs. He was obviously still ranting about his ugly, freaky daughter.

"I hate him," I whispered. "I can't *help* being ugly. He's my *dad*, he's supposed to *like* the way I look. He's supposed to be kind and funny and gentle, just like Rhona's dad. Oh, I wish wish wish I could swap places with Rhona."

Reginald Redted tilted his head at me. He seemed to be nodding. It looked like he longed to be back with Rhona instead of stuck with me.

Eight

Dad went off to golf again early the next morning. The minute he slammed the front door Mom jumped out of bed and pattered along the landing.

"Beauty? Are you awake, sweetheart? Hey, can I come and have a cuddle with you this time?"

"No, Mom! Don't come in!" I said.

"What? Why not? What is it?" said Mom, opening my bedroom door. "Are you still sleepy? Do you want to snuggle down by yourself?"

"Yes. No. Oh, Mom!" I wailed.

Mom came right into my room and switched on the light. I looked desperately at the mirror, wondering if it could have magically mended itself during the night. The crack looked uglier than ever.

Mom's head jerked when she saw it, her hand going over her mouth.

"Oh, lordy! A broken mirror, seven years' bad luck! However did it happen?"

"Don't be mad, Mom!" I begged.

"Don't be nuts, when am I ever mad at you?" said Mom, coming over to my bed. She put her arms around me and hugged me tight. "What did you do? Did you knock against it somehow? Don't worry, I know it was an accident."

"No, it wasn't, Mom. I did it deliberately," I said, in a very small voice.

"Deliberately?" Mom echoed, astonished.

"I threw my hairbrush at it—at *me*, my reflection," I said.

"Oh dear," said Mom, and she started crying.

"I'm so sorry, Mom. I'll pay for it out of my allowance," I said. "Please don't cry."

"I'm crying because your dad was such a pig to you, making you so unhappy. He was talking stupid rubbish, sweetheart. You look *lovely*. When your hair's natural it's all soft and shiny, you've got beautiful eyes, rosy cheeks, gorgeous smooth skin. Don't you dare let him put you down, baby."

"He puts *you* down."

"Yes, I know. Well, I'm going to try and stand up to him more. I know he's really worried about his work but that doesn't mean he can just be hateful and take it out on us," said Mom. She looked at the mirror, running her finger down the long crack.

"Could we mend it somehow?" I asked.

"Don't be silly," said Mom.

"So what are we going to *do*?"

"Simple. We'll buy another one and we'll sneak this broken one out to the dump."

"But they cost hundreds of pounds, Mom, you know they do. I've got seven pounds left out of my allowance after buying Rhona's birthday present."

"*I'll* buy the new mirror, silly."

"But you haven't got any money, Mom."

Dad didn't want Mom to go out to work now, not even at Happy Homes. He said her job was to make *our* home a happy one. He didn't give her an allowance out of his money. She had to ask for everything. Dad didn't even let her have her own credit card.

Mom was nibbling at one of her nails, thinking about it.

"I'll sell some stuff," she said. "Some of my rings, or maybe a necklace."

"But that's not fair to you, Mom. It was me that broke the mirror. Shall I sell some of *my* jewelery?"

I had a gold chain with a tiny real diamond and a silver bangle and some turquoise beads and a small gold signet ring with my initial on.

"I don't think your jewelery would get much, Beauty. I've got tons of stuff. I've sold one or two pieces to that jeweler's near the market before when I've needed to."

"Oh, Mom." I knew she spent the money on me. Every so often Mom took me up to London on Saturdays to go to art galleries. We never told Dad. He hated art: He said all Old Master paintings were boring religious stuff and all modern art utter rubbish and a con. I'm not sure Mom really liked going around all the galleries either. She often yawned and rubbed her back, but she still tottered around gamely in her high heels. She bought me postcards of all my favorite paintings and I pasted them into scrapbooks so that I had my own mini-gallery to look at whenever I liked.

"If I get to be an artist when I'm grown up I'm going to treat you to so many different lovely things, Mom," I said.

"I think artists are supposed to starve in attics," said Mom. "Maybe we'll both be living on dry biscuits and water. Ah, that reminds me! Do you fancy doing some baking this morning?"

"Baking?" I stared at Mom.

"Yeah, why not?" she said. "I thought I'd try making cookies. Then you could maybe take them to school, to share them around?"

I suddenly saw where she was coming from. "So they'll start calling me Cookie?"

"We could try it, eh?"

"Oh, Mom, you are sweet. But . . ." I hesitated. "Do you know how to bake cookies?"

"Of course I do," said Mom. "Well. It can't be that difficult. Remember that time we made cakes together?"

I remembered. They weren't proper cakes, they were just made from a cake-mix packet, and even so we got them wrong, adding too many eggs because we thought it would make them taste nicer. We put them right at the top of the oven, hoping that would make them go golden. They didn't do this at all, they burned themselves black, though the insides were all sloppy and scrambled. We still iced them and I ate them all up, insisting they were delicious. Maybe this had been a mistake.

"Have you got a cookie packet mix, Mom?"

"I'm not sure they make them. We'll just have to do it all from scratch," said Mom.

We had breakfast first, spooning down our cornflakes. Then we rolled up our sleeves and got cracking on the cookies. Mom found an old bag of flour at the back of the cupboard. It had been there since I used flour-and-water paste when I was at nursery school. Mom cracked in an egg and stirred in some milk. Then she kneaded and I kneaded. We both got our great lumps of cookie dough and thumped them around on the table until they were lovely smooth balls.

"Hey, they look good!" I said. "How shall we roll them out?"

We didn't have a rolling pin so Mom improvised with a bottle of wine. We didn't have any cookie cutters either but Mom twisted the lid off a jar of jam and started cutting out rounds in her flattened dough.

"I'm going to make mine into people," I said, starting to mold my dough.

"What, like a gingerbread man?" said Mom.

"Sort of." I made a dough woman, carefully cutting a skirt for her, then putting little dough high heels on her pale legs. I broke off pieces of dough and rolled them long, and then with my fingers I twirled them around and around, creating long curls. I stuck them on the dough woman's head. I found a safety pin and fashioned features on her dough face: two big eyes, a little nose, a cupid's-bow mouth smiling at me. I smiled back as I laid her carefully on a baking tray.

I started on another dough person, small and square. I made a dough dress for her and gave her a fancy hairdo. Her eyes went squinty when I scratched them into place, her nose went blobby and her mouth turned down. I stared at her, sighing. Then I pulled all her dough ringlets right out and gave her a radical haircut, chopping it tomboy short. It didn't look so bad now. I peeled off her party dress and made her dough overalls. She looked much better. I rubbed at her mouth and she started smiling.

Mom peered over at the finished figure on the baking tray.

"Oh, Beauty, that's so good! Is that me?" She came and stood beside me. "And who's this? Is it a boy? No, it's *you* with short hair! You look so cute."

"I wish I did have short hair," I said. "Do you think Dad would mind terribly if I had it all cut off?"

Mom rolled her eyes. "Don't even think about it," she said.

I put my dough girl beside her mom. Then I got started on a dough man.

"Is that Dad?" said Mom.

I didn't answer. I made the body and then rolled the arms and the legs. I made pin marks on the dough shirt to show it was checked and gave his long legs comfy jeans. I spent ages carving his face with my pin to give it the right gentle expression. Of course it wasn't Dad.

I started on a new smaller person, very fat, with four little legs. I fashioned long loppy ears. Then I carefully picked her up and laid her on my man's checked chest. He wrapped his doughy arms around her, holding her close.

My tray was full now. I patted my special pastry people, feeling bad as I put them into the hot oven.

"I hope it doesn't hurt," I whispered foolishly. "I'll try hard not to let you burn."

Mom put her tray of plain round cookies above mine and we shut them in the oven.

"Tra la!" said Mom. "Welcome to the world, Cookie Girl."

"Well, hi there, Cookie Mom," I said.

Mom switched on the radio and we started dancing to the pop music in our pajamas. We didn't disco dance like Skye; this was happy, mad dancing, leaping around the room, drumming a beat on the table top, tapping out tunes with the spoons. We sank into our seats exhausted when the music stopped.

"I can smell the cookies!" I said, my nose twitching like Lily's. "Do you think they're ready yet?"

"We've only just put them in the oven, sweetheart. They'll be ages yet. Come on, let's go and get washed and dressed while we're waiting."

I washed and dressed in double quick time, not quite trusting Mom's judgment. I decided to have a little peek in the oven. I just opened the door a tiny crack so as not to let the heat out. I stared. Then I opened it wide, peering at the two trays.

"Mom!" I shouted. "Oh, Mom, something really awful's happened!"

Mom came rushing into the kitchen in her underwear.

"Have you burned yourself? Have you broken something? What *is* it, Beauty?"

"Look at the cookies!" I wailed.

Mom's neat cookies had expanded in every direction, joining up so that her baking tray contained one long flat misshapen biscuit. My lovely cookie people had expanded too. They were now great grotesque caricatures. Sam was this bloated blobby man, all head and huge stomach, and lovely Lily had blown up into a beach ball. Little Mom was a great giant. Even her careful curls were ruined. Now she looked as if she had snakes writhing right out of her head.

I was the worst, so squat I was completely square, my jeans inflated into vast overalls, my short haircut making me look like a man. Not any old man. I looked the spitting image of my dad.

I put on an oven glove and pulled the baking tray out of the oven. I picked up the me-cookie even though it was red hot and snapped off its stupid head.

"Hey hey, stop it, Beauty! Don't burn yourself. And stop spoiling them. They might look a bit weird but I bet they taste yummy," said Mom.

We waited until they'd cooled down a little and then nibbled. They *didn't* taste good at all. They were as flat and hard and boring as cardboard.

"Oh dear," said Mom. She took the oven glove

and pulverized her own cookie. "They're horrible, aren't they?"

"Yep."

"Your dad's right. I can't cook for the life of me," said Mom, drooping.

"Yes, you can," I said. I hesitated. "Well, maybe you could *learn*."

"I'm useless at learning stuff. I was always in the bottom of the class at school," said Mom. "Thick as a brick, that's me."

"No, you're not. You're . . . pretty and witty," I said.

"OK, OK, so you're . . . cute and astute," said Mom.

"Maybe we need a proper recipe book?" I said, scraping the cookie crumbs into the trash can. "I think we need to get all the ingredients right. Maybe this is the wrong sort of flour? And perhaps we've left out something important? What would make the cookies softer and sweeter?"

"Butter and sugar!" said Mom. "OK, I'll look for a recipe book tomorrow. Number two on my shopping list. Number one will be the new Venetian glass mirror."

I quivered.

"Sorry! Forget about it now. Shall we go and watch some TV? Don't they have a Sam and Lily marathon on Sunday mornings?"

Mom and I curled up at either end of the sofa. We tucked our feet up cosily. We were never allowed to do that when Dad was around because he said it marked the sofa cushions. Mom flipped through the Sunday papers while I spun around and around into Sam and Lily world in the Rabbit Hutch. I'd seen all five shows during the week and so I could whisper all the right words. At the end of all the repeats there was a special five minutes of Sam and Lily on Sunday.

"Hey there!" said Sam.

He was holding Lily. She twitched her nose at me, but she was more interested in something down on the ground. She struggled a little in Sam's arms, not quite sure of herself.

"Hey, Lily, it's OK. It's only a little black cat come to say hello. Let me introduce you."

Sam bent down so that Lily's face was on a level with the cat's. They regarded each other warily.

"Lily, meet Lucky. Lucky, meet Lily." Sam looked out of the television set at me. "And here's my very special friend, Beauty. Say meow to her, Lucky."

Lucky obediently gave a tiny mew, lifting and licking one small paw.

"Oh, Lucky, you're so *sweet*," I whispered.

Lily stared at me reproachfully.

"Not quite as sweet as Lily, of course," I said.

"Lucky's come to live in the house next door.

She's just popped in to meet her new neighbor," said Sam. "Are you going to come and say hello on a daily basis, Lucky?"

Lucky gave a demure nod.

"Well, that's just fine and dandy, because that means you'll cross our path and if a little black cat does that then we'll have a lucky day."

"I wish you lived next door to me, Lucky," I whispered. "I need all the luck in the world to counteract seven whole years' *bad* luck."

"Seven *years*?" said Sam. "That's all the way until you're practically grown up! Whatever have you done to inflict such a curse upon yourself?"

"I broke my mirror," I confessed.

"Oh, Beauty, is that *all*!" said Sam. "Don't worry, you won't really get seven years' bad luck. That's just an old wives' tale."

I glanced at Mom, who was deep in a fashion article.

"OK, a *young* wives' tale," said Sam. "But it's just silly superstition. I think we make our own luck, Beauty."

"Well, I'm not very good at it," I said, sighing. "I wish I could come and live in the Rabbit Hutch with you and Lily, Sam."

"We'd love that too," said Sam.

"Do you think we'll ever meet?"

Sam looked straight into my eyes. "Yes, we'll meet."

"Really? Actually face-to-face?"

"Absolutely. Face-to-face. Or ear to ear in Lily's case."

Lily made a little snorty noise as if she was laughing. Then Sam reminded everyone that he'd love to see a drawing or a painting of their pet, and said good-bye.

"Bye, Sam, bye, Lily," I said out loud.

"Bye, Sam and Lily," Mom said, turning her page.

The television voice said, "Who have we just seen?"

"Sam and Lily in the Rabbit Hutch!" Mom and I said simultaneously.

I stood up. "I think I'll go and do some drawing, Mom," I said.

I sat cross-legged on my bed upstairs with my drawing pad and colored pencils. I propped Reginald Redted up beside me, telling him I wanted to draw his portrait.

"You can be my pet and then I can send your picture off to Sam in the Rabbit Hutch," I said.

Reginald Redted looked down his snout at me. He seemed offended at the idea that he was *my* pet. He wouldn't pose properly, falling forward, flipping backward, even tumbling head over heels over the edge of the bed onto the carpet.

"OK, *don't* cooperate then. I won't draw you. I'll draw Nicholas Navybear instead," I said.

I divided my page into four squares. I drew myself looking at Nicholas on the tray at Rhona's party. I was smiling from ear to ear as I saw his little furry face. Then in the second square I drew my hands gently cradling Nicholas. He lounged against my fingers, using my thumbs as a footrest. He was smiling from ear to ear too.

I drew great splashes of water in the third picture, with poor Nicholas thrashing wildly through the waves, mouth wide open, screaming for help. Then I drew the poor drowned Nicholas lying in an open coffin, paws crossed on his chest, with wreaths of daisies and dandelion crosses arranged all around him.

It was hard getting all four pictures properly balanced. I had to rub out quite a lot but at last it seemed OK. I colored it in very carefully, not going over a single line and keeping my pencil strokes as smooth as I could.

Mom came up to see how I was getting on and acted like I was an artistic genius.

"You have to send it in to Sam, Beauty," she said.

"No, Mom, I'm too old—and my picture's too weird," I said, closing my drawing book.

"You're *so* artistic, Beauty." Mom hesitated. "Shall we show it to Dad when he comes in?"

"No!"

"He'd be ever so proud."

"No, he wouldn't. He'd go off on a rant." I puffed myself up and put on a deep Dad voice. "Why don't you do a proper drawing of a teddy bear rather than this damn dumb cartoon rubbish."

Mom burst out laughing. "Oh, stop it! Yes, that's *exactly* what he'd say. OK, we won't show him."

Nine

I wanted to keep out of Dad's way when he came home from golf but he started bellowing for me the moment he got in the front door. I didn't dare hide in my room. I didn't want him thudding up the stairs and bursting into my bedroom. If he saw my broken mirror he'd explode.

I went downstairs, ducking my head, fiddling with my hair, so scared of what Dad might say to me this time. But he was in one of his determinedly jolly moods.

"Hello hello hello, here's my lovely little Beauty!" he boomed. His face was very red and he smelled of alcohol. "Who's my pretty girl, eh? You look lovely, darling."

I felt my face going red too. He was trying to make up for yesterday. It didn't make me feel better, it just made me go all squirmy inside. Dad patted the top of my head and then tapped me under the chin.

"My little girl," he repeated.

"I'm not that little, Dad," I said.

"I know, I know, you're growing up fast. Your birthday's just around the corner."

I held my breath. Mom came out into the hall.

"I've fixed it all up," said Dad, and he planted a wet kiss on my cheek.

"Fixed what, Gerry?" said Mom. She'd seen the expression on my face.

"Beauty's party, Silly Dilly!"

"Are you sure about this, Gerry?" said Mom. "Think of all those children running riot, sticky hands all over the furniture—"

"We're not going to have a party *here*. We're going to go out," said Dad. "I've been talking to a couple of guys at golf. One of them is part of some theatrical management company. He reckons he can get a whole block of front-row seats for that *Birthday Bonanza* musical. Isn't that great? It's solidly booked up for the next six months. It's always a matter of who you know, eh? And to make the day *extra*-special I've done a deal with another guy who has his own fleet of limos. You can ask all your friends, Beauty, and we'll fit them into a super-stretch white limo, how about that?"

I opened my mouth but no sound came out.

"Look at her, she's speechless!" Dad chortled. "There, trust your old dad to get you the best. Gerry the Fixer, that's me!" He turned to Mom. "I'll fix the Water Meadows deal too, just you wait and see."

"I know you will," Mom said mechanically. "So, Gerry, what about Beauty's birthday tea?"

"I've thought of that. They'll have a birthday buffet when they get here. None of that cheese cubes on sticks and jelly and trifle rubbish. This is going to be a real sophisticated buffet with canapés." He ticked each one off on his fingers. "Little tartlets and tiny vol au vents, chicken satay, sausages in honey sauce, crispy prawns, the works—and then instead of a birthday cake we're going to have a profiterole tower." He smiled at me. "Don't look so stunned, baby. You'll love it. Profiteroles are them little chocolate creamy balls—they taste just like éclairs."

"But, Gerry, who's going to make all this stuff?" said Mom.

"You are, of course," said Dad, and then he roared with laughter, redder than ever, wheezing and spluttering. "Your face, Dilly! Dear lord, you're practically wetting your pants. Calm down, darling, I'm only kidding you. We're going to get caterers in. They come along and lay it all out, even provide the fancy plates, and then they serve it all too. Won't that be grand, Beauty? Fancy having a proper waiter and waitress serving all your little friends, treating you all like grown-up ladies. Won't they be impressed!"

I felt faint. I could just imagine what Skye and Emily and Arabella would say.

"It's ever so kind of you, Dad, but won't it all cost an awful lot of money? You said we'd maybe be poor if your Water Meadows deal doesn't go through," I stammered.

"It will go through, one way or another. Just you leave it to your old dad. Who am I? Gerry the . . . ?" He put his hand to his ear, waiting for me to say it.

"Fixer," I whispered.

"That's right, little Beauty. There! I bet there's not another girl in your whole school who will have such a special birthday treat. Aren't you a lucky girl?"

"Yes, I'm very lucky," I said.

I made myself smile and bounce about though inside I was dying. I didn't *want* a party. I didn't want a posh buffet with profiteroles instead of a birthday cake. I didn't want a fancy stretch limo and front-row seats at *Birthday Bonanza*. I especially didn't want all my class at school to come to my party.

I took a deep breath.

"Dad, it all sounds as if it's going to be wonderful but I think I'd like it just as much—maybe even more—if I just had *one* friend, say, and you and me and Mom."

I thought of Rhona and me partying together. We could feast on our buffet and then go off to the show in a posh limo, playing we were celebrities. It would be such fun, just Rhona and me . . .

"Don't be silly, Beauty," said Dad. He was still smiling but there was an edge to his voice. "We don't want people to think you haven't got any proper friends."

"But I *haven't*, Dad, not really," I mumbled.

"I saw you just the other day with two lovely little girls—hanging on your arms, they were. And then there's that other gorgeous kid, the one with all the hair and the big blue eyes."

Skye.

"But Dad—"

"Stop all this butting! You're not a little goat! How many girls are in your class?"

"Nineteen."

"Well, you'd better get busy, little Beauty. You need to write out eighteen invitations. You can do it on my laptop or maybe hand-print them yourself, seeing as you're artistic."

I hand-printed the first one. I used special purple card and my silver italic pen. I didn't address it to Skye or Emily or Arabella. I didn't even address it to Rhona.

I wrote:

Dear Sam and Lily,
Please come to my birthday party next Saturday.
There will be a big buffet for you, Sam, and I'll
make special lettuce sandwiches and carrot cake
for you, Lily.
Love from Beauty xx

I drew a border of little silver rabbits chasing each other all around the edge of the card, and then I put it in a purple envelope and shook little silver hearts inside.

I didn't mail it. I put it in the folder where I kept all my Sam and Lily drawings. Then I sighed deeply and started on the real invitations. Eighteen of them. I used ordinary white cards and envelopes and a blue pen. I drew a birthday cake on each one, even though I wasn't going to have one. I saved Rhona's card till last. I used a red card for her and a gold pen. I drew four little teddy bears in each corner. I added, *Reginald Redted is of course invited. He can feast on his very own pot of honey.*

Then I thought of everyone opening their invitations at school. They would see that Rhona's was more elaborate. If they looked at what I'd written they'd laugh at me and think I was weird. I sighed again and wrote a new invitation for Rhona on a white card with a birthday cake, identical to all the others.

I gave her the invitation first, when I got to school on Monday morning. I made Reginald Redted hold it.

"He's had a good weekend but he wants to live back with you now," I said.

"Is he giving me a letter?" said Rhona, laughing.

"It's an invitation to my party," I said shyly.

"Oh, how lovely!" said Rhona, opening up the card.

"What's that you've got, Rhona?" said Skye, running over to her.

"Beauty's asked me to her birthday party," said Rhona.

"Oh, *gross*. Ugly's having a party. Well, that will be total freaky funtime," said Skye. "So who else have you invited to your party, Ugly? You've got a whole *wad* of invitations there. Just as well, because I bet very few girls will want to go to *your* party."

"I want to go," said Rhona, as I handed out invitations. "What sort of birthday cake will you be having, Beauty?"

"I'm not having a proper birthday cake," I said apologetically. "I'm having a profiterole tower."

"Oh wow!" said Rhona. "I've seen those cakes in a special shop in London. Are you *really* having one?"

"Yes. But you can't put candles on them."

123

"Who needs boring old candles?" said Rhona.

I wanted candles so I could blow them all out in one go and have a proper birthday wish. But my wishes didn't ever come true, so maybe I didn't need candles after all.

"What else are you having to eat at your party apart from this proffy thingy," asked Poppy. "My mom says I can have proper pizzas when I have my party, with all different toppings."

"I don't think there'll be pizzas," I said. "It's going to be like a buffet. Finger food. Canapés. Little tarts and sausages and stuff."

"Canapés!" said Rhona. "How *cool*, just like a real grown-up party."

"It sounds totally weird if you ask me," said Skye. "Are you going to have dancing at your party, Ugly, as you're such a good dancer—*not*."

"No, we're not having any dancing, Skye," I said.

Skye rolled her eyes. "So what kind of a dull party is it going to be? Are you all going to sit cross-legged and do spelling tests for fun?"

"We're going to the theater to see *Birthday Bonanza*," I said.

"Oh wow wow wow!" Rhona shrieked. "That group McTavish are in that—and Will Forman. They are *so* cool. I've been dying to see that show for *ages* but my dad can't get tickets."

"Well, my dad can," I said, suddenly proud.

"So who's going to *Birthday Bonanza*?" said Skye, narrowing her eyes. "Just you and Rhona?"

"Dad's got tickets for everyone," I said.

There was a great whoop from all the girls standing around.

"Am *I* going?"

"Are we really *all* going?"

"Are we sitting near to the stage so we can see McTavish and Will really close up?"

"Dream on," said Skye. "They'll be those rubbish seats right at the back where you can't see a sausage."

"We've got front-row stalls seats," I said. "My dad's fixed it."

"So how is everyone going to get there?" Skye said. "I suppose your famous fixer dad has hired a *coach*?"

"No, he's hiring a super-stretch limo," I said, with a little nod of my head.

Everyone squealed and clapped their hands, even Arabella and Emily. Skye stood there, arms folded, chin jutting.

"So, is *everyone* invited?" she said.

I still had her invitation in my hand. I so wanted to tear it into tiny pieces and say "Everyone but *you*, Skye."

She was staring at me, her blue eyes suddenly

anxious. I hated her, but I still couldn't do it to her.

"Of course everyone's invited, Skye. Even you," I said, and I pressed her invitation into her hand.

She didn't even thank me. She simply glanced at hers and then said in an off-hand manner, "I'm not sure I can make it that Saturday anyway." But we both knew wild horses wouldn't stop her coming.

She was still horrid to me all day long. In a way I respected her for that. Emily and Arabella still called me Ugly but they smiled at me in a new silly way and Arabella offered me some of her chips at playtime. Louise and Poppy started up a *Did-I-like-bears?* birthday-present conversation and some of the girls who hadn't said a single word to me since I joined the class last year started chatting away as if I was their new best friend.

It felt so weird. Dad really was Gerry the Fixer. I'd longed for them to like me and now it looked as if they did. But it wasn't *real*. They hadn't really changed their minds about me, they just wanted to keep in with me so they could come to my party. I smiled and chatted back to all of them but inside I despised them.

I didn't despise Rhona, of course. She'd been kind to me all along—and she was lovely now.

"You're so *lucky*, Beauty! Imagine your dad fixing all that for your birthday!"

"Yes, Dad's like that," I said.

"Can I sit next to you in the super-stretch limo, Beauty?" Rhona asked.

"Of course. And will you sit next to me in the theater?"

"You bet." She hesitated. "I suppose I'll have to have Skye on my other side, seeing as she's my best friend."

I took a deep breath.

"Is she *always* going to be your best friend, Rhona?"

Rhona shrugged awkwardly.

"Well, we've been best friends since that first day of preschool and we live on the same street so we *can't* really break friends. I hate it when she's mean to you. I've begged her to stop but she won't. You know what she's like." Rhona edged closer to me and whispered in my ear. "I wish *we* could be best friends, Beauty."

Ten

When I went to meet Mom after school lots of girls called good-bye to me. They said it nicely enough, but they still called me Ugly.

"I can't *stand* them calling you that," Mom muttered. "You wait, we'll get them calling you Cookie."

She looked unusually red and shiny, with her hair scraped back into a quick ponytail. She had white smudges all down her shirt.

"Have you been baking more cookies, Mom?"

"Wait and see," she said, grinning.

The whole house smelled like a baker's shop, though there was an underlying burning smell too. We went into the kitchen. I stared, open-mouthed. There were cookies everywhere, on big plates and little plates and three different baking trays. They covered the kitchen counter and spiralled around and around the table. Some were burned nearly black. Some were pale gray and sludgy. Some were great overblown monster cookies. Some were oval, some were square, some had no determinate shape at all. But the cookies on our best big green-leaf china plate looked perfect: round and smooth and golden.

"Take one," said Mom, proudly proffering the plate.

I picked one up and held it to my face. It smelled delicious.

"Have a bite, go on!" said Mom.

I nibbled. "Oh, Mom, it tastes so good!" I said, munching.

"They're OK, aren't they?" said Mom, whirling about the crazy kitchen. "I've been making them all day long. I found this old American recipe book for twenty-five pence in the Oxfam shop. It's got *lots* of cookie recipes, but I thought I'd stick to the very basic one to start with—and it's worked, hasn't it! I've actually made proper cookies. Eventually. I had to do three batches before they came right."

"You're the total Cookie Queen," I said, savoring each mouthful. "Can I have another one?"

"Of course you can! I'll have another too—and then we'll have to get going clearing up all this mess. Your dad will go nuts if he sees the kitchen like this."

I went upstairs to take off my blazer and dump my school bag—and then I stared at my Venetian glass mirror. It was glittering and gorgeous, the glass shining. No crack!

"Mom! You've got me a new mirror!" I shrieked.

"Yes, it's been a very hectic day," said Mom. "I sold that diamond collar thingy your dad gave me for our first anniversary. I only ever wear it for posh dances and I hardly ever go to them now. I didn't really like it anyway. I didn't like it being a *collar*, like I'm a little dog. Anyway, I got lots of money for it, enough for a roomful of mirrors, only try hard not to break this one, eh, darling?"

"You are just the best mom ever," I said.

I helped her get the kitchen spic-and-span. We threw away all the experimental cookies, but kept the plate of perfect ones.

Dad got home from work early. He started up his Happy Homes routine the moment he got in the front door:

"Happy *Homes,* Happy *Homes*
Where everybody smiles
And nobody moans.
There's a mommy—"

He burst into the kitchen and pointed at Mom. Then he got distracted. He sniffed.

"What's that *smell*?" he said.

"I've just been doing a little baking," said Mom.

"A little *burning*, more like," said Dad, laughing at her.

"I've made cookies," said Mom.

"You're the kookie one, you silly little Dilly, you know you're hopeless in the kitchen," said Dad.

"Mom's made lovely cookies, Dad. Try one," I said, offering him a plate.

"I don't really like home-madey stuff," said Dad, wrinkling his nose. "What sort of cookies are these anyway? I can't see any chocolate chips or sultanas."

"They're plain," said Mom.

"Plain but perfect," I said. "Do eat one, Dad. They're utterly delicious."

He picked one off the plate, mimed taking a bite, smacking his lips together, the way you pretend to a baby.

"Yum yum yum," he said, and he put the cookie back.

"Oh well, Mom, all the more for us," I mumbled.

"What's that?" said Dad. "Are you being cheeky, Beauty?"

"Oh, Gerry, she's just being sweet, that's all," said Mom. "How are things at work? What's happening with the Water Meadows situation?"

Dad's face cheered.

"Well, we seem to be making progress at *last*. One of the guys at the council, one of my golfing buddies, got back in touch and I feel we *might* be able to get planning permission after all. I just need to put a few things in place and we're *there*. Gerry the Fixer, eh?" He looked at me. "So, little

Beauty, what did your little pals say about your birthday celebration? I bet they're thrilled, eh?"

"Yes, they are. Ever so," I said.

"And how about my birthday girl? You're thrilled too, aren't you?"

Mom looked at me.

"Yes, Dad. Ever so, ever so, ever so," I said. I whirled around and jumped up and down in a little pantomime of excitement.

"That's my girl," said Dad. "I spoil you rotten, don't I? I've got a little idea up my sleeve for your birthday present too. You're going to be *so* surprised, totally bowled over."

My tummy churned, wondering what Dad had in store for me.

"What's Dad giving me?" I asked Mom later, when she was kissing me good night.

"I don't know. I've asked and asked, but he just taps the side of his nose and won't tell. I've suggested we get you a new outfit for your birthday. I know just how much you hate that pink dress."

"Oh, Mom, he won't choose it for me again, will he?"

"I said he'd maybe get the size wrong and I'd need to supervise as dresses are girly things—but he didn't seem to take any notice," said Mom, sighing.

I curled up with PJ, hugging her tight. It took me a long time to get to sleep.

Skye wasn't at school the next morning. Rhona said she had a dental appointment and wouldn't be back until the afternoon. Rhona played with *me* at lunch time. She gave me half her chips from her packed lunch and I gave her half my chocolate from mine. I gave her half my tangerine too and she shared her apple. We took careful alternate bites until we got down to the core.

Then we went and sat on the wall together. Rhona found a piece of string and showed me how to play cat's cradle. It was so special. I hoped Skye would stay at the dentist getting every single tooth filled and filled for ever.

"I don't know what to get you for your birthday present, Beauty," Rhona said. "You gave me lovely presents. I especially like my T-shirt. And I wear my bangles all the time. I love the way they *clink clink clink*."

"Have you started *A Little Princess* yet?"

"Well, I'm not really a great reader, not like you. I looked at the first chapter but it seems a bit . . . old-fashioned."

"It's a truly lovely story when you get into it," I said earnestly. "Maybe I could read you a bit?"

"Maybe," said Rhona. "*Anyway*, what can I get *you*? Do you want some books? You'll have to tell me the titles because I don't know all these weird old classics. I know what I *really* wanted to get you—another little teddy like Reginald Redted and poor Nicholas Navybear. I told Mom and she went looking for one yesterday, but the shop hasn't got any more."

"It was ever so nice of you to think of it though," I said, giving her arm a little squeeze. She squeezed me back and we smiled at each other.

"Isn't there anything else you really, really want for your birthday?" said Rhona. "I know you like books but they are a bit boring."

"No they're not!"

"Is that what your mom and dad are getting you too?"

"I don't know what I'm getting," I said gloomily. I felt so close to Rhona I wondered if I dared confide in her. "My dad's a bit . . . funny."

"So's mine," said Rhona, not understanding. "I was so embarrassed when he told all those silly jokes at my party."

"No, I mean my dad likes to be the boss. He likes to decide stuff, like what he's giving me for my birthday present. He went bananas when I asked him for a rabbit."

"A *rabbit*?" said Rhona. "I used to have a rabbit. A little gray one with blue eyes. He was so sweet."

"A *real* rabbit? Oh, you lucky thing. What did you call him?"

"Bunny."

"Oh, Rhona, didn't he have a proper name?"

"He *liked* being called Bunny. Mom let me have him in the house sometimes, though I had to promise to clean up after him if he did a poo. You're supposed to be able to house-train rabbits but Bunny did *lots* of poos."

"So what happened to him?"

"Oh, he died last winter. It was so sad. Mom and Dad said I could have another rabbit but I didn't want a new one, I just wanted Bunny back. I cried and cried whenever I saw a picture of a rabbit. I even cried when I watched some goofy baby show on television about a rabbit."

"*Rabbit Hutch*?" I said casually, though my heart was beating fast.

"That's the one. There's this big white rabbit with funny droopy ears."

"That's Lily."

Rhona grinned. "Yeah! And then there's this smiley man—"

"Sam."

"Do *you* watch *Rabbit Hutch*?" asked Rhona.

"Occasionally," I said.

Rhona giggled. "We're a pair of babies, aren't we?"

"Rhona! Rhona!"

It was Skye, running up the playground toward us.

"Don't tell Skye," I said quickly.

"As if!" said Rhona.

Then she jumped down off the wall and left me.

When I got home after school I switched on the television straight away.

"Who do we want to see?" said the voice.

"Sam and Lily in the Rabbit Hutch!"

"Hey there!" said Sam, and Lily twitched her nose to say hello too.

"Lily's got a little friend who's come to tea," said Sam. He squatted down and pointed to a little fat furry black-and-tan creature.

"It's Oliver the guinea pig. Hello, Oliver, how lovely to see you. Say hello to Oliver, Lily!"

Sam tried to put Lily down on the ground beside Oliver but she scrabbled her paws, trying to cling on. Sam smiled and stroked her. "Lily's a bit shy," he whispered to me.

"I know what she feels like. I feel ever so shy sometimes," I whispered back.

"There now, Lily," said Sam, easing her gently until she was nose to nose with Oliver. "It's dear old Oliver, Lily—you like him. He's your special friend. That's right, twitch your noses at each other. Shall we twitch noses too?"

Sam twitched his nose, looking wonderfully silly. I twitched mine back, giggling.

"Do *you* have a special friend?" Sam asked.

This was my opportunity.

"Yes I do! It's Rhona! You might know her, she watches *Rabbit Hutch* too."

"Oh, that's good," said Sam, nodding.

"She's *my* special friend but I'm not sure she'd say I was *her* special friend. Her absolute best friend is this girl called Skye. She is a truly *revolting* person. Why on earth Rhona stays friends with her I simply can't understand. But I think Rhona might like me second best. She sat with me at lunch time and it was *so* lovely and we chatted about all sorts of stuff and that's when she said she sometimes watches you too."

I babbled on to Sam while he nodded and played with Lily and Oliver. He had to interrupt every now and then to talk to all the other children but I didn't mind. I knew he was still listening to every word I was saying. I wasn't through when he said good-bye. I went to talk to Mom instead.

There was a wonderful warm baking smell in the kitchen. Mom smiled at me, flour sprinkled down her front like fairy dust.

"More cookies?" I said.

"I'm having another go. I'm making oatmeal-and-raisin cookies this time. I already made two batches this morning but they didn't come out quite right. The first lot looked weird, though they didn't taste too bad. The second lot looked fine but they weren't quite *munchy* enough." Mom patted her tiny waist ruefully. "I'm going to put on pounds and pounds doing all this baking. I went to the gym at lunch time but if I keep on stuffing cookies I'll need to go to the gym twice a day. And I *hate* that blooming gym, it's so boring."

"Maybe you could have your own personal trainer, Mom? That might make it more fun."

"I'll say," said Mom. "A young hunky guy putting me through my paces, eh? I wonder what your dad would have to say about that! You know what he's like."

I knew all too well. "Doesn't he trust you, Mom?"

Mom shrugged. "I don't know. He just doesn't want me getting close to anyone else but him. He'd go bananas if I got friendly with any man even if it was entirely innocent. He doesn't really like me having women friends either."

"Did you have lots of friends when you were at school, Mom?"

"Not really."

"Did you have a best friend?"

Mom nibbled her lip. "No, they didn't really like me much, the girls in my class."

"But you must have been the prettiest one!"

Mom shrugged. "They all teased me because I was a bit slow and dreamy. I was hopeless, I just let them walk all over me. I've never been able to stand up for myself."

She opened the oven door and had a peek at the cookies.

"Hey, I think they're done. They look pretty good, don't they?"

She took the baking tray out of the oven and showed me twenty-four raisin-and-oatmeal cookies, pale gold and perfect.

I reached out eagerly.

"Hey hey, let them cool down a bit, you'll burn your mouth."

"OK, but they smell so delicious! I can't wait!"

"We'll give all your friends cookies on your birthday and that'll be your new nickname, little Cookie Cookson."

Mom picked up an oatmeal-and-raisin cookie and popped it into my mouth. I chewed appreciatively. They were softer than the plain cookies, much chewier, with a spicy, nutty tang.

"Well done, Mom!" I said through my mouthful. "They're really, really gorgeous. How did you do it?"

"Just call me the Cookie Fairy," said Mom. "I wave my magic wand"—she mimed it—"and hey presto, cookie heaven. No, actually it's this recipe book. It told me to use cinnamon and cloves and chopped nuts as well as the oatmeal and the raisins, and then there's eggs and brown sugar and all sorts of stuff. You sift and sprinkle and stir like crazy. I think I'm getting the knack of it, Beauty!"

"You are, you are."

"Funny if I turn out to be a good cook after all these years of being so terrible at it," Mom said, nibbling one of her own cookies appreciatively.

"Maybe Dad doesn't need these fancy buffet people. Maybe you could do it all, Mom?"

"Maybe *not*," said Mom, laughing. "I think I'd better stick to cookies."

Eleven

"Surprise!" Dad shouted, bursting into my bedroom on Saturday morning.

I opened my eyes and screamed. An enormous shocking-pink hairy monster loomed above me, its horrible bug-eyed buck-tooth face inches from my own.

"Happy birthday to you,
Happy birthday to you,
Happy birthday, dear Beauty,
Happy birthday to yooooooou!" Dad sang.

Every time he said the word *birthday* he made the monster nuzzle my face grotesquely.

"Careful, Gerry darling, you'll smother her," said Mom.

"She's fine, she's fine! She's just having a happy romp with her birthday rabbit," said Dad. "Do you like him, Beauty? You said you wanted a rabbit, didn't you! I bet you never thought you'd get one this size. I had to get a taxi all the way home. I couldn't possibly struggle on a subway with him in my arms. Isn't he the loveliest bunny you've ever seen, Beauty? Why don't you give him a big hug? What's up with you?"

"She's still half asleep, Gerry. Give her a chance!" said Mom. She wriggled around the dreadful giant rabbit and gave me a kiss. "Happy birthday, darling."

I hugged her close. Then I sat up properly and hugged Dad. And then I took a deep breath and wrapped my arms around the rabbit. Its fur was coarse and tickly and it had an overpowering smell of wool and carpet.

"Don't you just love your birthday bunny?" said Dad.

I hated hated hated the monster rabbit but I pretended to be thrilled with him.

"So what are you going to call him, eh?" Dad demanded.

I didn't want to personalize the rabbit with a proper name.

"He's called . . . Pinky," I said.

"Pinky!" said Dad. "All right, so be it."

He lumbered around the room with Pinky, singing:

"My name's Pinky,
I'm not dinky,
I'll give you a winky
'Cos my eyes are blinky!"

Dad gave the rabbit a vigorous shake. His eyes revolved alarmingly.

"Come and join in the dance, Beauty!" said Dad.

144

I had to get up and caper in a circle with my crazy dad and the worst toy rabbit in the world.

"I *told* you she'd love the rabbit," Dad said to Mom.

"Yes, of course she loves it, Gerry. Now, Beauty, you'd better whiz along to the bathroom and then you can open the rest of your presents at breakfast."

"Special birthday breakfast! Scrambled eggs and smoked salmon. I'd better go and do it. Your mother still can't scramble an egg to save her life. Can't even *boil* a blooming egg for that matter, can you, Silly Dilly?"

"Mom *can* cook. She makes wonderful cookies," I mumbled, but Mom put her finger to her lips, shushing me.

Dad marched downstairs. The pink rabbit lounged on my bed, giant limbs sprawled, paws clenched like boxing gloves. Mom and I stared at it. Then I suddenly spluttered. Mom giggled too. We became helpless with laughter, our hands clamped over our mouths in case Dad heard us.

"Oh, Beauty, I'm sorry," Mom whispered. "I couldn't *believe* it when I saw it. You hate it, don't you?"

"Yes!"

"It completely fills up your bedroom. Dear God, it's going to give you nightmares."

"Maybe I can stuff it in my closet every night?"

I tried lifting it but I could barely drag it off the bed.

"Watch those massive arms! We don't want to break another mirror!" Mom hissed.

"It so spoils my bedroom," I said despairingly, suddenly near tears.

"Yes, I know. Maybe we'll sit him in a corner and drape a huge wrap over him when your dad's not around. But cheer up, there's a trade-off! As your dad bought you the pink rabbit I begged him to let me buy your birthday outfit as *my* present to you. He was fed up with shopping by this time, so he said OK. He even gave me a hundred bucks toward it. You go and get washed and it'll be waiting in your closet when you get back."

"Is it pink or frilly?" I asked anxiously.

"Not a single frill and it's not pink, OK?" said Mom. "Scoot."

I scooted—and when I got back I saw my new outfit hanging outside my closet. The dress was pearly-grey with long sleeves and a full skirt with a white broderie anglaise pinafore over the top. There were grey silky tights and amazing gray laced boots with little heels.

"I know you'd much sooner wear a T-shirt and jeans but your dad would never allow it, especially when he's turned your birthday into such a big do. He said you had to wear a proper party frock.

I was going bananas trying to find something you'd like. Then I saw this. I know it's very old-fashioned but I thought you wouldn't mind. It's like something Sara would wear in *A Little Princess*."

"Oh, Mom," I said, stroking the soft dress. "It's beautiful—but will I look funny in it? Will it fit me? I'm getting *sooo* fat."

"No, you're not, sweetheart. I think it'll look great. Try it on and see."

Mom had bought me new underwear too, white pants with lace and a wonderful whirly petticoat a bit like a ballet dress.

"Maybe I'll just wear this as a party dress," I said, doing wobbly arabesques all around my bedroom.

"Come and put your dress on, Sugar Plum Fairy," said Mom, unbuttoning it for me.

She acted like a Victorian maid, buttoning me into my dress, tying the sash of the pinafore and kneeling in front of me lacing my boots.

"There!" she said. "Look at yourself in the mirror!"

I went and stood in front of the Venetian glass. I looked so different. I really looked like a girl in a Victorian story book. I still didn't look *pretty*—but I didn't look hideously ugly either.

"Oh, Mom!" I said, my eyes shining.

"Oh, Beauty!" said Mom. "You look lovely, sweetheart. Maybe I ought to get a job as a stylist!"

Dad shouted impatiently from downstairs. "What are you two up to? The eggs are scrambling into sawdust!" he yelled.

"We're dressing Beauty in her finery. Come to the bottom of the stairs, Gerry," Mom called.

She took me by the hand and then led me downstairs. I walked down cautiously in my heeled boots, my petticoat and skirt swishing around my calves, making a lovely rustling sound.

Dad was frowning at first, still fussing about the eggs. Then he saw me—and he looked taken aback.

"Oh goodness! It's not really a *party* dress, is it? Still, you don't look bad in it, Beauty. The color's a bit insipid, mind you. A nice bright pink might have been prettier. And I'm not sure about the apron. It's certainly unusual. What do you think, Beauty?"

"I absolutely love it!" I said, twirling round.

I ended up changing out of my beautiful gray dress and pinafore to eat my breakfast just in case I spilled scrambled eggs all down me. I sat in my new petticoat and my Tracy Beaker dressing gown opening up my birthday presents. Dad's parents were dead, but Nana, my mom's mom, sent me pink nylon baby-doll pajamas about a hundred sizes too small.

"How lovely—*not*," said Mom. She bent close to my ear. "I wonder if they'd fit your new rabbit?"

We had a private snicker. There was a present from Auntie Avril, the first Mrs. Cookson. She always liked Mom because she thought she'd taken Dad away from the *second* Mrs. Cookson, Auntie Alysha. Auntie Avril *hated* Auntie Alysha. They couldn't even be in the same room together without starting a screaming match, but Auntie Avril and Mom were quite friendly.

Auntie Avril sent very good birthday presents. This time she'd given me a large tin of fifty markers, special Swiss ones with fine points, all the colors of the rainbow. Dad frowned when he saw them.

"You watch what you're doing with them crayons," he said, but mercifully he didn't confiscate them.

The present that made me smile the most was one wrapped in blue paper with a white rabbit pattern. The label was carefully printed TO BEAUTY, LOVE FROM SAM AND LILY.

"Oh my goodness!" said Mom. "Fancy Sam and Lily knowing it's your birthday!"

"Who on earth are Sam and Lily?" said Dad.

"They're special friends of Beauty's," said Mom.

Mom was my special friend. I knew her writing, even though she'd tried to disguise it. I ripped off the paper—and there was a DVD compilation of all the best *Rabbit Hutch* shows.

"Oh how *lovely*," I said.

"Looks very babyish to me," said Dad, glancing at it. He stood up, patting me on the head. "Glad your birthday's got off to a good start, Beauty. What's your favorite present, eh?"

I didn't have any choice.

"The toy rabbit," I said.

Dad chuckled triumphantly, rolling his eyes. He looked alarmingly like the rabbit himself.

"Now, girls, I've just got to dash to the office to meet up with this guy who's going to sort everything out for me."

"But it's Beauty's birthday, Gerry! The children are coming at twelve!"

"Don't worry, don't worry, I'll be back long before then, fusspot. You two girls get the living room in spit-spot shape. The caterers are arriving at eleven. OK, my darlings. Ready to show off our Happy Home?"

Dad went off whistling his silly song. Mom and I rushed around dusting and vacuuming. The house already seemed spotless but Dad winced at the tiniest scuff or smear. When it was all utterly perfect Mom sent me off to sit on her bed and watch Sam and Lily on her DVD player.

"While you're watching could you bear to write

150

some labels for me?" said Mom. "You did such a lovely job of the party invitations. It would be great if you'd write this out for me, eighteen times over."

She put the message in front of me, scribbled on her shopping-list pad:

Hears a little gift!
Cookies from Beauty Cookson!

"Is that OK?" she asked anxiously.

I wasn't going to tell her but she saw my eyes flicker. "What is it? Have I got it wrong?"

"I think 'here's' is maybe spelled differently, Mom," I said gently.

"Oh lordy! Good thing you're my little brainbox. Spell it properly for me then, sweetie, while I go and sort out all the cookies."

I wrote out the eighteen labels with Auntie Avril's markers while Sam and Lily chatted to me. They kept getting distracted from each little show to wish me a happy birthday. Sam even sang the birthday song for me, making Lily's ears sway in time to the music.

"Are you having a lovely birthday, Beauty?" Sam asked.

"I *think* so," I said. "I'm scared it'll all go wrong when all the girls come. You know how they all tease me. It would be OK if Skye and Arabella and

Emily weren't coming. Do you think they'll laugh at my new party dress? It's not a bit like the sort of stuff they wear."

"It's much, much nicer," said Sam. "We think you look stunning in your dress and pinafore and special boots. Your mom's chosen a wonderful outfit for you. We're not so sure about your dad's present though. You're a bit frightened of that great big pink rabbit, aren't you, Lily?"

Lily snuffled, nodding her head.

"*I* was frightened just at first," I said. "It's hideous, isn't it?"

We had a private chuckle together and then Sam and Lily went through the routine for their ten shows, pottering in the garden, clearing out the rabbit hutch, coping with a cold, smelling the spring flowers, getting wet in the rain. I especially loved that episode because Sam made Lily her own little sou'wester to keep her ears dry.

I finished off the labels and ran down to give them to Mom. She had eighteen special transparent gift bags lined up on the kitchen table. I stuck a label on each one and then Mom brought out four huge tins.

"These are the oatmeal-and-raisin cookies," said Mom, pointing. "And these are the plain, but I've iced them with lemon frosting and stuck those little silver balls on top so they look quite pretty, don't they? Then these are cherry cookies and *these* are chocolate chip."

"You're so clever, Mom! They look wonderful."

"They do, don't they!" Mom agreed happily. "We'll give each girl three of each kind, OK? You get filling and I'll tie the tops with ribbon."

Mom had brought beautiful thin satin ribbon, all different colors. When each bag was neatly tied up Mom washed her hands and then tied one lock of my hair into a tiny plait and secured it with the last of the green ribbon.

"There, it matches your eyes!" said Mom. "You'd better go and get into your party finery now, the caterers will be here any minute."

I went upstairs and put on my gray dress and pinafore and my lovely boots. I looked at myself in the Venetian glass and then I went to check in the long mirror in Mom's bedroom. Sam and Lily were still talking on the television. They stopped and looked at me.

"Oh, Beauty, you look lovely!" said Sam, and Lily's eyes shone as she stared at me.

I blew them both a big kiss and then switched them off. I imagined them snuggled up together asleep in the dark of the Rabbit Hutch, waiting until I wanted to wake them up again.

Mom came running in to change into *her* party outfit—a cream dress that showed off a lot of her

153

own creamy skin. Mom squinted sideways at herself in the mirror.

"Do you think I ought to wear a little camisole under this dress, sweetie?" she asked.

I lowered my voice, doing my best gruff Dad imitation. "If you've got it, babe, flaunt it," I said.

Mom cracked up laughing. "You are a card, Beauty." She cupped my face with her hands. "You're going to have the happiest birthday ever, just you wait and see."

The caterers arrived and started setting up the buffet on the dining-room table. Mom and I hovered, worried about getting in the way, but when they put the extraordinary profiterole tower in pride of place in the middle of the table Mom spoke up.

"Can we leave room for a plate of my homemade cookies, please?" she said.

She'd arranged all the leftover cookies from the tins on her best green-leaf plate. She laid them in circles, lemon iced cookies in the middle, then the cherry, then the chocolate chip, with the darker oatmeal around the edge. They looked like a beautiful biscuit flower. To make the plate even prettier Mom had scattered little white and purple freesia heads across the cookies.

"They look lovely, madam," said the head caterer—and Mom flushed with pride.

Then we heard the front door bang and Dad came

stomping into the dining room. He didn't pause to take off his shoes. It was immediately obvious he was furious about something. Mom took my hand and squeezed it.

"Hello, Gerry, darling," she said. "Look, doesn't Beauty's birthday buffet look wonderful?"

Dad barely glanced at it. He nodded curtly at the caterers, stretching his mouth into a grimace.

"What's the matter?" Mom murmured. "Is the super-stretch limo still coming? The theater has reserved the seats?"

"Oh, everything's fine and hunky-dory for Beauty's birthday," said Dad, ruffling my hair and pulling my ribbon out of place. "I've fixed *that* all right. I'm just screwed when it comes to the Water Meadows development."

"But I thought that guy was going to fix it all for you?" said Mom.

"That's what *I* thought. But he's gone and got cold feet. And not only that, he's blabbed to someone else about a little gift I gave him." Dad lowered his voice to a hiss so the caterers wouldn't hear. "And now there's ridiculous talk of *bribery*."

"Oh no!" said Mom, her hand to her mouth. "But . . . isn't that a criminal offense?"

"Shh! Don't act as if I'm about to be frog-marched off to jail. It won't come to that, but it might mean hiring lawyers and it's all going to be horrendously

expensive one way or another—and the Water Meadows deal is off now, whatever happens."

"Oh, darling, I'm so sorry," Mom said.

"I should think you jolly well are, because we're going to have to tighten our belts. No more fancy frocks and finery for either of you!" Dad turned to me. "Make the most of this birthday, Beauty. It looks like it'll be the last proper party you'll have in a long time."

I knew it wasn't the moment to remind Dad I'd never asked for a proper party. I looked at his red face and his twitchy eyelid and his clenched fists, all the warning signs. He was primed like a hand grenade. He was just about keeping it together because the caterers were here but all it needed was one tiny trigger—and then he'd explode.

The girls were due to arrive in twenty minutes. I thought of Dad screaming and shouting in front of Skye and Emily and Arabella and I wanted to die.

"Don't look so tragic, Beauty!" said Dad. He forced a smile to his face, teeth bared as if ready to bite. "Don't you worry about Daddy's little troubles. You're still going to have a grand time with your little pals. Look at this lovely spread, yum yum!" Then he frowned. "What's the big green plate doing smack in the middle?"

Dad marched up to the table and banged the

cookie plate. They all bounced out of their elaborate pattern and the freesias fell off.

"What are you doing, ripping me off with all these arty-farty fancy cookies? I didn't order them!"

"I know, sir. Your wife made them," said the chief caterer. "She asked us to put the plate there."

"My wife? Is *she* paying your company then? I think you'll find *I'm* the poor Joe Shmoe writing the check, and if that's the case you'll take your orders from me. Move that home-made rubbish off the table, pronto. Look at it, half the biscuits are broken anyway!"

They were broken because Dad had thumped them around. Mom picked up the plate and carried it into the kitchen. She kept her head held high but I saw the tears in her eyes. I followed her and gave her a big hug.

"I'm so sorry, Mom. They looked so lovely too," I said.

"Never mind," said Mom, swallowing hard. "We can still give the girls their own special bags."

"What are you two whispering about?" said Dad, following us into the kitchen. "Beauty, stop looking at me like that! Dilly, shove all that cookie muck in the trash where it belongs. I don't want you to start all these stupid cooking experiments, you're useless at it. Your job is to look beautiful, so brighten up and put a smile on your face, for pity's sake. You need a bit more sparkle. Put some jewelery on. That neckline's a bit bare. I know, wear your diamond collar."

I froze.

"Yes, good idea," Mom said calmly. "Or even better, my string of pearls. They'll look beautifully creamy with this dress. I'll go and put them on."

"No, pearls are a bit old-fashioned and understated. I want you looking flash, girl. Go for the diamonds," said Dad.

Mom walked out of the kitchen and went upstairs. I followed her, feeling frantic.

"Stop trotting after your mother, Beauty. You're acting like you're her little shadow. Come here, let's look at you. You're a bit *pale*. What's up with you?"

Dad didn't wait for an answer. He went to pour himself a drink and order the caterers around. Mom stayed upstairs. Then there was a ring at the door. It was only quarter to but one of the girls was here already!

"Go on then, Beauty, answer the door to your first guest," said Dad, prodding me out into the hall. "Dilly, what the hell are you doing? Get yourself down here!" he hissed up the stairs.

I went to the door. It was Arabella and her mother, both of them long and thin and jittery, like thoroughbred ponies.

"Happy birthday, Beauty," Arabella neighed.

It was the first time I'd ever heard her use my real name.

"Happy birthday, Beauty," Arabella's mother said in her high posh voice. She said my name as if it was in quotation marks, her eyebrows raised. "Where's Mommy, dear? I'd just like to check on all the arrangements. Is it right that all the girls will be brought back to their own homes?"

"Please come in. Oh yes, they'll be dropped off in a super-stretch limo," I said.

Mom came flying down the stairs. She was wearing a big gold heart locket. Dad joined her in the hall.

"Ah, Mrs. Cookson—and Mr. Cookson," said Arabella's mom. "This is Arabella."

"Hey, hey, Gerry and Dilly, please," said Dad, shaking hands. "Welcome to our Happy Home."

My throat dried. I thought Dad was going to start his Happy Homes song-and-dance routine. Mom obviously thought so too because she started talking hurriedly about car times and the theater seats and when we'd get back home.

"Dilly, Dilly, quit burbling," said Dad.

Mom flushed. Arabella's mom blinked. She smiled pityingly at Mom.

"Bless you, dear, you're just putting my mind at rest. We can't help worrying. It's a female thing, Mr. Cookson," she said.

Dad stared at her, not liking it that she'd called

him Mr. Cookson again—but he managed a wintry smile. He held his glass of whisky up.

"Oh no, nothing for me, thank you," said Arabella's mother, as if he'd offered her rat poison. She turned to Mom. "Who's going to be driving this limousine?" she asked.

"Oh, don't worry, there's a special chauffeur," said Mom quickly. "And of course Gerry and I will be there with the girls, keeping an eye on things."

"Mmm," said Arabella's mom. She pressed her hand on Arabella's shoulder. "Well, I'll be off, darling. Remember, you've got the cell phone if you need me at all. Have a lovely time."

"Bye, Ma," said Arabella. She thrust a pink parcel at me. "This is your birthday present."

I opened it. It was one of the *Princess* paperbacks. I'd read it last year.

"Oh, Beauty, how thoughtful. Araminta's given you one of them books you like so much," said Dad. "Say thank you, darling."

"Ara*bella*," I said. "Thank you."

"Dilly, can I have a word?" said Dad.

"In a minute, Gerry," said Mom. "Would you like some juice, Arabella?"

"That's what we've got the caterers for, Dilly. I need you." Dad took hold of Mom by the wrist.

She had to go with him. They went into the

kitchen and shut the door but I could still hear Dad clearly.

"Why the hell aren't you wearing your diamond collar?"

"Thank you very much for my *Princess* book," I said loudly. "It's very kind of you."

"No, it's not," said Arabella. "Someone gave it to me at Christmas and I've never been bothered to read it."

"You're to put it on now!"

"I love reading, I read all the time, I even read in the bath," I babbled.

"What's your dad getting so worked up about?" asked Arabella.

"Nothing. He just shouts sometimes, it doesn't mean he's really mad," I said.

"You've LOST it? What the hell do you mean, you ditsy cow?"

Arabella blinked. "Your dad just called your mom a *cow!*"

"No, he didn't. Shall we eat something? Or we could go out in the garden if you like?"

There was a sudden unmistakable sound from the kitchen, harsh and horrible.

"Was that a slap? Does your dad *hit* your mom?" Arabella asked, her eyes wide.

"No. No, of course not. I expect he just bumped into something. Look, do you see my profiterole tower? I wonder how they're going to cut it?"

Arabella shrugged. "I don't know. It *was* a slap. This is kind of weird." She fingered the cell phone in her pocket. "Maybe I'm going to phone my mom to come back."

"No, don't! You've only just got here."

"I wish Emily and the others were here," said Arabella.

Then the doorbell rang and there was a whole gang of girls on the doorstep. They all crowded into the hall. Dad came out to greet them, getting their names wrong, welcoming everyone to his Happy Home.

Mom stayed in the kitchen. She didn't come out for another ten minutes, when nearly everyone had arrived. One side of her face was still much pinker than the other and her eyes were red, but she smiled heroically at everyone and helped serve the food, even though Dad told her not to. He made himself another drink.

Arabella was huddled in a corner whispering to Emily and Skye. They kept looking around at my dad and rolling their eyes.

Emily gave me the very same *Princess* book as Arabella. Her eyes gleamed as she gave me her parcel. I knew they'd done it deliberately but I thanked her all the same.

I expected the exact same copy from Skye but

her present was a different shape. It was a little child's brush-and-comb set, painted with rosebuds. There were two words in swirly writing around the edge of the mirror and across the back of the brush. *Little Beauty*.

Skye and Emily and Arabella all grinned.

"There you are, Ugly," Skye said. "Your very own brush to get the tangles out of your corkscrews, and a mirror especially for you."

"I bet it cracks the minute she looks in it," said Emily.

"She looks *especially* weird today. What *is* that you're wearing, Ugly? Some kind of historical costume?" said Arabella.

"She's got her apron on, so maybe she's the maid," said Skye, sniggering. "Go on, give us a curtsy, Ugly-Wugly."

"What did you just say, Skye?" said Mom, pushing forward to stand beside us. Her voice was steely.

"Nothing," Skye mumbled.

"You just mind that mouth of yours," said Mom, and walked on.

Skye flushed scarlet.

"What a cheek!" Emily hissed. "You're not allowed to tell someone else's child off!"

"Especially an s-l-u-t like her," said Skye.

I stood still. I clenched my fists. "You say another

163

word about my mom and I'll drag you by your hair over to that table and shove you head first into that profiterole tower and I'll stuff profiteroles up your snobby nose and down your foul mouth until you're sick," I said.

Skye stared at me, shocked. She took a step backward, then another. Then she recovered a little and shook her head at Emily and Arabella, rotating her finger into the side of her head.

"Watch out, she's got a screw loose," she said shakily.

"I think I'm going to phone my mom," said Arabella.

"Maybe I'll phone mine," said Emily. "Where's Rhona, Skye? Isn't she coming?"

"She *said* she was," said Skye. "But she's obviously thought better of it. Clever her. I *knew* she didn't really like Ugly."

My heart started thumping. I thought she was simply trying to wind me up—but where *was* Rhona? She was half an hour late. Everyone had eaten the vol au vents and sausages and all the other buffet bits.

"Time to cut your birthday cake, Beauty," said Dad.

"But Rhona isn't here yet," I said.

"Which one's Rhona? I don't think she'll be coming now," said Dad.

"Yes she will. Rhona's my friend," I said desperately.

"Did you hear that!" said Skye. "As if!"

"Everyone knows Rhona's *your* friend, Skye."

"You and Rhona have been best friends for ever," said Arabella.

"Rhona's still my friend too—and she said she was coming," I said.

Mom put her arm around me. "Maybe she's not very well," she whispered. "Don't worry, Beauty. We'll save her some of the profiterole tower, and you can give her a bag of cookies at school on Monday."

"I wish she'd come *now*," I said.

There was a ring at the door.

"Rhona!" I said, and went flying.

It *was* Rhona, standing on the doorstep clutching a large box, her cheeks bright pink with excitement. Mr. Marshall stood beside her, hauling what looked like a wooden crate.

"Happy birthday, Beauty! Hey, what a lovely dress! And *wonderful* boots!" said Rhona. "I'm so sorry we're so late. We were all set to leave an hour ago but then your birthday present escaped!"

"It . . . escaped?" I said.

"It took ages and ages to catch him. Be very careful when you take the lid off! We don't want him to get away again."

Twelve

"A rabbit!" I whispered.

"It's your birthday bunny," said Rhona. "Dad's scrubbed out my rabbit's hutch for you, and we've got bedding and rabbit food. Mom's packaged up some lettuce and dandelion leaves too."

"Oh, Rhona!" I said. I shut my eyes tight but I couldn't stop two tears from spilling down my cheeks.

"What's the matter, Beauty? You did *want* a rabbit, didn't you?" said Rhona.

"Yes, I wanted a rabbit more than anything else in the world," I said.

"So there you are then!" said Rhona. "I can't wait to hear what you're going to call him."

"Call who?" said Dad, coming up the hall behind me. "Can you just lift that wooden thing off of the parquet flooring?"

"Certainly, certainly," said Mr. Marshall. "Shall I shove the hutch round the back?"

"The . . . hutch?" said Dad.

I swallowed so hard my head started spinning. I had one hand inside the box. I stroked the soft soft fur.

"Rhona's bought me a little r-r-rabbit for my birthday," I said.

I waited. I didn't dare look around at Dad. I heard his sharp intake of breath.

"I think our Beauty's been a bit of a naughty girl asking you to give her a rabbit," said Dad. "She knows she's not allowed to have pets."

"Oh, she didn't *ask*, Mr. Cookson," said Rhona, totally unfazed. "But I *knew* just how much she'd love a rabbit. It's just a little weeny baby rabbit. He won't make any mess at all, he'll just stay neat and cozy in his hutch. You'll let Beauty keep him, won't you?"

"I certainly hope you will, pal, because I don't want to lug this damn hutch all the way home!" said Mr. Marshall.

I waited, holding my breath. We all waited, Rhona and Mr. Marshall, Mom, Skye, Emily, Arabella, and every other girl at my party.

"Well, in that case of course Beauty can have her little bunny," said Dad.

"Hurray!" said Rhona.

"Cheers!" said Mr. Marshall.

There was an excited babble as everyone crowded around, wanting to see my rabbit.

"No, no, careful, we mustn't frighten him," I said firmly, feeling the poor little thing quivering.

I looked up at Dad. He was smiling at me. He

even said "Aaah!" as I lifted the little rabbit out of his box and cradled him in my arms. But I saw his narrowed eyes, his clenched jaw, the pulse beating in his forehead.

Mr. Marshall carried the hutch through the house and out of the French doors into the back garden. Rhona carried the bunny box and I carried the rabbit. Everyone else crowded around, wanting to see him and stroke him.

"Get back a bit! He's getting so frightened. He's little, he's worried you might hurt him," I said, fiercely protective.

They all moved back, even Skye. It was tricky transferring my rabbit into his hutch. He wriggled frantically and I had to hang on to him really tightly though I was terrified of hurting him. I knew how clumsy I could be—and yet somehow my hands knew how to cup and hold and soothe him.

"Let's tuck him up in bed," said Rhona, pulling his straw out of the box.

"Watch what you're doing, dear, that stuff's going all over the patio," said Dad. "Come on, girls, we've still got to eat the profiterole tower, and the super-stretch limo will be here soon."

"Hang on, Mr. Cookson. We've got to feed the rabbit first!" said Rhona. "I didn't give him any breakfast so he wouldn't do too many poos in his birthday box."

All the girls giggled and started chatting about what rabbits liked to eat. Dad's smile was so strained his lips disappeared.

"Buck up, then, dears," he said.

Skye had hold of the lettuce-and-dandelion parcel.

"Here you are, Bunny, here's your yummy greens," she said.

"No, Skye, it's not *your* rabbit. Beauty must feed him," said Rhona.

So I fed my rabbit. My hand was shaking and my tummy in knots because of Dad, but it was still the most fantastic feeling offering the leaves and seeing my rabbit's nose twitch, his soft mouth open, his little teeth starting to chomp chomp chomp.

I'd loved Nicholas Navybear but that was nothing like having a real soft breathing little creature nuzzling my fingers.

"He's the loveliest rabbit ever, Rhona," I whispered.

"So what's his name, your little birthday bunny?" she said.

"We'll *call* him Birthday," I said. "Because he's the best birthday present I've ever had."

"Apart from the gorgeous giant toy rabbit I gave

you, Beauty," said Dad. "Come on now, they're about to cut the cake. Back in the house everyone."

Mom made me wash my hands though I wanted to keep the feel of Birthday's soft fur and warm tongue on my fingers. I didn't get to cut the profiterole tower myself as it was such a complicated job but I handed out the plates to everyone. Mr. Marshall stayed to have a piece too.

"Yum yum, I got lucky," he said. "Happy birthday, Beauty. You look an absolute picture in that lovely dress."

I looked at him. He didn't seem to be making a joke. He was smiling as if he really meant it.

"Thank you," I said, smiling back at him. "It's my birthday present from Mom."

"Oh well, your mom's got the knack of looking lovely herself," said Mr. Marshall, nudging up to Mom and giving her a little pat. He was just being silly, wiggling his eyebrows and playing about— but Dad glared at him.

"Right, we'd better start rounding up the kids, the super-stretch will be here any minute," he said, peering at his Rolex. "I don't want to chase you out, chum, but we need to get cracking."

Mr. Marshall took this heavy hint and said good-bye. I wished he was coming with us. He was so kind and funny. I felt nothing really bad could happen when he was around.

"Now, girls, you'd better all make a quick trip to the little girls' room. We don't want any of you to have an accident in the super-stretch," said Dad.

I blushed scarlet. Some of the girls tittered, some rolled their eyes.

"Beauty, show everyone the bathroom. Don't worry, at the last count we had four toilets in our Happy Home, so you shouldn't have to stand around with your legs crossed too long."

"Honestly!" Emily muttered. "He's so *crude*."

"Vulgar," Arabella agreed.

"Why go on about all his toilets anyway? Does he think we don't have any at home?" said Skye.

"Oh stop it, he's just being funny," said Rhona— but I knew she was just saying it to comfort me.

She came up to my bedroom with me. She squealed when she saw the monster pink rabbit lurking in the corner.

"Oh my goodness! It's the biggest rabbit I've ever seen!"

"It's horrible," I said.

"What's it *called*?"

"Just Pinky. If I give it a proper name it'll start to get real." I suddenly gave Rhona a big hug. "Thank you so much for Birthday, Rhona. I really meant it, he's the best birthday present in the whole world."

"He's only a little bunny from the pet shop. Your dad isn't really angry about it, is he?"

"No," I lied. "No, he's fine." I sighed. "I do like *your* dad, Rhona."

"Oh, my dad's a silly old sausage," said Rhona fondly. "That's what I call him sometimes—and he calls me his little chipolata."

Rhona danced around my bedroom, gently touching all my Victorian doll collection and my little china animals and my musical box and all my glass snowstorms.

"You've got such a *lovely* bedroom, Beauty. And fancy having your very own bathroom! Even Skye hasn't got her own en suite bathroom and her family has got pots of money. It must be such fun to be as rich as you!"

Lulu and Poo-poo were clamoring to use my bathroom too so we let them in and then went downstairs. I heard a sudden squeaking.

"It's here! Look out the window! Oh goodness, it's *enormous*! Our own super-stretch limo!"

All the girls were dancing up and down, so excited. I had a peek too and my heart started thumping at the thought that it was *my* birthday super-stretch limo.

The caterers were starting to clear my birthday buffet already. There was no sign of Mom and Dad. I went looking for them to tell them the car was here. I opened the door of the kitchen. Dad had hold of Mom, his face contorted. I ran forward, terrified he was going to hit her again.

"Dad, Dad, the super-stretch limo is here! Come and look, it's so grand, I'm so lucky!" I blurted.

Dad didn't even seem to hear me.

"Never, never let me see you flirting with that creep Marshall again," he said, giving Mom a shake.

"She *wasn't* flirting, Dad!" I said.

"I'll thank you to mind your own business, Beauty," Dad said. "Did you say the car was here? Right, let's be off then."

Mom rubbed her wrist, blinking hard. She looked at Dad as if she wanted to say something—but then looked at me instead. She tried to smile.

"Come on then, birthday girl," she said, picking up a large carrier bag on the kitchen floor.

"What's that you've got, Dilly?" Dad asked.

"It's little going-home presents," said Mom. "Beauty can give one to each girl as we drop them off."

Dad breathed a little easier. "Nice touch," he said grudgingly. "So what are we giving them all? Bracelets, smelly bath stuff, cuddly toys?"

"Oh, it's just a little token," said Mom, walking to the door. "Come on, Beauty. A super-stretch limo, imagine! How exciting!"

But Dad grabbed at the carrier bag before she could get any farther. "Let me see!" he demanded.

He delved in and brought out a handful of the beautifully beribboned cookie bags.

"Are you *still* trying to palm them off with this muck?" he said.

"They're just little cookies, Gerry, so the children will start calling Beauty their little Cookie," said Mom.

"Don't talk such nonsense. You're not shaming us by doling out these. We'll be a laughing stock— and we'll probably give them food poisoning to boot," said Dad.

He picked up the carrier bag and bashed it to the floor. Then he stamped up and down on it dement-edly, smashing all the cookies into crumbs.

We watched him silently, wincing as if he was stamping all over us. Dad slowed down a little, out of breath, half glancing toward the door, obviously wondering if anyone could hear.

Mom gave him one long look and then she took hold of my hand.

"Come on, Beauty, let's look after our guests," she said.

They were huddled in the hall, nudging each other, looking anxious. Rhona came and slipped her arm round me.

"Come on, girls, let's get in the limo," said Mom.

She acted like nothing had happened, though her cheeks were burning and even her chest was flushed pink.

She opened the front door and the girls ran out eagerly, shoving over who was going to sit where.

"I'm sitting next to Beauty," said Rhona.

"No, you're sitting next to *me*," Skye insisted.

"I've got two sides, haven't I, silly?" said Rhona. "I'll be sitting next to *both* of you."

I looked at Mom. "Is Dad still coming?" I whispered.

"I don't know and I don't care," Mom whispered back.

Dad did come, rubbing his hands and humming *Happy Birthday to you* as if nothing had happened.

"Hands up who's ever been in a super-stretch limo before!" he said.

No one put their hand up. Dad nodded triumphantly. I saw Skye and Emily and Arabella roll their eyes at each other.

"He'll be telling us how much it cost to hire it next," Arabella whispered.

"He is so awful," said Emily.

"He's just plain nuts," said Skye.

Rhona shifted closer to me and started talking about Birthday.

"They had six rabbits in the pet shop. They *did* have a white one like Lily but it didn't have floppy ears and it wasn't anywhere near as little and cute as Birthday."

"He's the best rabbit ever. And you're the best friend ever," I said.

"Hello?" said Skye. "Rhona just happens to be *my* best friend."

"I'm best friends with both of you," said Rhona. "Now shut up, Skye. It's Beauty's birthday."

It *was* my birthday, and here I was with Rhona being lovely to me, on a fantastic birthday trip, and back home I had the present I'd been longing for. I should feel the happiest girl in the whole world— and yet every time I looked at Mom I wanted to burst into tears. She was terribly squashed up beside Louise and Poppy, trying hard to chat to them, giving barley sugar to someone who felt sick, pointing out places we were passing, being so *brave*. She smiled at me from time to time but she didn't so much as glance in Dad's direction.

He'd stopped going on and on about the super-stretch limo and had dozed off. I prayed he wouldn't start snoring.

He didn't wake up until we pulled up outside the theater. Then he sprang into action, assembling us all on the pavement, jumping around and joking. He made a great show of counting everyone, tapping each girl on her nose. He tried to tap Mom too but she ducked out of his way.

Birthday Bonanza started off wonderfully. There was a huge birthday party on stage with lots of singing and dancing. I liked McTavish, I liked Will Forman, I liked the actress playing the Birthday Girl, a beautiful slender girl with long red hair past her waist. But then she came to the front of the stage and asked if there were any other birthday girls or boys in the auditorium.

I turned around and saw lots and lots of hands waving.

"You wave too, Beauty," said Rhona.

So I stuck my hand up and waved feebly, thinking they were just going to sing *Happy Birthday*.

"Hey, there! You'd better come up on stage and share our birthday party," said the red-haired girl, beckoning.

Oh no! I saw ten or twelve kids rushing forward to get on stage. The girls were all pretty skinny Skye-type girls in short skirts or tight jeans. I imagined myself standing amongst them in my prim pearl gray dress and nearly died.

"Go on, Beauty," said Rhona.

"No way!" I said.

"Anyone else?" said the red-haired girl, peering in our direction.

"Beauty!" Dad hissed along the row. "Get yourself up there!"

"I can't!" I said, shrinking down in my seat. "I *won't!*"

"Well, if she's not going to, I am," said Skye, jumping up.

"But it's not your birthday, Skye!" said Rhona.

"They're not going to ask for my birth certificate, are they?" said Skye, shoving her way along the row.

I heard Dad hollering at me but I shook my head determinedly, knowing he couldn't push his way right along past eighteen girls to physically shove me on stage.

Skye was up there like a shot, tossing her blond hair and standing with one hand on her hip, totally at ease. They all had to join in a birthday song and then play a crazy game of musical chairs. Then disco lights started flashing and they all had to dance. I was so so so relieved I hadn't gone up on stage myself, even though Dad was madder than ever at me. He glared down the row at me but when he looked back at the stage he couldn't help smiling as Skye pranced and strutted up and down, arms up, hips shaking, toes tapping. It was obvious he'd give anything to have a daughter like her. Rhona's hand found mine and she gave it a comforting squeeze.

Everyone talked like crazy in the car going back, telling their favorite parts, arguing about which was the dreamiest boy in McTavish, singing snatches of song. Skye stood up to repeat her little dance routine but the chauffeur told her to sit right down again. Dad didn't tell Skye off. He winked at her. She winked back and then turned her head and sniggered at Emily and Arabella.

Dad wasn't in a winking mood with me. I knew he was furious because I wouldn't go up on the stage. I didn't want him to start ranting in front of everyone—but I was getting very scared about being left on my own with him.

We dropped Rhona off last and we gave each other a very big hug.

"Thank you so so so much for Birthday, Rhona," I said again.

"I'm so so so glad you like him," said Rhona. She paused and then whispered in my ear, "We'll let Skye still think she's my best friend but really I want to be *your* best friend, Beauty."

"Come on, girls, no need for all these grand farewells, you'll be seeing each other at school on Monday!" said Dad. "Off you go, Rosa."

"Rhona!" I said, giving her another hug.

Her mom and dad must have been watching out for her because her front door opened and Mr. and

Mrs. Marshall were there on the doorstep waving to her. Rhona gave me one last hug and then ran up her garden path to her home.

"Is she the one with the swimming pool?" said Dad. "It must be the size of a footbath because those houses haven't got any back garden to speak of. It's a tacky house too. Look at the state of the paintwork! Wouldn't you think that guy would take a bit of pride in his own house and keep it up to scratch? I don't know why you're acting so friendly with that little kiddie, she isn't anything special. Why on earth don't you make friends with that little blond doll Skye?"

Dad remembered *her* name all right.

"I don't like Skye," I mumbled.

"Don't be so silly! You could take a few tips from that girl. *She's* not backward in coming forward. She was off like a rocket when she got the chance to go on stage. Why wouldn't *you* go, Beauty? That's the whole blooming point of the show, to celebrate your birthday in style. Why the hell do you think I forked out a thousand quid for the tickets? You were supposed to get up there and enjoy yourself and show off to all your little friends, not sit quivering in your seat like a great fat pudding."

"Gerry!" said Mom.

"I'm sick to death of the two of you," Dad said,

181

his voice raising, not caring that the chauffeur could hear every word. "I work my butt off for both of you, flinging money at you like it was confetti and yet I never get one word of gratitude. You're both sitting there with your faces tripping you. I've spent a small fortune on your birthday, Beauty, and yet you haven't the wits to make the most of it. You stand in the corner like you're some little saddo no-friends while all the other girls bounce about and have a laugh and enjoy themselves."

"Please don't, Gerry!"

"You're no better, Dilly. You won't chat properly with the other moms. You act like you're scared of your own shadow half the time. I buy you lovely clothes and jewelery so you can show yourself off and what do you do? Only go and lose your diamond collar! How can you *lose* it, for pity's sake? I know you're a fool but surely even you can do up the clasp of a necklace?"

"I know I'm a fool," said Mom. "I'm a fool to let you talk to me like this. I'm even more of a fool to let you say such unkind things to poor Beauty."

"*Poor* Beauty!" Dad reached over and gave me a shake. "You're a little slyboots, miss. How *dare* you suck up to that Rosa like that and ask her to bring you that wretched rabbit."

"I didn't, Dad."

"Don't you lie to me, I won't have it," said Dad.

"And don't think you can get the better of me either. You've a long way to go before you can outwit your old dad."

He had an awful gleam in his eye. I didn't understand until we got home. I went running right through the house and out of the French doors to see Birthday.

The hutch door was swinging open. I stared at it. I *knew* I'd shut it up properly. I'd carefully checked the latch to see it was secure. I held my breath, bending down to see if Birthday was still there, huddled in his bedding. I scrabbled my hands through the straw desperately but it was no use. He was gone.

I looked wildly around the patio and then started searching the garden, going down on my hands and knees to peer under every bush.

"Beauty?" Mom came out onto the patio. She saw the empty rabbit hutch. "Oh no!"

"I left it latched up properly, Mom, I know I did," I cried. "I don't know how it came undone."

"I do," said Mom. "Gerry? Gerry! Come here!"

Dad came out onto the patio too.

"Quit bawling at me like I'm your pet dog, Dilly!" he blustered. "Beauty, what the hell are you doing? Stand up, you're getting your fancy new dress filthy!"

"I'm looking for Birthday," I sobbed.

"Who? Oh, that damn rabbit. Has it escaped already?" said Dad.

"You deliberately let him out," said Mom. "You must have snuck out here while Beauty and all the girls were getting into the limo."

"I didn't *sneak*," said Dad, putting his hands on his hips. He stuck his chin up belligerently. "Yes, I let the rabbit out. I've always made it plain, I'm not having animals all over the place."

"But he's *mine*," I wept. "How could you let him out, Dad? He's so little. He'll be so frightened. Oh, Birthday, where *are* you?"

"Stop talking nonsense. He'll be chomping grass somewhere with all his little bunny friends," said Dad. "That's the place for rabbits, out in the wild. Now stop that baby crying. You look a sight with your face all screwed up like that. There's no need to make such a stupid fuss. You've got your lovely pink toy rabbit to play with."

I barely listened to Dad. I carried on searching. Mom helped too.

"He must be here somewhere. He couldn't have burrowed all the way under the fence, could he?" I said.

"He might have squeezed out at the end, behind the shed," said Mom. "I think there's a bit of a gap in the fence there." She ran to look and then gasped. She staggered backward, her hands over her mouth.

"What? What is it, Mom?" I said, getting to my feet.

"Don't come any nearer, Beauty! Stay where you are," Mom said.

She was shaking all over, as if she was going to fall down. I couldn't help running to her, though she shouted at me to keep away. Then I saw why. Birthday was lying limply beside the shed, his little furry body and his soft paws. But his head mostly wasn't there.

I started screaming. Mom put her arms tight around me, pushing my head against her chest so that I couldn't see poor torn Birthday anymore. Dad ran over too.

"Oh God. How disgusting! A fox must have got it. That's animals for you," he said.

"You monster," said Mom.

"What? Look, *I* didn't tear its head off its shoulders. *I* didn't know a fox would get it. Still, that's what happens when you have pets. Come here, Beauty, have a cuddle with your dad."

I shrank away from him. "I bloody hate you!" I sobbed.

"*What?*" Dad stared at me, shaking his head. "Don't you dare talk to me like that! I'll wash your mouth out with soap."

"Stop your stupid threats, Gerry. You sicken me," said Mom.

"I *sicken* you?" said Dad. "How dare you say that to me! I dragged you out the gutter, spent a fortune on you, gave you this beautiful home—"

"It isn't a beautiful home, it's a living hell," said Mom.

"Well, if you don't like it then get out," said Dad. "Go on, push off out of it, you ungrateful cow."

"All right, I shall," said Mom.

"Mom!" I said, clutching her.

"And you can take the kid with you," said Dad.

"Of course," said Mom.

Dad stared at her and then folded his arms. "Right then. Get lost, both of you," he said.

"We will, just as soon as we've buried poor Birthday," said Mom.

"You're going to do *what*? You're not digging a hole in my lawn," said Dad.

Mom took no notice. She went to the shed and got a big garden spade and a smaller one for me.

"We'll dig here, Beauty," she said. "Go and change out of your dress and boots. Put your jeans on and come back and help."

I did what I was told, still sobbing. When I got back to the garden Dad was digging too, sighing and swearing. Mom carried on, digging as well, though her hands kept slipping and her spade didn't cut cleanly through the earth. She'd taken her high heels off but she couldn't put her bare foot on the spade and push down. I gently took the spade from her and started digging properly. Mom straightened up, staring over at the remains of Birthday.

"I won't be a minute," she said, going into the house.

I hated being left alone with Dad. He was crimson in the face and sweating badly.

"This is all your fault," he said to me. "You would go on and on about wanting a rabbit. Maybe this will teach you a lesson."

I didn't answer, I just went on digging. Mom came back with a pillowcase. She went up to Birthday's body.

"I'll do it," said Dad.

"No, I will," said Mom.

She retched as she touched Birthday, getting her hands all bloody, but she wrapped the pillowcase around him and carried him at arm's length over to us.

"Say good-bye to him, Beauty," said Mom.

"Good-bye, darling little Birthday," I said, touching the pillowcase.

I could feel him underneath, still and stiff. Mom let me lay him in the bottom of his grave and then we started covering him with earth.

"Let *me* do it, for God's sake. You've got to fill it in evenly so the turf fits back on top," said Dad.

"All right, you do it, Gerry," said Mom.

She took me by the hand and we walked into the house. Mom looked at me.

"Go and pack a suitcase, Beauty. Three or four outfits, a few of your favorite things, shower stuff, pajamas, just as if we're going on vacation," she said.

"So we're really leaving?" I said shakily.

"Yes, we are," said Mom. "You don't want to stay, do you?"

"No, I want to go with you!"

"Then that's what we'll do," said Mom. "Quick then!"

I chose my new gray dress and boots, my other jeans, a denim skirt, three T-shirts and a thick jumper. I packed my new markers and my drawing book, my Sam and Lily folder and my new DVD, and *A Little Princess*. The giant pink rabbit leered at me in a corner as I snatched things frantically and squashed them into my suitcase.

"Ready, babe?" said Mom.

She'd got her suitcase packed too. She carried them both out to her car.

"Let's go now, Mom, while Dad's still around the back."

"No, we'll say good-bye properly," said Mom.

We waited in the hall, both of us trembling. Dad came in from the garden at last, his shoes in his hand.

"What are you two doing, lurking there?" he said, walking down the hallway. "Get those shoes off, you'll be walking mud all over the carpet."

"We're going, Gerry. I'll keep in touch, obviously, as you'll want to see Beauty."

"What? You're not really going?" said Dad. "Because I set the damn rabbit free?"

"Because of many, many things," said Mom.

"Now, listen. I've had enough of this. Walk out of here and you're never coming back, do you understand? And if you think I'm setting you up in another Happy Home you're very much mistaken. I'll sue you for desertion and I won't pay you a penny. I won't *have* any money anyway, not if I'm done for bribery. I'll probably end up in *jail*."

"I don't care where you end up," said Mom. "Don't worry, I'd sooner live in a pigsty than one of your Happy Homes. Good-bye."

"Good-bye, Dad," I whispered.

Dad was still shaking his head, looking utterly baffled, as we walked out of the house.

Thirteen

Mom started the car and we drove off.

"Where are we going, Mom?" I asked.

Mom didn't answer for a minute. I thought she was just concentrating on her driving. Then she gave a shaky little laugh.

"I don't know!" she said.

"Oh!" I said.

Mom carried on driving. I bit my lip, thinking hard.

"Well, there's *your* mom, my nana," I suggested.

"No," said Mom. "Not if she's still with that same boyfriend. I left home at the age of sixteen on account of *him*. My mom didn't seem to care much. She certainly wouldn't welcome me back with open arms."

"OK. Not her then," I said quickly, because Mom was sounding like she might burst into tears any minute.

My other granny was dead. We didn't really seem to have any proper relations.

I thought about friends. I thought about my best friend Rhona. My heart started beating faster.

"We could go to the Marshalls'!" I said.

"Who?" said Mom.

"Rhona's family."

"Oh, Beauty, we don't know them properly. I don't even know Rhona's mom's first name. I've only ever said hello to her. We can't just turn up on their doorstep," said Mom.

"I know Rhona," I said stubbornly. "And Mr. and Mrs. Marshall are ever so kind. They really like me. I know they'd like you too."

"No," said Mom. "Get real, Beauty. We can't just uproot and go and live with the Marshalls. This isn't just for one night. This is forever. Well, if we want it to be forever." Mom slowed down. "We could go back."

I thought hard. I was nearly crying too. It was so frightening having to make decisions. Dad had always told both of us what to do. *Should* we go back to Dad? If we got down on our knees and said sorry enough times he'd welcome us back with open arms. But then I thought of those arms swinging through the air and smashing all those cookies Mom had made so lovingly. I thought of his hands unlatching Birthday's hutch and shooing him out into the garden.

"We're not going back. We're going forward," I said.

"Right," said Mom, and she reached out and squeezed my hand. "Two girls together."

"Driving on and on and on into the sunset," I said. "Driving and driving and driving until . . ." I let my voice tail away. We were both silent. I took a deep breath.

"I suppose we can always sleep in the car, Mom."

"Oh, Beauty, bless you. No, we're definitely not doing that. I'll make sure there's a proper roof over your head. I'll sell some more of my jewelery. It's just tonight and Sunday that are the problem. But don't worry, I'll think of something."

Mom drove on, staring straight ahead. She was gripping the steering wheel so tightly her knuckles looked about to burst through her skin.

"What's that song, 'Don't Worry, Be Happy'?" she said. She didn't know all the words so she sang the same line over and over again.

I stared out of the window. Everything looked so astonishingly ordinary and everyday. Street after street, shops, restaurants, houses, a Happy Homes estate . . .

"Mom! I know where we can go! Auntie Avril!"

Mom slowed down, thinking. "But she's your dad's ex-wife," she said.

"Well, you're going to be his ex-wife too. And she likes us. She's just sent me those lovely markers.

Oh, Mom, let's go to Auntie Avril's. She lives on the Fruitbush estate and that's just over there, look!"

"Well, maybe we could try," Mom said doubtfully.

She reversed into a side entrance and drove back to the Happy Homes Fruitbush estate.

"Are you sure it's this one? There are so many blessed Happy Homes estates," said Mom.

"She lives at Seven Cherry Drive. I know it from writing her thank-you letters." I peered out of the car window. "That's Lime Avenue. And Grape Lane."

"All these fruity names! I wonder what else your dad made up? Do you think there's an Apple Alley?"

"What about a Banana Bend? Or Raspberry Road?"

We started giggling hysterically as we drove around the estate.

"Hey, look! Cherry Drive!" I said.

"Well done, Beauty."

Mom pulled up outside number Seven. It was less than half the size of our own house, a small shrunken semi-detached Happy Home with a narrow strip of grass at the front, but Auntie Avril had put trellis up on her brickwork so that clematis and wisteria hung lushly, softening the red of the brick. She'd planted pansies and geraniums in her garden and there was a hanging basket of pink petunias swinging above the blue front door. Her doormat said WELCOME. We hoped Auntie Avril would say welcome too.

"Right, ready, steady, go!" said Mom.

She opened up her handbag and peered at herself in her mirror. "God, I look such a mess!"

"No you don't, Mom, you look lovely," I said. "Come on."

We got out of the car and went up the drive together. I rang the bell. We waited, holding hands. Then the door opened and Auntie Avril stared at us in surprise. She looked older than I remembered, and she was a lot plumper. Her hair was a very bright yellow blond.

"Good Lord! Dilys and Beauty!" She peered behind us. "Where's Gerry?"

Mom and I looked at each other uncertainly.

Auntie Avril put her hand to her mouth, smudging her red lipstick. "Oh God, he hasn't *died*, has he?"

"No, no, he's fine," said Mom. "It's just . . ." She swallowed. "Can we come in, Avril?"

"Yes, of course, only I'm going out in about half an hour. Still, there's plenty of time for a cup of tea. In you come."

We trooped in after her. We automatically took our shoes off by the front door. Auntie Avril kept her high heels on and laughed at us.

"I see Gerry's got you well trained," she said. "Come into the living room."

It was a warm little room with a dark crimson carpet and a black leather sofa with furry cushions as pink as the petunias. There was a big white cat curled decoratively at one end.

"You've got a cat!" I said.

"That's my Cream Puff. Give her a gentle shove and she'll make room for you," said Auntie Avril. "Goodness, you're getting to be a big girl, Beauty. Of course, it's your birthday today, isn't it? Happy Birthday!"

"Thank you ever so much for my lovely markers, Auntie Avril. They were just what I wanted," I said, nestling near Cream Puff. I delicately ran my fingers down her soft fur and she sighed and quivered.

"You've brought her up very nicely, Dilys," said Auntie Avril.

"Oh, she means it, Avril. She loves drawing. She's ever so good at art. Well, Beauty's good at most things. Not a bit like me," said Mom.

"Not much like Gerry either!" said Avril. "Well, he's bright enough, no flies on him. I'll go and make us that tea then. Or would you like something stronger, Dilys? You look as if you could do with a pick-you-up. Shall we have a little gin?"

"It'll have to be a *very* little gin because I'm

196

driving," said Mom. "Unless . . ." She didn't dare say the rest.

Auntie Avril bustled around, making two gin and tonics and a special lemonade for me with a couple of cherries and a weeny paper umbrella, just like a real cocktail.

Cream Puff crept right onto my lap and started purring when I stroked her.

"It's lovely to see you both," said Auntie Avril. "We'll have to get together more often. After all, we're family, sort of."

I started to dare hope we might be at the start of a wonderful new life together, Auntie Avril, Mom, and me. I imagined living in this cozy little house, playing with Cream Puff every day, sipping cocktails every evening, all of us dancing up and down the carpet in our outdoor shoes with no one to yell at us ever.

"Come on then," Auntie Avril said, glancing at her watch. "Tell me why you've come around out of the blue. It's Gerry, isn't it?"

"Well, yes," said Mom. "We've split up."

Auntie Avril sighed and downed the rest of her gin and tonic. She reached over and patted Mom's knee. "You poor little darling. Still, you know what it feels like now. So who has he left you for? Not another little blond?"

"No, no, Gerry hasn't left me." Mom took a deep breath. "I've left *him*."

"*What?*" Auntie Avril looked astonished. "When?"

"Just now. We packed our bags, Beauty and me, and walked out."

"But *why*?"

"I just couldn't stand it anymore," Mom said shakily.

"What did he *do*?"

"He just kept shouting at us, belittling us, telling us what to do all the time," Mom said, starting to cry. "I know he's very stressed about his work, it's all going wrong, there's even some talk of bribery, I suppose he could be in really big trouble—but that's no excuse for being so mean to us."

I eased Cream Puff off my lap and went to put my arm round Mom.

"Oh, don't you worry about our Gerry," said Auntie Avril. "He's always stressed, he's always in trouble, but he'll fix it, just you wait and see. I know he can be a royal pain at times. That's just the way he is. The way most men are, come to think of it. But he's not such a bad egg, Dilys. He thinks the world of you and Beauty, he's set you up in a lovely home, he's lavished money on you. What more could you want?"

"He was terrible today, humiliating me in

front of Beauty's party guests. He organized this ridiculous stretch limo and tickets for *Birthday Bonanza*."

"Oh yes? Well, that doesn't sound particularly humiliating! It sounds like he was doing his best to give Beauty a lovely birthday treat. Grow up, Dilys. Gerry's got many faults, as I know all too well, but you could do a lot worse."

"He broke all the cookies Mom made especially and let my birthday rabbit out of his cage and a fox killed it," I said, starting to sob too.

"Oh dear, oh dear. That's a real shame, darling—but you don't break up a happy home just for that."

"It isn't a happy home, even though it's got that stupid name," said Mom. "We've not been happy there, Avril. It's getting to Beauty as well as to me. I've never been able to stand up for myself very well but I *can* stand up for my little girl. She needs a fresh start, somewhere quiet and peaceful where she's not shouted at all the time."

"And where's that?" said Auntie Avril.

There was a silence.

"You don't mean . . . you don't mean here with *me*?" she said.

"Well, if we could just stay a few days, until we get on our feet and I've found myself a job?" Mom suggested timidly.

"You have to be joking! You can't stay here. Whatever would Gerry say? Well, I have a rough idea what he'd say, only I'm not using that sort of language in front of Beauty here. Don't forget Gerry's given me this house. I'm not risking putting his nose out of joint. I don't want to find myself shoved out on the streets, homeless."

"But *we're* homeless now," said Mom, snuffling. "We haven't got anywhere else to go. What are we going to *do*, Avril?"

"*I* don't know, darling." She looked at her watch again. "I'm going to be late. I'm meeting three of my girlfriends in town for a pizza and then we're all going to the Gala Bingo. It's not exactly a wild night out for a Saturday but it's not likely a tall dark stranger is going to come calling at my time of life. Do yourself a favor, Dilys. Gerry's not tall and he's not dark and he's certainly not a stranger, but he's all man and if I remember rightly he can be fun to be with. Stop this nonsense and get yourself back there pronto."

"No," said Mom. "I know you mean well, Avril, but we're not going back. We'll just have to find someplace else."

"*Where*, exactly?" said Auntie Avril.

"Perhaps . . . perhaps we can go to the welfare council on Monday and they'll find us a little apartment," Mom said desperately.

Auntie Avril laughed at her. I was starting not to like her now.

"They've got a waiting list a mile long, you silly woman. You and Beauty would never qualify in a million years. You've got a luxurious six-bedroom house. You've deliberately made yourself homeless."

"Well, there are still refuges, aren't there?" said Mom.

"For battered wives. So has *Gerry* battered you?"

"He slapped my face. And he twisted my wrist."

"Oh, get a grip, Dilys! Most of those poor women in those places have been beaten to a pulp. They'd give their right arms to swap places with you. If I'm honest *I* still would, even though I know Gerry's no angel."

"Well, you have him then," said Mom.

"I don't stand a chance. I'm way past my sell-by date as far as Gerry's concerned. And most men too, apart from the crazy old fools. You think twice, Dilys. It's a lonely life without a man."

"It's a lonely life with the *wrong* man," said Mom. She drained her glass and then stood up. "Well, thank you very much for the drink, Avril. We must let you be off to your friends."

"*You* don't have to go. Look, you can stay here tonight by all means, if you really won't go back.

There's lots to eat in the fridge, you just help your-selves. Have another drink or two, watch a bit of TV, whatever. I've only got one bed in my spare room, but I'm sure you won't mind squashing up together. I'll be back around half past ten or eleven. Then we'll talk about things in the morning. I'm sure you'll see things differently then. You've got to consider Beauty and what's best for her. Think about it, Dilly. Ta ta then."

She kissed Mom, she kissed me, slipped on her lilac leather jacket, and rushed off. Mom and I sat on either side of Cream Puff, neither of us saying a word. Mom nibbled the edge of her fingernail, staring down at the deep red carpet.

"Are you thinking about it, Mom?" I asked in a tiny voice.

"I'm thinking so hard my flipping head's going to burst," said Mom. She bit harder, breaking one of her lovely manicured nails.

"*Don't*, Mom!"

"What?" She hadn't even realized what she was doing.

"You'll chew right down to your knuckles if you don't watch out," I said. "I don't want a mom with fingers all frayed at the edges."

I said it to make her laugh but she still looked as if she was going to cry.

"Avril thinks I'm bonkers," she said shakily.

"Maybe I *am*. Oh, Beauty, I don't know what to do."

"Let's stay here tonight. I like it here," I said, stroking Cream Puff. She stretched herself lazily. She obviously liked it here too. "Maybe Auntie Avril will change her mind and let us stay for a while. I could do all sorts of errands for her, feed Cream Puff, and make cups of tea and do the vacuuming. And you could . . ."

"Yeah, what could I do?" Mom said tearfully.

"You could make us cookies," I said.

I was serious, but this time Mom snorted with laughter, even though the tears were still running down her face.

"A fat lot of use that is," she said, blowing her nose. "No, Beauty, we'll have to go somewhere else tomorrow. Avril's right, your dad would be furious. It's very kind of her to let us stay now. Come on, let's go and see what's in the fridge."

There were lots of special ready-meals for one. We heated two in Auntie Avril's microwave and ate them at her tiny kitchen table. I'd hardly been able to eat any of my special birthday buffet. I realized I was starving now. I wolfed my meal down *and* most of Mom's, because she just stirred her food around and around with her fork. She was thinking again, frowning hard at her plate, twisting her knife and fork around and around like the hands of a clock. I leaned forward and rubbed her frown lines with my fingers.

"We'll be OK, Mom," I whispered.

"Yes. Of course we will," she said. "Tell you what—shall we see if Avril's got some flour and sugar and stuff? We could make her some cookies as a thank-you present. Do you think she'd like that?"

"I think she'd love your cookies, Mom."

"You start looking for all the ingredients, then. I'll go and get the suitcases. I remembered to pack my recipe book," Mom said proudly.

We made sugar and spice cookies, raiding Auntie Avril's spice rack and sifting cinnamon and cloves into the cookie dough. We washed up carefully while the cookies were baking, looking anxiously at Auntie Avril's oven every two minutes in case it might misbehave and burn them. When we opened the oven door we breathed a great sigh of relief. The cookies looked perfect and smelled delicious.

"We could have one each, just to make sure they're all right," said Mom.

It was getting near my bedtime now but I didn't want to go to bed and leave Mom sitting worrying all by herself.

"Oh, you might as well stay up if you're not sleepy. After all, it *is* your birthday," said Mom.

I'd totally forgotten it was still my birthday. It seemed to have lasted for weeks already. Mom switched on Auntie Avril's television but we couldn't settle to watching anything for more than two minutes.

"I know," said Mom. "You packed your Sam and Lily DVD, didn't you?"

"You bet I did."

"Well, run and fetch it then."

I slotted Sam and Lily into the DVD player. Mom and I curled up together to watch. Cream Puff woke up to watch too.

"Who do we want to see?" said the voice, as Sam and Lily spun around and around.

The little children sang, *"Sam and Lily in the Rabbit Hutch."* Mom and I sang it too.

"Hey there!" said Sam, directly to me.

He looked surprised to see me squashed up on a slippery leather sofa in a completely strange room. Lily blinked at Cream Puff.

"How are you doing?" asked Sam.

"I'm fine," I said.

Sam put his head to one side.

"Well, maybe I'm telling fibs," I whispered. I glanced at Mom. She was frowning again, nibbling at her nail, clearly not concentrating on the show.

"Sam, Mom and I have left Dad. Something terrible happened. I can't say it in front of Lily. We're at Auntie Avril's now but we can't stay here and we haven't got anywhere else to go," I mouthed.

"Oh dear, oh dear," Sam said softly. "I think you and Mom need a little break. How about a vacation?" He raised his voice, asking everyone now. "Where do *you* go on vacation? Do you go to the seaside?"

"We don't really go anywhere on vacation," I said. "We went to Marbella once but Dad got all fidgety and bored on the beach and said it was a waste of time."

"Lily doesn't like to go on holiday much," said Sam. "She doesn't like too much sun, she doesn't like getting her paws all sandy, she doesn't like swimming—she doesn't even like ice cream! Isn't she a funny bunny? I *love* sunbathing, I *love* building sandcastles, I *love* swimming in the sea—and I especially love ice cream!"

"So do I!" I said.

"I should have a little vacation right now," Sam said, just to me. "You and Mom. You'll have a lovely time. It will all work out, you'll see."

I nodded, snuggling up to Mom and Cream Puff, suddenly soothed. My head went on nod-nod-nodding and then Mom was gently shaking me awake.

"Your DVD's finished, pet. You've had a little doze. Let's pop you up to bed. I think I'll go to bed too. I don't really want Avril lecturing me when she comes home."

We had a quick wash in Auntie Avril's bright turquoise bathroom. Mom had forgotten to pack a nightie so she wore one of my T-shirts. She looked more of a little girl than ever.

The spare room was very grown up and glamorous, with a leopard-skin throw over the bed and a great china leopard baring its teeth at us in a corner.

"Watch out he doesn't bite," said Mom.

"He looks almost as scary as that giant pink rabbit!"

We got the giggles again and tried to jump into bed quick, but Auntie Avril had tucked the sheets in so firmly you had to pull for all you were worth to pry your way in. They felt icy too so Mom and I had to cuddle up close. We were both shivering though it wasn't *that* cold.

"I can't quite believe we're here," said Mom. "It feels so strange. I wonder what your dad's doing now."

"He'll be ranting," I said.

"But he's all by himself," said Mom.

I imagined Dad stomping up and down the house in his socks, bellowing abuse. I saw him very big at first, but he started to get smaller and the empty house got bigger until he was scampering about like a mouse, squeak-squeak-squeaking to no one at all.

"Mom?"

"Yes, darling?"

"I feel kind of sorry for Dad."

"I know. So do I."

"But if we went back he'd just start all over again."

"I know that too."

We were quiet for a little. I thought of Dad bashing the cookies. I thought about Birthday.

"Beauty? Don't cry, darling."

"Oh, Mom. Look, this sounds dumb, but do you think baby rabbits go to heaven?"

"Yes, definitely," said Mom.

"And do you think he'll be . . . whole there? His little head will be back in place?"

"Yes, of course. He'll be skipping about with all the angels. They'll be having little arguments over who gets to have him as their special pet," said Mom.

We were quiet again. We heard the front door open and Auntie Avril come in. We heard her go into the kitchen and give a little gasp. We nudged each other, knowing she must have spotted the plate of cookies. We heard a glass clinking downstairs, and then after ten minutes or so she came upstairs. We stayed quiet until she'd been in bed awhile.

Then I whispered in Mom's ear, "Are you still awake?"

"Yes."

"I know you're right. Auntie Avril's OK but we can't stay here," I said.

"Mm."

"So have you thought where we can go?"

"I've thought and thought and thought, but I haven't come up with anything just yet," said Mom.

"I think I know where we can go!"

"Where, darling?"

"The seaside!"

"But we don't know anyone at the seaside, do we?"

"It doesn't matter, does it? We could pretend we're going on vacation. We haven't had a vacation for ages. We've got a *bit* of money. Let's just go to the seaside and swim and sunbathe and it'll all feel easy and normal. We'll just be like everyone else, on our vacation."

I was cuddled up so close to Mom I could feel her heart beating fast.

"OK," she said. "That's what we'll do. For tomorrow, anyway. Well done, Beauty, it's a great idea."

Fourteen

Auntie Avril didn't look as if she thought it was a great idea when we told her over breakfast the next morning.

"For pity's sake, this isn't a *game*, Dilys. You can't just take off with your child and pretend you're on vacation."

"Why not?" said Mom. "Beauty and I *need* a vacation. You know what Gerry's like, he'll never leave the firm for more than a couple of days and he's hopeless at relaxing anyway. We just need to chill for a bit."

"Chill!" said Auntie Avril, shaking her head.

But when we said good-bye to her she pressed a large wad of notes into Mom's hand.

"Here, this is for you, Dilys."

"I can't take your money!"

"Well, how else are you going to do this 'chilling'? I know Gerry. I bet you're not even allowed your own credit card. You take it, my dear. Just don't ever tell Gerry I helped you out."

"Oh, Avril, you're a star," said Mom, giving her a hug.

"You're my all-time favorite auntie even if we're

not exactly related," I said, giving her a hug too.

I wanted to hug Cream Puff as well but she was busy gobbling up her breakfast and wouldn't be distracted.

We lugged our suitcases into the car and thanked Auntie Avril for letting us stay overnight.

"Well, if you get into totally dire straits you'd better come back, Gerry or no Gerry," she said. "And thanks for the cookies, girls. They were a lovely surprise. They're very good, Dilys. I thought you couldn't cook!"

"Mom's the greatest cookie cook in the whole world," I said. "And I'm learning fast, so maybe I'm the second greatest!"

We drove off, Auntie Avril standing on her doorstep under her hanging basket of petunias, waving and waving until we turned the corner.

"So, which seaside shall we pick?" said Mom. "Brighton's fun."

I remembered Brighton from a day trip.

"It's too big and busy and the beach is all pebbles," I said. "Let's find a sandy seaside place."

"OK," said Mom. "Well, we'll drive due south and see what we find. If we tip over into the sea we'll know we've gone too far."

We couldn't go directly south all the time because the roads wiggled around and once or twice we had to stop the car and look hard at the map. I couldn't read it when we were driving along because it made me feel sick. I wasn't much better sorting out the route when we were stopped. I kept squinting at red roads and yellow roads and little spidery black roads, trying to work out which one we were on.

"Don't worry, babes, we'll make it to the seaside somehow," said Mom. "Bournemouth's very sandy. And Bognor. Which one shall we aim for?"

I peered at the map. A name in tiny print suddenly swam into focus.

"Oh, Mom! Not Bournemouth, not Bognor. I've found a place here right by the sea and guess what it's called: Rabbit Cove! Oh, Mom, *please* let's go to Rabbit Cove!"

"I've never even heard of it. Let's see where it is." Mom squinted at the map. "It's obviously a very *small* place, not a proper town. I wonder why it's got such a funny name? You don't get rabbits at the seaside, do you?"

"I think it must be because of the shape of the cove. See those two sticking-out bits of land? They look like rabbit's ears!" I said.

"So they do! OK, OK, we'll go and have a look at Rabbit Cove if you've set your heart on it, though I'm not sure there'll be anywhere to stay there."

I tried hard to keep us on a direct route now, peering at the map as Mom drove, though I started to feel horribly car sick.

"Open your window a bit—and sit back and close your eyes," said Mom.

I did as I was told because all the world outside the window had started spinning and I kept yawning and swallowing spit. It seemed to be spinning inside my own head now. I was falling down and down and down into a scary black nothingness.

I called and called for Mom but she wasn't there. And then I called for Dad and I could hear him calling back. I struggled to get closer to him, reaching out, but then a light flashed on his face and I saw it was screwed up with rage.

"You don't want me and I don't want *you*, because you're ugly ugly ugly," he shouted.

He shoved me hard and I tumbled on downward, mile after mile, but I could still hear him shouting *ugly*. Other voices joined in. Skye and Arabella and Emily were shouting it, all the girls in my class, even Rhona, and I started crying, my hands over my ears . . .

"Beauty! Beauty, sweetheart, wake up. It's all right, Mom's here."

I blinked in sudden dazzling daylight. Mom leaned over and pulled my head onto her shoulder.

"Oh, Mom, I couldn't find you!" I sobbed.

"It was just a horrible nightmare, darling, that's all. You were crying out and tossing about. I had to stop driving," said Mom.

"We're driving?" I said stupidly. Then everything snapped properly into place. "Oh yes, we're going to Rabbit Cove!"

"Yes, we are—and we're nearly there! You've been asleep a long time. OK now, pet?" Mom wiped my nose with her tissue as if I was two years old.

"I'm sorry to be such a baby," I said, feeling ashamed.

"You're not a baby, darling! You're ever so grown up, much more than me. There now, let's get cracking. Rabbit Cove, here we come. Penny for the first one to see the sea."

I sat up properly and we edged off the shoulder back onto the road. I still felt a bit weird but Mom had the window right down and I breathed in deeply. We were on one of the yellow roads now, surrounded by fields of corn and barley, gentle rolling hills purple in the distance. And then I saw a dazzle of brilliant blue . . .

"The sea, the sea! I spotted it first! You did say a *pound* for the first one to see it, didn't you?"

"No, I didn't! A penny, you cheeky girl."

Mom slowed down when we got to the next road sign. We could stay on the main road and go to Seahaven—or turn down a little lane marked Rabbit Cove!

"OK, OK, we'll make for Rabbit Cove," said Mom.

"You bet!"

"Don't be too disappointed if there's nothing much there, sweetheart," said Mom. "We can just have a little wander and then make for Seahaven. I think that's a proper seaside town so we should be able to find a little bed-and-breakfast place there."

We turned down the lane for Rabbit Cove. There were tall trees growing on high banks on either side of us, their branches joining to make a dark green canopy overhead. Then there was a sign to a little farm, and then driveways to houses, then a whole street of little terraced houses with pebbles stuck on the walls. Then the shops started, a small supermarket, a dress shop, a little gallery, a newsagent's, a liquor store, an antique shop with a rocking chair outside, and a tearoom called Peggy's Parlour.

"Oh, we'll definitely go and have a cup of tea in Peggy's Parlour," said Mom, giggling. "It all looks so old-fashioned. I do hope Peggy herself is a little old lady in a black dress with a frilly white apron, tottering around writing everybody's orders in a little notebook tied to her waist."

"You are silly, Mom. Don't let's go there yet though. I want to see the sea."

"OK, OK, stop bouncing around in your seat!"

We drove on past a proper restaurant, a pub,

and a white hotel with a big green lawn and several swings.

"See, there *is* a hotel! Oh Mom, can we stay there?"

"Maybe. It might be a bit expensive."

"But Auntie Avril's given us lots of money."

"It might have to last us a long time until I manage to get a job," said Mom. She nibbled at her lip. "Beauty, what can I do? Jobwise, I mean. I've only ever been a receptionist, and I was hopeless."

"You could do *lots* of things, Mom," I said. "You could . . . be a cookie baker."

It was a little joke to make Mom laugh. She smiled at me. "OK, that's what I'll do," she said.

She turned down a steep little lane toward the seafront. There were more houses now with sloping gardens. Some of the houses had BED AND BREAKFAST signs.

"We *could* stay in one of these," I said.

"OK, we'll pick one later," said Mom.

We drove downward, round another bend, Mom's foot hard on the brakes—and then we were at the seafront.

"Oh, Mom!" I said.

"Oh, Beauty!" said Mom.

Rabbit Cove was perfect. There was a high cliff on either side (the rabbit's ears) sheltering a

217

beautiful cove of soft golden sand. There was hardly anyone on the beach, just a few families with little kids running about trailing seaweed and sticking flags in sandcastles. An old-fashioned artist with a beard and a baggy blue shirt was sitting up on the little white wall, painting. At the other end of the wall there was a small car park, a little wooden hut for toilets, and a beach shop-cum-café festooned with buckets and spades and an old tin ice-cream sign spinning outside.

"It's just like a picture in an old story book!" I said. "It's so lovely!"

I couldn't be sure I wasn't making it all up. I closed my eyes, counted to three, and opened them again. Rabbit Cove was still there, serenely beautiful.

"I'm so pleased it's lovely," said Mom. "I was hoping and hoping it would be and yet sure it would be this ramshackle old pebbly place, all gray and ugly."

"Maybe I'm still dreaming?" I said. "And you're dreaming it too, Mom."

"Well, let's park the car and then we'll have a little run on the beach. If you can feel the sand between your toes you're definitely wide awake," said Mom.

We put the car in the little car park. I delved into my suitcase for my drawing book and new markers and then we went on the beach. I kicked my shoes off and wiggled my toes in the soft powdery sand.

"I'm definitely not dreaming!" I said.

Mom kicked her own sandals off and did the same. "Doesn't it feel great!" she said. "Here, roll your jeans right up, Beauty. We'll go and dip our toes in."

We ran across the sand, slowing as it became hard and damp, and then both of us shrieking as the first wave washed around our ankles.

"It's absolutely *freezing!*" Mom said. "I think you can be the chief water-babe. I'll sit and watch."

Mom sat back on the soft sand looking after my markers for me while I waded around up to my knees, jumping waves, stooping to search for shells, walking up and down the little ridges in the wet sand. When I went back to Mom I was soaked right up to my bottom but she just laughed at me.

"They'll dry soon enough. That's what the sun's for! Are you hungry, sweetheart? Shall we have a picnic? Wait here!"

Mom sprang up and went skipping over the sand, not bothering to put her sandals on. She went into the beach shop. When she came out she was carrying two huge ice creams with a big carrier bag over her arm.

"The ice creams are for dessert but we'll have to

eat them first or they'll melt."

Mom sat down cross-legged and we licked our ice creams appreciatively. Each cone had two chocolate flakes and a little blob of raspberry sauce.

"They're a Rabbit Cove special," said Mom. "The chocolate flakes are meant to be ears and the jam blob is a little bunny nose."

"Yum!" I said, eating all the distinguishing features of my rabbit face.

When we'd finished our ice cream, Mom produced two cheese salad rolls, two packets of salt-and-vinegar chips, two mini chocolate donuts, two apples, two bananas, and two cartons of orange juice.

"This isn't a picnic, it's a veritable feast!" I said, clapping my hands. "There's only one thing missing—cookies!"

"We should have kept a few of Avril's cookies. I'm sure she's not going to munch her way through the whole batch," said Mom. "Oh well, I'll have to try and make some more some time."

We ate all our wonderful lunch and then Mom lay back on the sand, using her handbag as a pillow. I trickled sand on her feet and she giggled sleepily, shutting her eyes. She was asleep in seconds. I thought about burying her legs in the sand, but it was too soft and slithery to cling.

I tried to make a sandcastle, using my hands as scoops, but I needed the damp sand near the sea and I didn't want to leave Mom alone. I got out my drawing pad and markers and *drew* a sandcastle instead. I made it a huge sand palace with pinnacles and domes and towers. I had a sand princess with long golden hair peering out of her tower window, waving at the mermaids swimming in the moat around the castle. All the mermaids had very long hair right down to their scaly tails. I had a blonde, a brunette, and a redhead and then experimented with emerald green, purple, and electric blue long wavy hair. I gave them matching jewelery and fingernails and thought they looked gorgeous, if a little unusual.

I studded the mermaid moat with starfish and coral flowers and decorated the palace with seashells in elaborate patterns. The princess looked a little lonely even though she had the mermaids for company, so I drew more people looking out of the windows. I drew a queen mother with even longer golden hair, a best-friend princess with short black hair, and a handsome prince with a crown on his floppy brown hair. He was holding a very special royal rabbit who had a tiny padded crown wedged above her floppy ears.

Mom turned on her side, opened her eyes and yawned.

"Have you been drawing? Let's have a look. Oh, darling, that's lovely! It's so *detailed*. I must have been asleep ages." Mom sat up and stretched. "Shall we go and have a little walk around and explore Rabbit Cove?"

We stood up and brushed ourselves down. We didn't have a towel with us to get all the sand off our feet but when we got to the little wall Mom sat us down and rubbed our feet with the hem of her dress.

"Here," said the artist, holding out one of his painting rags. "Use this. I've got loads."

"That's very sweet of you," said Mom. "This is a lovely spot, isn't it?"

"Yes. I must have painted it hundreds of times but I never get sick of it," said the artist.

He was quite old and quite fat, with a smiley face and a little soft beard. He wore a big blue shirt and old jeans dappled with paint and surprising scarlet high tops.

"Are you admiring my funky sneakers?" he said, seeing me staring.

"I'd like a pair like that," I said shyly.

I stuck my feet in my own boring sandals and sidled toward him, keen to see his painting. It was very bright, the sky and sea a dazzling cobalt blue, the sand bright ochre yellow. I wondered if that was the way he really saw the soft gray-blue and pale primrose cove. He'd painted the children swimming, the families chatting—and right in the middle of his canvas there was a lovely blond woman lying asleep, a plump little girl by her side, her head bent over her drawing pad.

"You've painted us!" I said.

The artist smiled.

"Oh, God, let's have a look," said Mom, banging her sandals together and slipping them on her feet. She peered at the canvas, giggling.

"Oh dear, you've painted me fast asleep!" She squinted closely at the painting. "You've drawn me with my mouth open, like I'm drooling!"

"No I haven't! And anyway you looked lovely lying back like that." He turned to me. "You were drawing a long time."

"Oh, Beauty *loves* drawing. She's ever so good at it," said Mom.

"No I'm not," I mumbled. I wished Mom hadn't told him my stupid name.

"Yes you are. I shouldn't wonder if she ends up a proper artist like you," said Mom.

"I'm not a *proper* artist. I wish I was! No, I just *like* painting." He looked at me. "You've seen my work. Can I see yours?"

"Oh no, mine's silly. It's just made-up stuff," I said shyly.

"Go on, show him, Beauty," said Mom.

I opened up my drawing pad and flashed my sand picture at him bashfully.

"Oh my goodness! Let's have a proper look." He took the drawing back from me and peered closely at my picture.

"I know it's silly and babyish," I said. "I was just sort of fooling around. I know you don't really get rabbits with crowns and mermaids with green and purple hair. Well, mermaids aren't real anyway, obviously."

"That's the whole point of painting though. We can imagine the world the way we want it," he said. "I think you're very talented, Beauty. Is that your real name?"

"Poor Beauty hates her name," said Mom. "You can call her Cookie if you like. That's her new nickname."

"I think Beauty's much more distinctive," said Mike. "What's *your* name? Total Delight? Ravishing? Gorgeous?"

Mom laughed. "I'm Dilys—but everyone calls me Dilly."

"I'm Mike."

We all nodded and smiled and then stood a little foolishly, not knowing what to say next.

"So . . . are you here for a day out?" Mike asked.

"We're here on a little holiday," said Mom.

"Oh, lovely. You're staying here in Rabbit Cove?" said Mike.

"Oh yes," I said.

"At the hotel or a guest house?" Mike asked.

Mom and I looked at each other.

"Sorry! I didn't mean to be nosy," said Mike.

"No, no, it's just we haven't quite decided where we're staying yet," said Mom. "Maybe we should go and do that straight away, Beauty? Oh heavens, I hope they're not all fully booked."

"It's not the proper holiday season yet. You should be fine," said Mike. "There's just the one proper hotel in Rabbit Cove but there are lots of bed-and-breakfast guest houses."

"That's what we'd prefer. Could you recommend a particular one, seeing as you're local?" said Mom.

"I'll do my best," said Mike. "There's a row of them just up the hill in Primrose Terrace. I'll come with you if you like. I've finished my painting for today."

He let me help screw up all the tubes of oil paint and fit them carefully in their box.

"I *love* the smell of oil paint and the way it's so thick and shiny," I said.

"Have you ever used oil paints yourself?" Mike asked.

"No. Dad doesn't let me have paints," I said without thinking.

I wished I hadn't said *Dad*. It suddenly stopped being a vacation. I started to feel scared and sad all over again.

Mike was looking at me carefully.

"Tell you what—if you're around the beach tomorrow you can come and paint with me. I'll give you your own little bit of canvas, OK? Is that all right with you, Dilly?"

"It's very kind of you."

We went to get the car, Mike walking with us.

"Do you think the bed-and-breakfast places will have their own parking lot?" said Mom.

"There's a little alleyway behind the terrace of houses. You can park the car there. I'll show you if you like."

He got in the car beside Mom and directed her to the alleyway. It was a tight squeeze to get the car slotted in the space and Mom's always been terrible at parking. She made one attempt. Two attempts.

"It's OK," Mike said gently. "How about swinging the steering wheel around, backing in—no, no, the other way!"

"Oh God, I'm hopeless!" said Mom.

"No, you're not. It's blooming difficult parking here. It takes ages to get used to it. Do you want another go—or would you like me to back it in?"

"You do it, please!"

Mike had the car properly parked in a matter of moments. He didn't boast though, he just shrugged and smiled when Mom thanked him. We got the two suitcases out of the trunk, and Mike insisted on carrying them for us. I carried his paints and his art folder and his folding easel, feeling very important. I hoped people would look at me and think I was the real artist.

"OK, here we are, Primrose Terrace. Which guest house do you fancy?"

We gazed up and down the street. They were tall narrow Victorian houses painted in pretty pastels, pale yellow, pink, peach, and white.

"Which do you think, Beauty?" said Mom. "What about the one that's painted primrose yellow to match the name of the terrace?"

"That's *quite* a good choice," said Mike. "But maybe . . . ?"

"There's the pink one," said Mom.

"Not pink," I said, and Mike nodded in agreement.

"OK, OK, the peach one. That's got lovely roses in the garden," said Mom.

"Mmm. Maybe," said Mike. He was looking toward the white house at the end. I laid his art stuff down carefully and ran to have a proper look at it. It had a shiny green door and green willow-leaf curtains and there were white flowers painted on a sign above the door. I read the name—and came flying back to Mom and Mike.

"We have to stay in the white one at the end. It's called Lily Cottage!"

"*Excellent* choice," said Mike. "Let's see if they've got any vacancies."

We walked up to Lily Cottage. I rang the bell. We waited. I rang again. Nothing happened.

"They're obviously not in," said Mom. "Maybe we'd better go next door after all."

"Or maybe *I* can let you in?" said Mike, producing a key. He put it in the lock and opened the door with a flourish.

"It's *your* house!" said Mom, laughing.

"It's how I earn my living," said Mike, grinning. "I've got a double bedroom free with an en suite bathroom and a sea view. It's my best room and very cheap. Come and take a peek. I hope you like it."

It was a lovely old-fashioned room with a patchwork quilt on the bed, a rocking chair in the corner, two comfy armchairs with flowery cushions, a scarlet Chinese storage chest—and Mike's bright paintings all around the white-washed walls.

"We'll definitely take it!" said Mom.

"Make yourself at home," said Mike. "I'll go and

228

put the kettle on. I'm sure you'd like a cup of tea."

"I wish this *was* our home," I said to Mom, when he'd gone downstairs.

"Oh Beauty!" Mom sighed and opened her handbag, taking out her cell phone. "I think we'd better phone home."

"What? We're not going back, are we?"

"No, no. But it's only fair to let your dad know where we are. You're his daughter. I can't just whisk you away and not let him keep in contact."

"Not yet though, Mom. We're on *vacation*."

"Well, I think we should just reassure him that you're all right."

Mom switched on her phone. It immediately started beeping and beeping with many messages. Mom held it at arm's length, as if she thought it might explode. She pressed the first text message, the second, the third, so quickly that I couldn't read them. She listened to the first recorded message. She kept the phone pressed to her ear but I could still hear a few words. They were mostly rude swear words.

"Oh dear," said Mom. "Maybe we'll wait until tomorrow," and she switched the phone off again.

Fifteen

I woke up to see the sun streaming through a chink in the curtains. It was going to be another lovely sunny day in Rabbit Cove! I lay quietly beside Mom, fingering the stitching on the patchwork quilt, looking at each seaside picture in turn. Then I heard a loud mewing right outside the window. I jumped up and pulled back the curtains. Two seagulls were balancing boldly on the window ledge, tapping their beaks on the glass in a jaunty fashion.

"Shoo!" I said, tapping back at them.

They flew off and I wondered what it would be like to soar effortlessly up into the sky. I spread my arms and whirled around and around the bed.

"Whatever are you doing?" Mom mumbled.

"Just having a little fly," I said.

"You are such a funny kid," said Mom, sitting up and stretching. "Are you happy, babes?"

"Ever so, ever so, ever so. I simply love it here. Can we go on the beach again and have another picnic?"

"Of course we can."

"And do you think Mike was serious about letting me do oil painting?"

"I think so."

"He's so nice, isn't he?"

"Yes, he's a sweetheart. I'm sure he's not charging us the full rate for the room—but I'm not going to argue!" said Mom. She sniffed. "Can you smell bacon? Mmm!"

We washed quickly and then went downstairs to the breakfast room. There were two sets of couples wearing jeans and big woolly socks over their boots, obviously all set to walk along the coast path, and a family with a little boy and a toddler.

Mike rushed in and out of the room in a big navy-striped apron, bringing veggie sausage breakfasts for one walking couple, bacon and egg and black pudding for the other, baked beans on toast and boiled eggs with toast fingers for the family. Mom just wanted a bacon sandwich but I had a big plate of everything—and it was delicious. Mike was too busy to chat much, though he found the walkers a special map and he gave the two little boys some tiny cars to race up and down their arms and around and around their plates.

When the walkers and the family had all finished Mike came and sat down at our table and had a cup of tea with us. It made us feel special.

"What are you two ladies planning for today?" he said.

"The beach!" I said.

"Well, I've got to clean all the bedrooms and do a spot of shopping this morning," said Mike. "But this afternoon I'll be down on my usual patch with my paints, and you're very welcome to come and do a bit of painting too, Beauty."

Mom and I had another lovely lazy morning at Rabbit Cove and a picnic on the beach. The family with the two little boys were on the beach too. I built a real sandcastle down on the damp sand near the sea and they came and "helped" me, finding shells and seaweed to decorate it and pouring water from their buckets to make a moat.

Then Mike arrived and he had a small canvas especially for me! He'd even brought me a piece of board to mix my colors on and two different brushes, one fat, one thin.

"OK, what are you going to paint?" said Mike. "A seascape?"

"I think I'd like to do a portrait, a made-up one. Is that all right?" I asked.

"Of course it is, funny girl! You can paint whatever you want."

So I sketched out a big figure that nearly filled the whole canvas. I squeezed dabs of blue and black and brown and red and white paint on my palette and got started. It was such *fun* sploshing on the thick paint. It stayed obediently where I put it; it didn't slop all over the place like watercolor. If I made a mistake I could just wipe it off or decide to paint over it later.

I painted a man with shiny brown hair and lovely blue eyes. I gave him blue jeans and I fiddled around with the smaller brush, trying to give him a plaid shirt. It was tricky work, but not a lot of it showed because the man was holding a big white rabbit in his arms. It was hard making her *look* like a rabbit rather than a huge blob of marshmallow, but Mike showed me how to make a pale gray and do little dabbing strokes of the brush to look like fur. I mixed up a perfect pink for the rabbit's little nose, and I gave my man matching rosy cheeks.

"That's fantastic, Beauty," said Mike. He hesitated. "So . . . is that your dad?"

"No!" I said. "It's Sam and his rabbit Lily. They're on the television. It's a little kids' show. I'm a big baby." I hung my head.

"Beauty, you're looking at a man who used to watch a little kids' show called *The Magic Roundabout* every single day. In fact I have a daughter called Florence named after one of the *Roundabout* characters. Luckily she hasn't got a funny face and very big feet like the Florence puppet."

"I didn't see any girl at Lily Cottage," I said shyly.

"Oh no no, she's grown up now and lives in London, near her mom," said Mike.

"Oh," I said, nodding.

"We split up several years ago. My wife hated it here."

"How could you *possibly* hate Rabbit Cove?" I said, astonished.

I started doing the sky behind Sam, realizing that it might have made sense to fill it in first.

"Oh, Jenny likes city life, bright lights, lots going on, lots of shops. She found it incredibly boring when I took early retirement and we moved down here. I think she probably found *me* quite boring too," said Mike.

"You're not a *bit* boring," I said.

Mike laughed at me. "You're an incredibly polite girl, Beauty. You've obviously been impeccably brought up by your mom and dad. So . . ." He hesitated again. "Where *is* Dad?"

"Back at home," I said. I hesitated too. "I think maybe he and Mom have split up too. Just the day before yesterday, on my birthday, actually."

"Oh dear! So where are you going to go after your vacation here?"

I didn't say anything, painting green grass under Sam's feet. It went a bit blobby and lumpy, but I pretended the biggest lumps were lettuces for Lily.

"I was prying again," said Mike. "I'm sorry, take no notice. I'm so nosy." He tapped himself on his big cherry nose, scolding himself. I giggled, because he left a big smear of sand yellow paint on the tip.

"I think maybe you should wipe your nose, it's all painty now. Here, shall I do it?" I said, brushing at him. "I'm not really sure *where* we're going to go next."

"But Mom knows?"

"Nope. We did go to Auntie Avril but she couldn't have us for more than one night."

"I see. Well, what would you like to do, Beauty?"

I hung my head.

"Do you want to go back to Dad?" Mike asked gently.

"No! He tries to be a kind dad and he spends lots of money on me but he gets so scary sometimes. He gets mad at Mom and me and he broke all the cookies and he let my birthday rabbit out of its hutch and it *died*," I said, all in a rush.

I suddenly couldn't see my canvas anymore because my eyes were blurry with tears.

"Oh, Beauty, I'm so sorry. I didn't mean to upset you," said Mike, dabbing at my eyes with the much-used paint cloth.

I'd thought Mom was asleep down on the beach but she came dashing over the sand toward us.

"What have you said to upset her?" she demanded of Mike.

"It wasn't Mike's fault, Mom, honest," I snivelled. "I just thought about my *rabbit*."

"Oh. Yes. Poor darling," said Mom, giving me a big hug.

"It *was* my fault," said Mike. "I was asking stuff about her dad. I'm sorry, it was unforgivable of me. I was worried because Beauty let it slip that you haven't got anywhere to go."

"We'll be absolutely fine," said Mom. "And you needn't worry about us not paying for our room and breakfast, I've got more than enough."

"Oh Dilly, stop it. You *know* that's not what I'm worrying about."

"You don't have to worry at all," said Mom. "Come on, Beauty, I think we'll go for a walk."

"But, Mom, I haven't finished my Sam and Lily painting," I said.

"Oh, for heaven's sake, I'm getting a bit sick of stupid Sam and his Lily," said Mom. "Come on. Now."

I glanced despairingly at Mike.

"Better do what your mom says," he said.

So I miserably followed Mom along the seafront and up a little winding chalk path to the clifftop. I walked behind her, glaring at her back. She walked faster and faster, swinging her arms, her fists clenched. I lagged behind, out of breath.

"Keep *up*, Beauty," Mom hissed.

"I don't want to," I said, and I suddenly sat down.

"Oh come on, don't be a silly baby," said Mom.

"Stop bossing me about! Why are you being so *horrid* all of a sudden? You were so rude to Mike and he was just trying to be *kind*."

"He made you cry. I'm not having that."

"You *know* why I was crying—it was because of my rabbit."

"Beauty, you spent five minutes maximum with that blessed rabbit," said Mom, squatting down beside me.

"I still loved it—and it was so terrible seeing it without its poor little head," I said, my voice going shaky again. "I'll never forgive Dad for that, never never never."

"Your dad didn't mean that to happen. I know he undid the hutch but I'm sure he just meant Birthday to escape. You mustn't blame him."

"Why are you sticking up for *Dad*? Yet you were being mean to Mike who's ever so nice. And being mean to me too."

"I'm not being mean. Don't be so childish."

"I'm a *child*, how else am I supposed to act? And you *are* being horribly mean. Why are you being so nasty, even saying Sam and Lily are stupid."

"Well they are. And you're stupid being so obsessed with them. You're a big baby," said Mom.

"I am *not*," I said, and I shoved her, hard.

She was still squatting and so she lost her balance. She fell backward, legs in the air.

"Don't you *dare* hit me!" she said. "Do that again and I'll hit you right back."

"I *didn't* hit you, I just shoved. *This* is a hit," I said, and I punched her shoulder.

It was only a token punch, a feeble little tap, but Mom smacked me hard on my leg. I stared at her, shocked. She'd never ever smacked me before.

Mom seemed stunned too. Her face suddenly crumpled and she burst into tears.

"I don't know why you're crying. *I'm* the one who should be crying—that really hurt," I said.

"I'm sorry," Mom sobbed, her head in her hands.

She cried and cried. I edged closer and then put my arm around her. She cried even harder, clinging to me.

"Oh, Beauty, I'm so sorry," she gasped. "How could I have slapped you like that? You're right, I was being horribly mean. It's just I'm so *scared*. I don't know what to do for the best. I was awake half the night worrying about it. I think I've gone crazy, running away with you like this. I haven't got an idea in my head what we're going to do. I couldn't stand Mike looking at me like that, acting so kind and concerned, when he must think I'm the worst mother in the world."

"He doesn't think that at all. He *likes* you. Don't you like him?"

"Of course I do. I feel embarrassed that I was so snotty to him. I think we'd better be on our way tomorrow."

"Oh *no*, Mom. I love it here."

"I know, darling, but we can't stay here forever."

"Why can't we?"

"This is just our little vacation, you know that. We've got to make proper plans. I've been trying so hard, but my head just goes whirling around and around. I've got so used to your dad telling me

what to do I can't seem to think for myself anymore."

"So I'll think for you. We'll stay here in Rabbit Cove and you'll get a job, and we'll find our own little place—"

"Oh, Beauty, we couldn't even afford a blooming beach house."

"Well then, I'll build us a blooming sandcastle and we'll live in that, happily ever after," I said.

Mom burst out laughing and hugged me tight. "Oh, thank God I've got you, babe. We'll be fine, you and me, just so long as we stick together. I'm sorry I was so crabby."

"Are you going to say sorry to Mike too?"

"Oh, lordy. Yes, I suppose so. He *has* been sweet to us—and it was lovely him showing you how to paint."

"I'm quite good at it, aren't I! We don't really have to go tomorrow, do we? I so want to paint some more."

"We'll see," said Mom.

When we walked back arm in arm we saw Mike still perched on the wall, painting away.

"I don't think we'd better disturb him just now," said Mom.

"Oh, Mom, stop being such a coward! Let's get it over with," I said.

I practically had to pull her over to Mike. Her cheeks went very red as we got nearer. He didn't look up, even when we were standing right next to him. He carried on dabbing paint on his canvas in determined fashion.

Mom made an agonized face at me. I gave her a nudge. She swallowed hard.

"Mike, I'm very sorry for being so rude and off-hand with you," she said in a tiny voice.

Mike paused, paintbrush in mid-air. He looked up at last.

"I don't blame you. I was asking Beauty all sorts of silly questions which were none of my business," he said stiffly.

"Not at all," said Mom.

Mike nodded awkwardly. Mom made little shuffling movements, about to stride off again. I couldn't bear leaving it like that.

"So to make friends properly we'd like to ask you out to supper tonight," I said.

Mom and Mike stared at me, looking equally astonished.

"*Where?*" Mom mouthed at me.

We'd discovered that Peggy's Parlour closed on the dot of six last night so we'd bought cod and fries from the fish shop and eaten them on the beach.

"That's very sweet of you, but I was actuall planning a meal in tonight, with friends," said Mike.

"Oh," I said, drooping.

"Yes. I do a great fish pie. Fancy trying it, you two?"

"Well, we wouldn't want to intrude, not if you're having your friends around," said Mom.

Mike looked at me. I rolled my eyes.

"*Mom!* I think *we're* the friends," I said.

So we had supper with Mike. We did wonder if he'd invited any of the other guests, but the two walking couples drove off to some gourmet pub and the family went to try the evening meal at the hotel.

"So it's just us," I said, smiling. "Mom, can I wear my gray dress and pinafore and my new boots?"

"Oh, Beauty! It's just supper. Just pop a clean T-shirt on and wear it with your jeans."

"No, I want to look lovely. Well, I know I look terrible no matter what, but I *feel* lovely in my gray dress."

"Oh, sweetheart. You don't look terrible at all. But OK, you wear your gray outfit if you like. *I'm* not going to make a big effort though."

Mom wore her jeans—but she changed into her little pink clingy top with pearl buttons and she wore her pink strappy high heels. She even bothered to paint new nail polish on her toes.

We went downstairs at seven as Mike had suggested but the breakfast room was empty, all the tables set ready for the morning.

"Oh goodness, maybe he's changed his mind," Mom whispered.

But Mike came into the breakfast room, beaming at us.

"Through here, ladies. I thought we'd be cozier in the kitchen, and it won't give any of the other guests ideas if they come back early."

Mike had on his stripy apron, but underneath he was wearing a big blue flowery shirt and clean jeans without a single paint smear, and his big high tops shone scarlet. He had obviously made a *big* effort.

"Oh, Beauty! *Is* it you, Beauty?" he said. "You look so grown up. And you look even younger, Dilly. You're just like sisters."

We were used to people saying this but it was still good to hear. We followed him into the kitchen. I'd expected it to be a big formal stainless-steel working kitchen, but it was a glorious colorful old-fashioned room with a great wooden dresser hung with willow-pattern plates. Old toby jugs jostled each other on the windowsill and there were big blue luster vases on the wooden table, containing red asters, white daisies, yellow lilies, and pink rosebuds.

The stove itself was big and green and spread a cozy glow throughout the kitchen. There was a red and yellow and blue rag rug on the tiled floor with a black cat stretched out, comfortably dozing.

"I didn't know you had a cat, Mike!" I said, squatting down beside it and stroking its sleek head.

"I don't. It's next door's, but she's got a sixth sense whenever I make fish pie. She comes on the hunt for the scraps," said Mike. "Right, sit yourself down, girls. What would you like to drink? White wine, Dilly? And I thought you'd like a special *red* wine, Beauty." He grinned and poured us each a glass. Mine was the most beautiful deep red. I knew it couldn't really be wine but I felt wickedly grown up sipping it all the same.

"It's wonderful!" I said. "What *kind* of wine is this, Mike?"

"Oh, the very best. Vintage pomegranate," said Mike. "Now, you ladies talk among yourselves while I do the finishing touches to the meal."

He popped some runner beans and asparagus into a pan of boiling water and then had a peek at the fish pie. It was golden brown and smelled wonderful. The cat raised her head from the mat and looked hopeful again.

"No, you've had your share, greedy-guts," said Mike. "It's our turn now."

It truly was delicious—soft creamy mashed potato with a crispy cheese topping and large chunks of haddock and cod and curly pink prawns. I ate my entire plateful and then had a second helping. Mike didn't frown at me and make comments about my weight. He seemed delighted that I appreciated his pie and congratulated me on my appetite. Mom couldn't quite clear her plateful because she's got the appetite of a bird at the best of times, but she told Mike he was a brilliant cook.

"I'm not so great when it comes to desserts, I'm afraid," he said, producing a bowl of red apples, some purple grapes and an orange cheese. "I'm not sure I've got any sweet nibbles for you, Beauty. There might be a cookie or two in that tartan tin."

"Are they home-made?" I asked.

"Beauty!" said Mom.

"No, sorry, I don't do that sort of baking," said Mike.

"Mom does," I said proudly. "She makes the most fantastic cookies, all different sorts, iced and chocolate chip and cherry and oatmeal raisin."

"Mm! So you're a good cook, are you, Dilly?"

"No! I've just got a very sweet daughter," said

Mom. "I can't cook for the life of me, apart from cookies. I *can* make good cookies though."

"What about breakfasts?" said Mike. "I'm going to need a hand in the kitchen now the summer season's starting up, and I usually employ a student to come in and do cleaning. It's a bit of a boring job but you'd be finished and free by lunch time. You don't fancy trying it for a few weeks?"

Mom looked stunned. She just stared at Mike, not saying a word. So I answered for her.

"Yes, *please!*" I said.

"No, no, hang on, Beauty. Mike's just being kind, trying to be helpful," Mom muttered.

"No, I *need* help. It's not a great job and I can't pay much, but it'll give you time to think out what you really want to do. The only trouble is I can't let you keep the first-floor double, not if you're here as staff. If I have a live-in girl she usually sleeps up in the attic, but it's a bit basic, I'm afraid."

"The attic!" I said, clapping my hands. "Oh, can we see? I've always wanted to live in an old house with a proper attic."

So Mike led us up the three flights of stairs to his attic. It was a dark narrow little room with just one very small window, but it was still beautiful. The small bed had a navy patchwork quilt with silver stars and moons appliquéd all over it. There was a squashy ruby velvet armchair with a matching footstool and a red-and-blue tapestry curtain hiding a clothes rail.

"Oh dear, I don't think it's anywhere near big enough for you," said Mike worriedly.

"We can easily scrunch up together. It's great!" I said.

I ran to the window, rested my elbows on the sill, and looked out over the red tile rooftops to the sea. "I feel just like Sara Crewe in *A Little Princess. She* lived in an attic!"

I knelt down, examining the baseboard.

"Whatever are you doing, Beauty? Get up!" said Mom.

"I'm just seeing if there are any little rat holes," I said.

"What? There are absolutely no rats in this house, I promise," said Mike. "You won't find so much as a mouse's whisker!"

"Oh, I'd *love* my own pet rat like Sara's Melchisedec," I said.

"You might, Beauty, but I definitely wouldn't," said Mom. She smiled at Mike. "We'll be great here, Mike, Beauty and me. I'll bring our stuff up here and start work in the morning, how about that?"

"No, no, you must have your little vacation first."

"Please. I'd like to get started right away. Shall we shake on it?"

Mom stuck out her hand and they shook, sealing the deal.

Sixteen

Mom was up extra early the next morning, wearing her checked shirt and jeans, her hair pulled back into a ponytail.

"Do I look like a breakfast chef?" she asked me anxiously.

"No, you need checkered trousers and one of those big floppy white hats," I said, laughing at her.

"Don't, Beauty! I'm so scared. I'm sure I'm going to mess up royally. Your dad always says I can't even boil an egg and I *can't*—they always come out rock hard or so soft they ooze everywhere. Mike's being so kind but he'll so regret it when I muck everything up for him."

"Mom, you *can* cook."

"I can't give folk a plate of cookies for their blooming breakfast!"

"I don't know, oatmeal raisin cookies might be just the ticket."

I went down with Mom to the kitchen, though she told me not to.

"I'm like the kitchen maid. I promise I'll be useful and not get in the way," I said to Mike.

"You're child labor and I'll get sent to jail for exploiting you," said Mike, but he patted me on the head and told me to stay.

He sent Mom into the dining room to take the breakfast orders. She got in a terrible fluster at first and couldn't remember which walkers wanted veggie sausages and which black pudding, and whether they wanted tea or coffee, but I'd been lurking in the doorway and knew exactly. Mike asked Mom to keep an eye on the sausages and bacon while he made some porridge for a new pair of old ladies. Mom's hand shook as she tried to turn the sausages so that three of them shot straight out of the pan and skidded across the floor.

"Oh God, I'm so sorry!" she said, nearly in tears.

"They can be *your* breakfast, Dilly!" said Mike cheerily. "Never mind, shove some more under the grill, there's a dear."

He didn't get the slightest bit angry, dancing around the kitchen, laughing and joking. Mom was soon laughing and joking back. She had to serve up the little boys' breakfasts and she made them each a face on a plate: a sausage cut in two for the eyes, a tomato nose and a bacon mouth, which they both loved. She made a smiley golden syrup face in both bowls of porridge too and the old ladies clapped their little claw hands in delight.

Mike seemed pleased when we all had break-fast together—but Mom and I *really* came into our own when it came to making the beds and doing the cleaning. We were used to living in a home where everything had to be pin-neat perfect. I'd followed Mom around when I was a toddler, doing my own "dusting" with a hankie and riding on the vacuum cleaner. Now I could tackle housework properly myself. We worked together in each room, making beds, cleaning the bathroom, vacuuming the carpet.

We were astonished at everyone's untidiness. We didn't like to tidy things up too thoroughly in case people thought we were meddling with their things, but we couldn't help playing little games. The walkers had left big woolly socks strewn all over the floor so we hung them in a row at the foot of the bed like Christmas stockings. The little boys had thrown their teddy bears every-where so I collected them up and tucked them all into the cot, the covers pulled up tight to their button noses.

Mike did a tiny tactful inspection in our wake and grinned appreciatively.

"I've got two girls for the price of one—and you've both done an excellent job. I *knew* it was my lucky day when I spotted you on the beach."

"*Our* lucky day," I said happily. "Can we do some

more painting together this afternoon, Mike?"

"You bet we can," said Mike.

Mom and I went up to our little attic room to gather our things together for the beach. We were running out of clean clothes now but Mike said we could use his washing machine.

"I wish I'd packed more sensibly," said Mom. "I filled half my suitcase with your baby photos and all the pictures you've ever drawn for me—and yet I forgot my nightie and my good underwear and I didn't even think to take any tights. Oh well, I can always buy some more when I get my first wages. Unless we ask your dad if we can go back to collect some more stuff? No, maybe not."

"*Definitely* not!"

"We'll have to phone him though." Mom took a deep breath. "Now!"

"*No*, Mom."

"Come on, we've got to. It's only fair and responsible."

"But he'll spoil it all."

"Beauty, he's your *father*."

"Yes, but I wish he wasn't."

"Now don't be silly."

"He wishes I wasn't his daughter."

"Now that's totally out of order. Your dad thinks the world of you."

"He's ashamed of me. He'd swap me for Skye quick as a wink."

"That's crazy," said Mom, but she was nibbling her lip, not looking me in the eye. "You mustn't ever think that, babes."

"I don't just think it, Mom, I *know* it."

"And *I* know you're just chattering away so I'll lose my nerve and put off phoning your dad. But I'm not going to!" Mom's fingers darted over the phone keypad and she pressed the green button before I could stop her.

"You're through to the desk of Gerry Cookson," said Dad in his brightest and best Happy Homes tone.

Mom and I stared at each other. He sounded so cheerily normal, as if nothing had happened.

"He's fine, Mom! Hang up now!" I hissed—but Mom had already started talking.

"Hello, Gerry darling," she said, and then made a face. The "darling" had obviously slipped out from force of habit.

"Dilly? Dilly, what the *hell* are you playing at?" Dad's voice revved up. I could hear him; Mike all the way downstairs could hear him; even kids down on the beach could hear him.

"I'm not playing, Gerry. This isn't a game," said Mom.

"You've been gone three *days*. You've made your point. Now pack your gear and get yourself home, pronto."

"We're not actually coming home," said Mom.

"*What?* Don't talk such total trash. Of course you are. What sort of a mother are you, flouncing out of your lovely home and dragging poor little Beauty with you?"

I tried to take the phone to stick up for Mom but she wouldn't let me.

"You were the one who told us to get out, Gerry," Mom said.

"Because you were totally out of order, you hussy," Dad bellowed.

"Well, nice to know what you think of me," said Mom. "Now listen, Gerry, I'm trying to be as responsible as possible. I know you need to know where Beauty is—"

"No! *No! NO!*" I said, jumping up and down.

"We're staying at a little spot on the coast called Rabbit Cove. It's lovely here. I promise you Beauty's very happy."

"Stop babbling this nonsense! Now come back home this *instant!*"

"We're going to stay here for a while, Gerry, at least for the summer season."

"And what exactly are you going to live on,

256

you little fool? You needn't think I'm sending any money for you and the kid."

"I've got a job," said Mom proudly.

"*You've* got a job?" Dad said. "What is it? The Useless Ageing Dumb Blonde Page Three Pin-Up job?"

Mom took the phone away from her ear, stared at it a moment, and then ended the call.

"About time," I said.

"Oh God," said Mom, starting to shake.

"I *told* you so," I said.

"Don't, Beauty," said Mom, and her eyes went watery.

"I'm sorry. I *hate* people who say I told you so. I didn't really mean it," I said, giving her a hug.

We stayed hugging hard, glancing anxiously at the phone. It started ringing again almost immediately. Mom switched it off quickly, keeping the phone at arm's length as if Dad could wriggle right out of it and grab her.

"OK, babes, let's go to the beach," said Mom.

We left the phone shut up in our dressing-table drawer and went down to the sands. We were both hot and flushed. We longed to cool down by going in for a swim. We hadn't packed bathing suits but Mom felt I'd look perfectly decent in my T-shirt and underpants.

"I can't go swimming in my *underpants*!"

"You wore them with your T-shirt on the beach the other day."

"Yes, sitting down. I can't go gallivanting into the sea dressed like that. Everyone will stare at me and laugh."

"No they won't! Don't be so silly. Look, *I'll* go in wearing my underwear. I've got my old red bra and panties on. They look *kind* of like a bikini. OK, get ready, *strip*!"

Mom ripped her top and jeans off. I gaped at her—and then pulled my own jeans off. We went charging into the sea. It was incredibly cold but we didn't hang around shrieking. We plunged straight in and splashed around like crazy.

We saw Mike setting up his easel by the wall and called to him to come and join us. He was an old spoilsport and wouldn't even come in wading. He painted us instead, bobbing about in the sea, Mom in her red "bikini" and me in my big T-shirt.

When I'd dried off I went to paint with him too. I did another Sam and Lily portrait: Sam was sunbathing in a funny long stripy costume and Lily was hunched up on a deckchair, licking a carrot-flavored popsicle, with sunglasses hooked onto her ears. I sang the *Rabbit Hutch* song under my breath as I painted, and I made Sam say, "Hey there," to me.

"Hey there," said Mike, thinking I was talking to him.

"Hey," I said again, giggling.

Mom put her clothes back on when she'd sunbathed herself dry. She gathered up our beach stuff and came to join us up on the wall.

"Do you want to do some painting too, Dilly?" Mike asked.

"You have to be joking!" said Mom. "No, I'm going to pop back to Lily Cottage if that's OK. I'm planning a little surprise."

I had an idea what Mom's surprise would be. Sure enough, when Mike and I went back to the guest house with our finished canvases there was a wonderful warm sweet cookie smell the moment we opened the door. Mike breathed in deeply.

"What's your mom been up to?" he asked.

"Cookies!"

They were the most amazing ice-cream cookies: sugar cookies for the cones with different colored frostings on each one, white, pink, and pale brown.

"Oh Mom, *ice-cream* cookies!" I said. "How did you cut them all into such neat shapes?"

"There was this funny little sandcastle-making

kit in the beach shop and they had three different cutters, starfish, mermaids, and ice-cream cones!" said Mom. "It was only one pound fifty so I thought I'd treat us. And I bought the flour and sugar and eggs myself, Mike. I wanted to give you this little present to say thank you for being so kind to us."

"That's truly lovely of you, Dilly! They look wonderful. Gosh, you've made so many!"

"Well, I thought we could offer all the guests a cookie and a cup of tea when they come back from the beach or wherever. I thought they might like it," said Mom.

They all *loved* Mom's cookies—and not just the children. The two very old ladies were particularly appreciative and asked Mike where he'd bought such lovely novelty cookies.

"I didn't buy them. Dilly here made them with her own fair hands," he said.

"My goodness! Well, they're excellent, my dear. We used to run a little teashop and we'd have been so proud to serve your cookies, Dilly," they said earnestly.

Mom went bright pink with pride and I wanted to hug her. She practically danced up to our little attic bedroom.

"I'm good at cookies now, *really* good at them!" she said, lying back on our bed and bicycling her legs in the air. "I've never been good at anything in my life, Beauty, but now I can say I'm a top cookie-maker! I'm so happy!"

"So am I, Mom, so am I," I said, leaning my arms on the windowsill and gazing out across the rooftops at the glistening sea.

Then I glanced down at our road, and saw a silver Mercedes draw up at the end. I stared, telling myself it couldn't possibly be Dad. There were hundreds and hundreds of silver Mercedes all over England. But then the door opened and a man stamped out, a small square balding man with a salmon-pink face. It *was* Dad.

I opened my mouth but no sound came out. I watched him marching up the path and hammering on the door of number one Primrose Terrace. Someone answered the door, Dad said something, waited, then stormed back up the path and tried number two. He was systematically searching for us.

"Mom!" I croaked.

"What, darling?"

"It's Dad! He's here and he's going to every guest house and he'll be knocking at our door in a minute or two! Oh quick, Mom, we've got to get out of here!"

Mom jumped up and ran to the window.

"Oh, God! Look at his face, he's *flaming*!" Mom took a deep breath. "But we're not running, sweetheart. We're going to stay here. We'll see him and . . . we'll talk quietly and sensibly and maybe Dad will understand."

"Are you *nuts*, Mom? Dad never understands. Come on, please!" I said, shaking her, but she wouldn't be budged.

"We're not going to skulk in our room. We'll go and meet him," she said, taking hold of my hand.

We went downstairs hand in hand, up the hallway, and opened the green front door. We stood in the porchway of Lily Cottage, waiting. We heard Dad's footsteps, his abrupt knocking, his demands. *Have you got a Mrs. Cookson staying here—Mrs. Cookson and her daughter, Beauty?* Then he pounded back up next door's path and burst through our gate. He was so intent on finding us that he wasn't quite focusing. He stamped halfway up the path staring at us but somehow not *seeing* us. Then he stopped still, mouth open.

"Hello, Gerry," said Mom calmly—although I could feel she was trembling.

He stared at us, his face flooding purple.

"Right. Come on. Get yourselves out of this dump *now*. You're coming back home with me."

I hung on tight to Mom's hand. Dad looked so crazy I was scared he'd pick us both up and stuff us head first into the trunk of the Mercedes.

"We're not coming. This is our home now," said Mom.

"This isn't a home, it's a tacky little B and B—and a right dump it looks too," said Dad. "Why didn't you stay in the hotel up in the village?"

"It's a *lovely* home, Dad," I said.

"You shut your mouth, Beauty. I'm sick of you. If you hadn't started begging for that bloody rabbit then none of this would have happened," Dad shouted.

The two teashop ladies came into the hall behind us, coughing discreetly to let us know they were there.

"Come on, I haven't got time to mess around discussing the pros and cons of guest houses," said Dad. "Get your stuff and get cracking—*now*!"

The two old ladies gasped.

"Are you all right, dear? Shall we go and get Mike?" one enquired timidly.

"Mike? Who the hell's *Mike*?" Dad asked.

"I'm Mike," said Mike, coming into the hallway. He put his arms around the elderly ladies.

"Don't worry, my dears. I'll look after things here. You should go up to your room," he said. Then he walked forward and stood beside Mom and me.

"I gather you're Dilly's husband? Would you like to come in?" he said.

"No, I'm not bloody coming in! I'll thank you not

to interfere. Just who the hell do you think you are?" Dad shouted.

"I'm Dilly and Beauty's friend," said Mike.

"Do you think I'm stupid? Friend! You won't make a fool out of me," said Dad, and he punched Mike right on the nose.

"For God's sake!" said Mike thickly, blood dribbling. He felt his nose gingerly. "Have you gone crazy?"

"Oh, Mike, I'm so sorry. Here, have a tissue," said Mom frantically.

"Do you think I was born yesterday? How long have you known her? So this was all a put-up job! I *knew* you didn't have the nerve to leave me and strike out on your own, Dilly! But is *he* the best you can do? He's an old man, for pity's sake—and he doesn't look like he has a bean to his name."

"You're right on both those counts," said Mike. "But totally wrong when it comes to any kind of relationship between Dilly and me. We are simply friends, plus I'm technically her employer."

"You *what*?" said Dad. "What do you employ her *as*, might I ask?"

"She's my breakfast chef," said Mike.

Dad stared—and then he started spluttering with laughter.

"Well, if you want to kill off all your guests then

set our Dilly free in your kitchen! She can't cook to save her life. All she can make is crappy *cookies*."

"Very, very good cookies," said Mike. "Would you like to come in and calm down and have a cup of tea and one of Dilly's cookies?"

"Don't take that patronizing tone with me! This is a private conversation between me and my wife." Dad took a step nearer Mom. Mike did too, protectively.

"Now listen up, Dilly. You obviously cleared off because you thought the whole business was going down the toilet, and me with it. But I've got a lot of pals in the right places. They're dropping the bribery nonsense, and now this guy's tipped me off about riverside council site that's going to be pulled down. It could be even bigger than the Water Meadows deal and I'm pretty damn sure I'm going to get it. Do you understand what I'm saying?"

"Yes, you're probably going to make a lot more money," said Mom.

"So I'm giving you one last chance, girl. Come back now and make the most of it—or I'll cut you off without a penny, you and the kid."

"Gerry, I don't want your money," said Mom. "That wasn't the reason I married you. I wanted you to look after me. But I'm not that stupid little girl anymore. It's time I learned to look after myself, and Beauty too, of course."

"Well, to hell with you," said Dad. "I can do a lot better than you. You're already losing your looks." Then he looked at me. "And *you*'ve never had any looks to speak of. You're just a waste of space, both of you. I wasted my time driving all this way to find you. You can stew here in this little seaside dump for ever for all I care."

Dad spat on the doorstep and then stamped off. Mom and I stood watching, still holding hands tightly.

"Phew," said Mike. "Well, come inside my little seaside dump, my dears. *We'll* have that cup of tea and another cookie—and I need to bury my poor nose in a bag of frozen peas!"

"I'm so, so sorry, Mike. I feel so terrible. Do you think you need to go to hospital? It could be broken!" said Mom.

"I very much doubt it. It's been broken twice before in football accidents so it's no big deal even if it is. It'll be fine. We'll all be fine, once we've stopped shaking!"

We stayed chatting to Mike and eating cookies, Mom and Mike talking about anything under the sun—apart from Dad. But when Mom and I went upstairs she made a *"help"* face at me.

"It looks like there's no going back now," she said.

"We'll stew here for ever, hurray, hurray, hurray!" I said. "So, Mom, *is* this home now?"

"Yes, I suppose it is."

"Then can I write to Rhona to let her know where I am?"

"Of course, darling."

I got out my best card and Auntie Avril's markers. I drew a picture of myself on the front, painting with Mike. I did a teeny weeny picture of *my* picture on Mike's easel, and a picture of Rhona holding poor dear Birthday on my canvas.

I wasn't quite sure what I was going to write to Rhona so I spent a long time coloring everything in. I even did the sea in the background all different blues and greens, leaving a little white tip on the top of each wave.

When the page was shiny and stiff with color I had to turn over and write my letter. I'd been rehearsing what to say inside my head but it was so difficult. In the end I just scribbled:

Dear Rhona,

Oh dear, I think this card will come as a shock as Mom and I have moved to the seaside. Rabbit Cove is lovely and we are staying at Mike's guest house and he has been teaching me how to paint (see front). I am happy to be here but so sad I can't see you anymore (though it would be GREAT if you ever came on vacation here!). I do hope you still want me to be best friends even though I'm here and you're there.

Give Reginald Redted a kiss and a spoonful of honey from me.

Love from Beauty xx

P.S. Something very very very sad happened to dear Birthday. It's so awful that I can't write it. But he will always be the best birthday present in the world.

I put Lily Cottage as my new address but I didn't really expect Rhona to write back. She wasn't really a girl for writing letters. But in two days' time I got a little *package* from her. It was small and soft and when I slid my little finger under the wrapping paper I felt *fur*.

I thought Rhona was sending me Reginald Redted to keep me company, but when I ripped the paper open I found a tiny droopy bear in a very wrinkled, faded navy outfit.

"Nicholas Navybear!" I whispered. "But you *drowned!*"

I opened Rhona's note.

Dear Beauty,

Oh I will miss you so! Guess what, Dad drained our swimming pool yesterday to clean it out and Nicholas Navybear was stuck in the drain!!! My mom washed him and steamed him dry but he still looks a bit weird. I hope you will still like him.

Love from your best friend, Rhona x x x

P.S. I hope nothing too dreadful happened to Birthday, but never mind.

Seventeen

"**I**think we'd better get you into a school here, Beauty," said Mom, as we had a cup of tea together after serving breakfast.

I stared at Mom, appalled.

"I don't want to go to *school*!" I said. "I can't! I've got to do my share of the guest-house work—and then I paint with Mike. I'm *working*, Mom."

"Don't be such a noodle, you know you've got to go to school."

"Yes, *some* day, but not *now*. It'll be summer vacation soon anyway. I can start school in September, if I must."

"You'll start *now*. I want to do everything properly. What if your dad starts suing for custody of you and it comes out in court I didn't send you to school. I don't want to be declared an unfit mother! No, you're going, sweetheart, and that's final. We'll ask Mike where the Rabbit Cove elementary school is."

"That's simple," said Mike, coming in to load the dishwasher. "There isn't one. It closed down five years ago because the numbers were dwindling."

"Hurray!" I said. "Then I can't go, Mom, can I?"

"Yes, you can. You'll have to go to the nearest school, that's all," said Mom determinedly.

It turned out the nearest primary school was in Seahaven, a good six miles away.

"Then I can't go," I said.

"Yes, you can. You have to," said Mom. "It's the law."

"But how on earth could I get there?"

"I'll have to drive you."

"You can't, not if you're serving breakfast."

"Well, maybe there's a bus. Although I don't want you going on a bus on your own. Oh, God, how can I be in two places at once?" said Mom.

"Don't worry, Dilly," said Mike. "There are kids at number two and number seventeen. They go on the bus. Beauty can go with them."

"It's not *fair*," I raged. "I won't go. You can't *make* me, Mom."

"Stop it, Beauty. You're giving me a headache," said Mom.

"Here, Beauty, leave your mom in peace," said Mike. "Come shopping with me. I need to stock up on lots of flour and sugar and stuff. Your mom's cookies are getting incredibly popular. Mrs. Brooke next door has got wind of them and wants to buy a batch to offer to *her* guests, if you please!"

Mike kept on chattering as we walked up the hill to the little supermarket. He kept asking for advice as we went around all the shelves, getting me stretching and bending and balancing and adding up in my head. He didn't mention the dreaded *S* word until we were trailing home, with huge grocery bags in both hands.

"Now then," he puffed. "About school . . ."

"You think I've calmed down now and I'll be reasonable. But I'm still—" I tried to think of the right word. "*Adamant!*" I finished triumphantly.

"Does it not occur to you that a girl intelligent enough to use a posh word like *adamant* might be in need of a good school?"

"There's no such thing as a good school. I think they're all bad bad bad."

"You didn't like your last school?"

"It was awful, the worst ever. It was ever so posh—and I'm not."

"But you must do OK in most classes?"

"That's partly the problem. If you have top grades that's another reason for everyone to tease you and call you Brainbox and Cleverclogs," I said gloomily. "I *did* try to act thick when I first went to Lady Mary Mountbank but the teacher got annoyed with me and said I wasn't trying. She got really upset and I hated that and so I worked hard and she was pleased so *then* I got called a teacher's pet too."

"Well, they could call you worse things."

"Oh, they did, they did! There was this one girl called Skye—she was ever so pretty and popular but the meanest girl *ever* and she invented a new nasty nickname for me nearly every day. It was just like a game to her. The worst nickname of all was . . ." I swallowed, still scarcely able to say it. "Ugly," I mumbled, my eyes stinging.

"What was that?" Mike said apologetically. "I didn't quite catch it."

"Ugly!" I said, shivering with the shame of it.

"Oh dear," said Mike, but he didn't sound shocked. "That's not very nice."

"It's a silly take on my name, Beauty. Skye laughed and laughed at it because I'm the exact opposite of my name. I *am* Ugly," I said.

"Oh *dear*," said Mike, more sympathetically. "You're not the *slightest* bit ugly, Beauty. You're not a pretty-pretty curly-wurly sort of girl, I grant you, but I think you look bright and intelligent and interesting. However, I'm not going to waste my breath trying to convince you, because I know what you women are like! And this poisonous Skye seems to have done her best to demoralize you. What about the school before this last one? Was that posh too?"

"It wasn't posh, it was quite tough, but they didn't like me there either. They all had a belly laugh at my name too."

274

"And you're worried that's what will happen at Seahaven?"

"Yep. Unless I can make them call me something else, like Cookie."

"Cookie's a cool nickname, but I'd stick with Beauty. It's great to have a distinctive, unusual name."

"Oh, Mike, I do like you ever so much and I don't mean to be rude but you do talk nonsense sometimes. How would you like to be called Handsome?"

"I'd love it!" said Mike, chuckling. "And why would that be funny, Miss? I *am* handsome!" He struck a silly pose as if he was being photographed, big belly right out in front. I couldn't help laughing as he intended, though I was still feeling very upset.

"I'm sure you'll like it there once you've settled in," said Mike.

"That's what my dad said about my last school. I didn't *ever* settle."

"Perhaps it's time to think *positive*, Beauty. I'm sure it's a great little school."

"Did your children go to this school, Mike?"

"No, no, they were both grown up when I moved here," said Mike.

"So how do you *know* it's a great school?"

"Sometimes you just have to take things on

275

trust," said Mike. "You and your mom didn't know anything about Rabbit Cove, right—but you *knew* you'd like it here."

I lightened up at last. "OK, OK, you've got me now," I said, laughing.

I didn't feel like laughing next Monday morning. Mom had phoned Seahaven Elementary and they said they'd squeeze me in somehow. Mom asked about a uniform and they said they didn't have one, just a sweatshirt. Mom and I had a long discussion about what I should wear.

I had very few clothes now so I didn't have much choice. I obviously wasn't going to wear the gray party dress and pinafore and my gray heeled boots—that outfit was far too grand for school. I wanted to wear my jeans and a T-shirt but Mom said they might look too scruffy. I was left with my denim skirt and the blue stripy top that went with it.

"I can't wear it every single day though, Mom," I said.

"I know. We'll maybe go shopping in Seahaven next week and buy you another couple of outfits. I've been saving my wages," said Mom. She ruffled my hair. "And we'll have to get you to a hairdresser, you're starting to look like a Shetland pony."

"Mom . . . Can I have it *all* cut off?"

"What? You want a crew cut? Are you *crazy*?" said Mom.

"No, I'd like it just ordinary short. So I don't have to bother with stupid bows and clips and stuff. They always fall off anyway. Oh *please*, Mom."

"But your dad won't let you—" Mom stopped herself.

"We're not *with* Dad. We're just us—and you don't really mind if I get my hair cut, do you?"

"All right. If that's what you want."

"Whoopee! Will you do it for me? I'll go and find some scissors."

"No, no, we'll get it cut *properly*. There's a hairdresser's card in the newsagent's window. We'll phone her up."

The hairdresser was named Dawn. She was a lovely large lady with a plump baby who smiled and waggled her legs in her baby chair while her mom did her hairdressing. The baby had very cute hair in little dandelion tufts.

"Do you think mine would go like that?" I asked.

"Maybe *not* a good idea," Mom said quickly. "I think a bob would suit you, Beauty. What do you think, Dawn?"

Dawn played around with my hair, draping it up and under.

"Oh *yes*! Perfect. Right, dear, hop up on a chair and we'll start snipping," said Dawn.

Mom winced as she cut the first lock of hair, peering at me worriedly, but by the time Dawn was making the last little tidying up snippets she was smiling.

"It looks lovely! Look, Beauty!" said Mom.

She held up her powder-compact mirror so I could see for myself. I stared at the face in the mirror. I didn't look a *bit* like me. I stuck my tongue out just to make sure it *was* me, and the mirror girl stuck her tongue out too. I looked so different. My face seemed so much smaller with its smooth cap of honey-colored hair. I didn't look especially fashionable or grown up, but for the first time ever I felt I looked like *me*.

Mom smiled, Dawn smiled, the baby smiled—and Mike mimed that he was struck dumb by this vision of beauty before him.

I wondered if I really was a new person now. Maybe this was the start of a whole new me. Cookie, cool and confident . . .

But on Monday morning I felt the old scared shaky Beauty—and I looked *awful*. Even my new hairstyle looked dreadful. I'd tossed and turned so much in the night it was all sticking up sideways, and it wouldn't lie down properly, even when I drenched it with water.

"Come *on*, Beauty. You need to get a bit of breakfast down you. You've got to leave at ten to eight. Hurry, sweetie," Mom urged me.

I stood in front of the mirror, brushing dementedly.

"It won't go *right*," I said, stamping my foot, almost in tears. "I look ridiculous!"

"Hey, hey, don't hurl that hairbrush whatever you do. You're a menace when it comes to mirrors," said Mom. "Your hair looks *fine*. Tell you what, I'll slap some gel on it. Don't worry, I won't turn you into a totally punky girl."

"I look a totally *pukey* girl," I said.

"Don't use that horrible word," said Mom, fussing with my stupid hair.

"I *feel* like I'm going to puke. I don't want my breakfast. I feel so *sick*." I felt my forehead. "And I'm all hot. You feel, Mom. I'm sure I've got a temperature. You can't send me to school when I'm *ill*, they'll think you're a terrible mother."

"Sweetie, you're *not* ill. You just don't want to go to school and I understand, but you *have* to go. There! Look at your hair! It looks great now, truly."

I glared at my reflection. Mom had made my hair look a lot better, admittedly, but the rest of me still looked ultra-depressing.

"Stop scowling!" said Mom. "You must *smile*

at everyone in your class, then they'll all want to make friends."

"I don't want to make friends with any of them," I said. "I've *got* a friend already, Rhona."

"Maybe there'll be someone at your new school you'll like even more than Rhona," said Mom.

"Don't be so *stupid*, Mom," I said sulkily.

"Hey!" Mom caught hold of me by the shoulders. "Don't you be so rude to me! You've been so good and grown up until now. *Please*, give this school a chance."

"OK, I'll try, but it won't work. They won't like me, I *know* they won't."

Mom shook me in exasperation.

"Look, get your Sam and Lily DVD, go and sit in Mike's living room and watch it for five minutes. It'll calm you down. I'll bring you a little bowl of cornflakes and some juice, OK?"

I did as I was told. Mike was busy in the kitchen so I had the living room to myself. I skipped along the Sam and Lily DVD to an episode right at the end, called "Starting School." It was aimed at very little kids going to school for the first time, but inside I *felt* like a very little kid. I couldn't even sing the Sam and Lily song when the episode started.

"Hey there!" said Sam.

Lily looked up at me, her nose twitching.

"Are you about to start school?" said Sam.

I nodded mournfully, spooning up cornflakes.

"Are you getting excited?" Sam asked.

I stared at him. Even Sam was being stupid today.

"OK, maybe you're just a little bit scared," said Sam softly. "I don't blame you for feeling like that, Beauty. I wish you could go to Lily's school, you'd absolutely love it. There's just five other rabbits in her class and they have such easy-peasy lessons. They learn how to groom their fur and make a comfy bed and how to lap water delicately so it doesn't dribble down their front. They run races with each other all around the vegetable patch and they have a little snack every ten minutes.

"Lily was a little bit shy her very first day and wouldn't talk to the other rabbits in her class. She crept around by herself at playtime and sucked the tip of her ear for comfort but she soon made friends with the others. Now they're *all* best friends. When they're playing they all go into a huddle together, cozying up close, little white puffball tails in the air."

"*How* did she make friends, Sam?" I whispered.

"She sidled up to the rabbit she liked best, a funny friendly one, and snuffled her nose at him."

"Hmm. Well, if I sidle up to some funny friendly boy in my class and snuffle my nose he'll think I'm a total lunatic," I said.

Mike came into the room, a big paper bag in his arms. I blushed and switched off the DVD player quickly.

"Hi, Beauty. Did you finish your cornflakes? Your mom's fussing. Are you just about ready?"

"I suppose."

"Let's have a look at you," said Mike. "Mm, cool hair, nice T-shirt, cute skirt. Your sneakers are a bit scuffed and grubby though."

"I know. I've tried brushing them but they still look terrible," I said.

"Well, see if these fit," said Mike, throwing the paper bag at me.

I opened it up—and found a pair of scarlet high tops, little versions of Mike's own funky boots.

"Oh, Mike! Oh, I *love* them! Can I really wear them to school?"

"That's what they're for, kiddo. Do they fit OK? I got a half-size bigger than your sneakers so that they'd last you a while."

They fit perfectly and looked incredible.

"There! Maybe your new nickname will be *Booty*," said Mike, laughing.

I gave him a hug and I gave Mom a kiss. I clutched my carrier bag—my own school bag and lunchbox were at home so I had to make do for the moment. Mom wanted to go with me to call at number two and number seventeen but I was scared the kids would think me a baby so I went by myself.

A red-haired freckled boy about my own age opened the door of number seventeen. I'd seen him several times rollerblading along the terrace. He'd always made a hideous face at me. He made a hideous face now.

"Yuck, are *you* the girl I've got to go to school with?" he asked.

I certainly wasn't going to snuffle my nose at *him*. I felt like bursting into tears—but I didn't. I made a face back at him.

"Yuck, are *you* the boy I've got to go to school with?" I said.

"Come on then. My mom says your name's *Beauty*. Is that right?"

"Yeah, so what?" I said, pretending I didn't care in the slightest. I felt horribly shaky and peculiar inside.

He ran full-tilt down the terrace and banged at the door of number two. Another boy came tumbling out, smaller, with curly hair.

"Hi, Toby!" he yelled excitedly.

"Hi, Ben," Toby said, and they did this silly high-five routine.

Ben totally ignored me. I didn't know if this was better or worse. Either way, I hated the thought of going back and forth to school with these two boys. But then a girl came out of number nine, much older, about fourteen, a big bouncy girl with spiky black hair and a lot of black eye makeup. I blinked at her, biting my lip. She smiled at me.

"Hi, I'm Angie. You're Beauty from Lily Cottage? Mom said you'd be coming on the bus with us. I hope for your sake you're not in Ben or Toby's class! They both drive me absolutely nuts. It will be so great to have a girl to go to school with. I'm in seventh grade at Seahaven High. It's right next to the elementary school. Hey, I *love* your boots! Where did you get them from?"

"They were a present," I said shyly.

I wondered if Angie was somehow messing around with me, ready to start teasing me any minute—but she chatted away happily all the way to the bus stop. There were some girls from the High School already on the bus and they called to Angie to join them, but she just waved and said she was sitting with me.

"It's OK, you don't *have* to sit with me," I mumbled.

"I want to! I can't stand those girls, they just want to chatter on about their boyfriends all the time. They're so boring. You don't have a boyfriend, do you, Beauty?"

She *was* teasing a little now, but in a sweet way.

"No, I haven't got a boyfriend!" I said.

"Well, we could maybe fix you up with Toby? Or even Ben, if you like younger men?"

"No thanks!" I hesitated. "I like *older* men, actually. There's this guy Sam . . . but he doesn't even know I exist."

"Oh well. I expect you'll be in Mr. Pettit's class with Toby, and Mr. Pettit is *definitely* an older man, but I don't somehow see him as fanciable. His glasses are all smeary and he wears knitted ties and those terrible trousers with an elasticated waist."

I made a face. "Is he strict?" I asked anxiously.

"No, he's OK. He can be quite sweet, actually. He tells the funniest stories if he's in a good mood. Tell you what, I'll come in the school with you and we'll find him and I'll introduce you. Toby's supposed to take care of you but he's hopeless."

Angie was *so* lovely to me. She got off a stop early at Seahaven Elementary and came into school with me. It was such a relief. Toby and Ben tore off in different directions without a backward glance. Angie took me to the school secretary and then led me up two steep flights of stairs, along a corridor, through some swinging doors, and around several corners.

It was all so much bigger than I was used to. There were kids charging around everywhere. I wanted to take Angie's hand like a baby.

"I don't think I'll ever find my way on my own," I said shakily.

"Yes, you will, it'll be easy-peasy," said Angie. "Ah, here's Mr. Pettit's class. Oh, look at all those sunflower paintings. *I* did one of them!"

She led me into the classroom, which was half full of chattering children. A man with smeary glasses, a red knitted tie, and terrible trousers was sitting on his desk reading some papers, his big thick-soled comfy shoes propped on a small chair. He looked up as we came in.

"Hello, Angie!" he said, smiling. "My goodness, you're so grown up now!"

"Hi, Mr. Pettit. This is Beauty. She's come to live on our road in Rabbit Cove. She's meant to be in your class, isn't she?"

"She is indeed. Hello, Beauty."

I ducked my head shyly.

"I'll be off then, Beauty. When school finishes this afternoon just go to the bus stop. Wait for me if I'm not there, OK?" said Angie. She put her head close to mine and whispered, "Good luck!"

I smiled at her gratefully, wishing she was my age so that she could be in Mr. Pettit's class with me.

"Now, where can we sit you, Beauty?" said Mr. Pettit. He took off his glasses, wiped them ineffectually on his tie, and popped them back on his nose. "We're all a bit crammed together, but there *is* a spare chair—this one!" He took his foot off it and dusted it down with his cardigan sleeve. "Now, whose table shall you join? There's a space at the boys' table at the back with Toby and all his friends—"

"No way, Mr. Pettit! We don't want *girls*," Toby protested.

Mr. Pettit laughed at him. "You are so *predictable*, Toby. I'd never dream of inflicting your company on Beauty."

"Beauty!" said Toby, sniggering.

Two of his friends started chortling too.

"I think maybe you could park your chair next to Princess, Beauty," said Mr. Pettit.

Princess! Mr. Pettit was pointing toward a big smiley girl with elaborate little plaits in rows all over her head. She was wearing a bright pink T-shirt with *Princess* in sparkly silver lettering— the same T-shirt I'd given Rhona for her birthday!

I maneuvred my chair toward her table. Princess squashed into a corner to make room for me. I sat down next to her, breathing in a beautiful rosy smell.

"Are you wearing perfume?" I whispered. "It's lovely!"

"It's my mom's Red Roses cologne. She'd kill me if she knew I was wearing it," Princess giggled. She sniffed her own wrists appreciatively. "Mmm, I smell gorgeous!"

"Is your name *really* Princess?"

"Yeah. See, it's on my T-shirt too!"

"I gave that exact same T-shirt to a friend at my old school!" I said.

"So was she called Princess too?"

"No, no, she was called Rhona."

"That's cool. I like being the *only* Princess. Well, Jordan's little girl is called Princess too, but I tell everyone she copied me." Princess chuckled. "And you're Beauty. That's an unusual name too. I don't think I've heard of *any* other Beauty so your name's even more unusual than mine. Hey, maybe we can start an unusual name club, you and me? Would you like that?"

"Oh yes!" I said.

We got it all sorted out at lunch time. Princess and I were UNCles—founder members of the Unusual Name Club. We discussed letting other children join too. There was an Anastasia in our class, and also a Britney-Lee but we decided these weren't quite unusual enough. There was a boy called Ezra which definitely qualified as unusual, but we decided we didn't really want boys in our club.

I designed a special logo and Princess put it carefully in her folder. She had a special badge-making kit at home and said she'd bring two UNCle badges to school the next day.

Then we shared our packed lunches. Princess had chicken in hers, and a special little pot of rice and peas. I just had cheese sandwiches and an apple—but Mom had made a special batch of cookies on Sunday. She'd found a little rabbit cookie cutter in amongst a whole load of kitchen junk at the Sunday flea market at the Rabbit Cove community center. She'd made her first bunny batch of cookies last night and given them white icing fur. I had two in my lunch bag so I gave one to Princess.

"Oh wow, bunny cookies!" she said. "They are so *cute*! They taste great too. I'm so glad you're my friend, Beauty."

Eighteen

No one called me Ugly at Seahaven Elementary, not even Toby. At first they called me the New Girl, which was a perfectly acceptable description. But after a little while they called me the Cookie Girl!

I started off just sharing cookies with my best friend and fellow UNCle, Princess, but soon I started taking a little bag of cookies each day and handing them around to anyone who seemed left out or lonely. Then the whole school got involved in raising money for some poor children in Africa. We were told to bring in cakes and cookies to sell to each other at lunch time.

"Right!" said Mom, rolling up her sleeves.

She started making an enormous batch of bunny cookies, all different flavors, every one lovingly iced with raisins for eyes and a dab of glacé cherry for a mouth. Nearly everyone brought cakes and cookies—but mine were the most popular! I sold them for ten pence per cookie, and they sold out in five minutes flat!

We had a summer fair for school funds at the end of June and Mr. Pettit actually wrote to Mom begging her to run her own cookie stall. She made us both little lacy white aprons out of curtains. She got me to paint a sign for the stall.

"What shall I put?"

"I don't know. Dilly's Cookies?"

"That sounds too much like those cookies you can buy, Millie's Cookies. People will think you're copying. How about Bunny Cookies? Then I can draw little white rabbits scampering around and around at the edges of the sign."

"OK, then, Bunny Cookies it is," said Mom.

She made cookies all afternoon, all evening, and half the night. I made cookies too, mixing and rolling and cutting alongside Mom. Mike helped too, finding endless tins to store them. He came with us on Saturday to help Mom set up the stall.

Princess was helping *her* mom on the raffle stall. Her sisters and brother were there too: Julep, Precious, and little baby Marley.

"We're going to have to enrol your entire family in our UNCles club," I said. "What's your mom called, Princess?"

"She's called Petal so she's in too! What about your mom?"

"Everyone calls her Dilly. That's kind of un-usual, isn't it?"

Princess was looking at Mike, who was arranging

hundreds of cookies on plates. He absent-mindedly nibbled the ears off one of the bunnies and Mom pretended to smack his hand.

"What about your dad? I thought you said your mom and dad had split up?" said Princess.

"He's not my *dad*," I said.

"Well, I did think he was a bit old," said Princess. "Is he your grandad?"

"No, no, he's just Mike. He's lovely. We live with him," I said.

Princess nodded, eyebrows raised. "So he and your mom are, like, a couple?"

"No!"

Princess stared at Mom and Mike. They were still fooling around, pairing up the rabbits on the plates so that they were giving each other Eskimo kisses.

"They *look* like a couple," she said.

"Well they're not," I said, but I started to wonder about it. *Dad* had thought Mom had a thing going with Mike—but then Dad was so crazy he thought every other guy in the world was after Mom.

He was still leaving angry messages on her phone, demanding to know what was going on. He kept asking when we were coming back. He actually said it was lonely at home without us, which made Mom cry. But Auntie Avril rang to see how we were getting on and she told us she'd called round at Dad's and she said he seemed quite cheerful.

"We had a glass of wine or two and a nice little chat. It was almost like old times," said Auntie Avril. "You don't mind, do you, Dilly?"

"I don't mind a bit, Avril," said Mom. "Why should I?"

"Well, dear, he is still your husband."

"Yes, but I'm not with him now, am I? You do what you want, Avril. Go for it, girl!"

Maybe Mom and Dad would get a divorce now and then Mom would be free to marry Mike if she wanted. *I* wanted it more than anything. I knew Mike would be the most magical stepdad in the whole world.

Mom's cookie stall made a positive fortune for the whole school. Mike made his special fish pie for supper and we opened a bottle of champagne to celebrate. Mom let *me* have half a glass. It was lovely, though the bubbles went right up my nose and tickled. Mom had much more than half a glass and went to bed quite giggly.

"You are funny when you're drunk, Mom," I said, giving her a hug.

"I'm *not* drunk! I've only had two glasses of champagne, silly," said Mom. "Well, maybe it was three. Anyway, I'm just *happy*, OK?"

"Are you *really* happy, Mom?"

"Yes. Well, sometimes I still wonder if I'm crazy,

if we've done the right thing. I worry about what's right for you."

"I think we've done exactly the right thing."

"Well, we've certainly been so lucky, coming here, finding Mike—"

"Yes, Mike. I *do* like Mike, Mom."

"Yes, so do I. He's been so kind, and he's such fun to be with. And he never ever seems to get angry," said Mom.

"He likes you too, ever so. So what would you do if—if he wanted to—to be your boyfriend?"

"Goodness! Well, Mike's lovely, I know, and I'm very fond of him, but . . ."

"I know he's quite old, Mom, but that doesn't really matter, does it?"

"No, no. I mean, I fell for your dad, didn't I?"

"And Mike isn't terribly good-looking, though I *like* the way he looks."

"I like the way he looks too."

"So, do you think you'll get together, Mom?"

"I don't think so, Beauty," Mom said gently.

"It's not because he hasn't got much money, is it?" I whispered.

"Oh, Beauty!" Mom sounded shocked. "As if that matters! I *like* it that Mike isn't rich and doesn't give a hoot about money. He's become a very special friend. If you must know, he did sort of hint that he'd love to be *more* than just good friends, but he was very understanding when I explained why I wanted things to stay just the way they are."

"But *why*, Mom?" I asked, exasperated.

"Because I want to be on my own for a bit. No man in my life. Independent. I got together with your dad when I was fresh out of school. I've never learned how to stand on my own two feet. I want to prove I can cope. It's still a bit scary but it's exciting making decisions for myself. I always thought I was absolutely thick but now I seem to be doing OK. Do you understand, darling?"

"Well. Sort of," I said. "But I hope you might change your mind later on!"

"I know one thing," said Mom. "I'm not *really* on my own. I've got you, babes. I couldn't manage without you. We're a team, you and me, Beauty."

Mom and I were a real team when it came to cookie baking. Suddenly our bunny cookies were absolutely in demand. We spent Saturdays and Sundays up to our elbows in cookie dough in an attempt to please all our customers. Mom had been supplying cookies for all the guest houses on Primrose Terrace for weeks, but now the big White Hotel wanted their own batch to offer to guests for afternoon tea, and Peggy's Parlour wanted a big jar of assorted iced cookies every single day. We'd had enquiries from several Seahaven hotels and teashops—and we were asked to provide a *hun-*

dred bags of bunny cookies for the big Seahaven Carnival in July.

I designed a special bunny label to stick on each bag: a white rabbit on a bright green background. Mom and I set up a big cookie stall at the carnival and dressed up in our white lacy aprons. The local television news came and filmed us. I didn't even know they were doing it. I was just busy selling cookies and then this guy jumped in front of me and told me to eat a bunny cookie and go "yum yum" so I did—and then I saw the camera pointing in my direction! I just about died—but it was all over before I could object. My heart started thudding like crazy in case I looked stupid when Mom and Mike and I switched on the local news that evening, but to my great relief I was only on for two seconds! They said I made the cookies all by myself, which made me fuss, but Mom just laughed.

The next morning Mike came charging into the kitchen, eyes popping.

"There's a phone call for our little television star. It's *Watchbox*, that kids' show on Saturday mornings. They want to have you on their show," he said.

"What? Oh, Mike, you are a tease," I said, shaking my head at him.

"Stop kidding, Mike, you're very bad," said Mom.

"I-am-NOT-kidding! Come to the phone, Beauty. Dilly, they need to talk to you too. I *promise* I'm not joking."

I went to the phone, Mom following me.

"Hello? It's Beauty speaking," I said uncertainly, still not quite believing Mike.

"Hello, Beauty. My name's Jules Latimer. I'm a researcher on *Watchbox*. Do you know our show? I've been watching various news items and I saw your little spot on the piece about the Seahaven Carnival. So you make all these wonderful cookies?"

"Well, my mom makes most of them. I just help out when we're really busy," I said.

"And did you design the bunny logo?"

"The logo? Oh, the picture on the bags. Yes, I did that."

"Well, we'd love to have you on our show. You could maybe show our presenters Simon and Miranda how you make the cookies? Would you like to do that?"

Would I like to go on *television*? Oh goodness, it might be so scary. I'd have thousands and thousands of children watching me, Ugly Beauty. They'd all laugh and snigger at their television sets, saying horrible things about me . . .

"No thank you very much," I said.

"What?" said Mom beside me. "Don't be silly, Beauty! Of *course* you want to go on *Watchbox*!" She snatched the phone away from me. "Hello, I'm Dilys Cookson, Beauty's mom. I think she's a little bit overwhelmed. I'm sure she'd *love* to go on *Watchbox*—it's her second favorite television show."

I heard the researcher laughing and asking something.

"Oh, her *favorite* has to be *Rabbit Hutch*. She's absolutely nuts on Sam and Lily," said Mom.

"Shut *up*, Mom! They'll think I'm a terrible baby!" I hissed.

Mom wouldn't shut up.

"That's why she painted that lovely white rabbit for our bunny cookies. It's because she loves Lily," she said.

She listened to the researcher for a while and then laughed. "Yes, yes! OK, what day do you record the show? Tomorrow!"

"*No*, Mom, I'm not going to," I said, struggling to get her off the phone—but she held it out of my reach.

"Can you give me the full address? That's London, right? I'm afraid I don't know London very well. Will I be able to park at the studio or should we get the train? You'll send a special *car* for us?

What, all the way to Rabbit Cove? Oh wonderful. It's Lily Cottage, nineteen Primrose Terrace. At nine o'clock? We'll be ready and waiting."

Mom hung up and then gave me a huge hug. I stayed stony still, not responding.

"*You* can be ready and waiting. *I'm* not going," I said.

"Oh, Beauty, don't be so silly!"

"I don't want to *look* silly on television."

"But you *won't*. You were fine on the local news, completely natural."

"Yes, because I didn't know what they were doing. But I'm *not* going on *Watchbox*. I'd *hate* it."

"You'll *love* it, especially when you know what they've got lined up for you. I'd give anything to tell you but they want it to be a total surprise," said Mom.

"I know what they want me to do: show Simon and Miranda how to make cookies. Simon is this big fat jolly guy who shouts all the time and Miranda is little and very bouncy and beautiful. I couldn't possibly make cookies with *them*. I'm not going on *Watchbox*, Mom, no matter what you say."

"But—"

"Look, you're getting just like *Dad*," I said, starting to shout. "He was always always always making me do stuff I didn't want to do. *Please* don't you start, Mom. I'm sorry, but I'm not the sort of pretty show-off girl who'd be great on television. I'd be awful. You don't understand me one little bit, do you? You're a totally useless mom."

Mom stared at me. Her eyes filled with tears and she rushed upstairs. I glared after her.

I was still glaring when Mike found me, kicking the baseboard in his living room.

"Are you looking for those rats again?" he said. "Hold on, you'll scuff the paintwork—and it won't exactly enhance your new sneakers either."

"I'm sorry," I said, feeling bad.

"That's OK, kiddo. Fancy saying sorry to your mom too? I think you were shouting at her—and when I listened on the stairs just now it sounded as if she might be crying," said Mike.

"Well, it's not my fault," I said. "Just because I don't want to go on *Watchbox*."

"What *is* this show anyway? I've heard of it but I don't think I've ever watched it."

"Oh, they have these two presenters on every day, and all these kids come on and do stuff, dance and sing and play around. All the girls at my old school were desperate to be on *Watchbox*, Skye especially."

"Is she the one who was particularly mean to you? There, don't you want to be on the wretched show, just to be one up on her?"

"Yes, but I'd make such a *total* fool of myself. Everyone would laugh."

"What makes you think that?"

"I just can't *do* stuff in front of people. They'd say my silly name and every child watching would give a double take and go, *"Beauty*—as if!'"

"Like they did at Seahaven Elementary?" said Mike, with a little edge to his voice. "You were so certain they were all going to laugh at you and tease you and make your life a misery, remember? And did that happen?"

He waited. I fidgeted. He cupped his ear, wanting a response.

"All right, they're all lovely at my new school," I said. "Well, except for Toby and Ben. And actually they gave me some of their perfectly disgusting home-made toffee that sticks your teeth together the other day, hoping I'd give them bunny cookies in exchange."

"So you were *wrong* about Seahaven school and its pupils?" Mike persisted.

"Yes, OK, I've admitted that."

"So don't you think you might just be wrong about this television show? You could go on it and actually be a little superstar."

"No I wouldn't!"

"Yes, you *would*. But even if you come over all shy and can't say a word, does it really matter? At

302

least you'll have had a go! And you'll have given your mom's cookies an enormous plug too. Do you know how much it costs to have an advertisement on television, Beauty? Thousands and thousands and thousands of pounds. Yet you can advertise Bunny Cookies for nothing on the most popular show on kids television. Don't you see what this could mean for you and Dilly? She could expand properly, take on some staff—there are lots of moms in Rabbit Cove who'd love to do a bit of baking part-time. It's her chance to turn Bunny Cookies into a quality product sold nationwide, Bunny Cookies in every up-market food emporium—Fortnum and Mason, Harrods, Selfridges . . ."

I stared at Mike open-mouthed. "Do you really think that could happen?" I asked.

"Well, I'm maybe going a bit over the top to prove my point. I'm not sure Dilly would want to develop the business to such an extent. But she's taking it very seriously, Beauty. She's getting some confidence in herself at last. You should feel so proud of her."

"I am," I said.

"So you know how much this means to her. Though *you* mean much more to her than her precious cookies. In a way she's doing all this for you—and yet what did I hear you shouting at her just now?"

"I said she was a useless mom," I said, my voice going all wobbly.

"And do you really think that?"

"No, of course I don't. I just said it because I was angry and wanted to hurt her. Because I truly still *don't* want to go on *Watchbox*—but I will if you really make me."

"I'm not going to make you do anything, sweetheart," said Mike, putting his arm around me. "But I'm hoping like anything you'll say you will! I'll be so proud of you, Beauty."

I gave him a big hug.

"You're very clever, you know. You don't shout and yell, you don't even really tell me off. You just say stuff that makes me do exactly what you want. You must have been a great dad, Mike."

"I think I was rather a useless dad, actually. Not much good as a husband either. I just wanted to do my own thing and expected everyone else to fit in. I try not to think about the past too much. I'm not very proud of the way I behaved. Maybe I've learned my lesson now. That's the only thing I've really learned about life. You don't have to go on making the same old mistakes over and over again. You can't change other people but you *can* change yourself. There! Wise old Mike has done enough mumbling in his beard. Scoot upstairs and make up with your mom, doll."

I ran up to our room. Mom was lying on our bed, sobbing into her pillow.

"Oh, Mom, don't! I'm sorry," I said, lying down beside her.

"I'm sorry too, Beauty. I just got so excited I forgot you'd find it a terrible ordeal. It's OK, you don't have to go on the silly old show."

"But I will," I said. "I'll do it, Mom—for us. To advertise Bunny Cookies. I'll probably be absolutely terrible on the TV and you'll die of embarrassment, but I'll give it a go, OK?"

"Oh, you darling!" said Mom. "You're the best daughter in the whole world."

"And you're the best mom," I said.

I was glad I'd changed my mind and made Mom happy and Mike proud—but in the middle of the night, wide awake, I wished wished wished I didn't have to. I kept imagining what it would be like. I'd be in a studio with a lot of cool, confident, talented, beautiful girls like Skye. They'd all dance and sing and I'd make a muck-up of my cookies and they'd all stare at me and chortle—and children from John o' Groats to Land's End would stare and chortle too.

I didn't get to sleep until about five o'clock. Mom bounced out of bed very early. I huddled under the comforter while she got ready. She seemed to be making a big performance of it, swishing clothes along the rail, opening drawers, snapping her suit-case . . .

She woke me up with a cup of tea at eight o'clock.

"Rise and shine, my little television star," she said, giving me a kiss.

I sat up in bed, looking Mom up and down. She looked lovely, wearing her cream dress, her hair newly washed and fluffy around her shoulders. I took a sip of tea and made my voice gruff.

"Your neck looks a bit bare, Dilly. Why don't you wear your diamond collar?" I said.

"Oh *don't*!" said Mom, and we both laughed shakily.

"Do you think I should tell your dad you're going to be on the television?" said Mom.

"No, because I know I'll muck it all up," I said. "I wish *you* were doing it. You look fabulous, Mom, really."

"Do you really think so, babes?" Mom glanced at her suitcase. "I've got another outfit in case they all look casual. I don't want to let you down, darling. Now, I've ironed your gray dress and your white pinafore and polished your gray boots. We don't want them to get all creased in the car so we'll pop them on a hanger and you can wear your comfy jeans and stuff for the trip, OK?"

I nodded, touched that she'd gone to so much trouble. I still wasn't sure I'd actually be able to stand there in front of the cameras. My tummy flipped over at the thought and I could barely swallow my tea.

Mike insisted on making breakfast by himself. He made Mom and me sit down as if we were ordinary guests on holiday at Lily Cottage. All the other guests made a great fuss of me and when the big black car drew up outside they all crowded on the doorstep and patted me and kissed me and wished me luck.

Mike gave me a big hug and whispered in my ear, "Good luck, kiddo."

He gave Mom a hug too and whispered in *her* ear. She blushed and giggled. I wondered if they *might* just get together, in spite of what Mom said.

Then Mom and I got in the back of the car. The chauffeur was a nice fat man called Harry who hung my dress and pinafore on a special little hook inside the car and stowed Mom's suitcase in the trunk.

"Are you comfy now, ladies? You just sit back and relax," he said.

I felt a horrible pang as we drove out of Rabbit Cove. I knew it was silly but I was scared I'd somehow made it all up, and once we were back on the main road to London it would vanish into the sea, a never-never land we'd never be able to reach again.

I knelt up on the seat and peered back.

"It's OK, babe. We'll be back this evening," said Mom softly. "Rabbit Cove's our home now. We're going to live there all summer—and winter too."

"And the *next* summer and winter, forever?" I said.

"Yes, yes, if that's what we both want," said Mom.

I turned around and cuddled up to her.

"You bet it is," I said.

Harry let us choose CDs to play in his car and we sang along for a while, but then my head started nodding. When I woke up again we were in London.

"Oh no!" I said, suddenly horribly scared. "Oh, Harry, are we nearly there?"

"Five minutes away."

"I don't want to go now!" I said.

"It'll be fine, Beauty," said Mom, holding my hand—but *her* hand was cold and clammy too.

"You'll *love* being on *Watchbox*, young lady,' said Harry. "That Simon is a right laugh—and as for Miranda—*phwoar!*"

We drove into the studios. I couldn't help feeling a *little* bit thrilled when Harry told the security man at the gate: "Here's Miss Beauty Cookson and her mom for *Watchbox*." We were let through straight away. Harry parked the car, handed over my gray outfit and the suitcase, and promised he'd be waiting to take us all the way home after the show.

"Wish us luck, Harry," said Mom.

"Oh, yes. I wish you *lots* of luck—but you won't need it. You'll be brilliant."

"Well, if Beauty makes a batch of bunny cookies we'll make sure we'll bring you some," said Mom.

We were met by Jules, the researcher. She was much younger than I'd imagined, with a ponytail and a very short skirt. I thought just at first she might be one of the child performers on the show. She took Mom and me to our very own dressing room. It even had our names on the door!

"Now, we'll probably have a little rehearsal and you'll meet Simon and Miranda and all the other kids in the show," she said. "You're going to start the show, Beauty, making cookies. You'll be showing Simon and Miranda what to do. Then while the cookies are baking—we have our own little oven, no expense spared on *Watchbox*!—all our other guests will do their turns. We've got a singer, a magician, and two different dancers, and then we'll finish with you, Beauty, taking the cookies out of the oven. We were wondering if you'd maybe draw a little rabbit for us, seeing as you designed the Bunny Cookies logo."

"Oh yes, that would be great," said Mom. "Look, I've brought lots of Beauty's drawings. She's even done some oil paintings."

She unfastened her suitcase. She didn't have spare clothes in there at all. She had all my Sam and Lily drawings and paintings.

"Oh, Mom!" I said, terribly embarrassed. "They don't want to see all that silly old stuff."

"Oh yes we do!" said Jules, seizing an armful. "Do you mind if I take them away to show the producer? They'll fit in brilliantly with the special finale."

"What special finale?" I asked.

"Oh, we've just thought of a good way of rounding off the show," said Jules. She winked at Mom and Mom winked back.

"What's all the winking about?" I asked Mom, when we were left on our own in the dressing room.

"What winking?" said Mom. "I just had something in my eye, that's all."

I didn't have time to quiz her further, because we were called to go into the studio for a run-through rehearsal. It was a great room full of cameras with cables snaking all over the floor. There were two big red squashy sofas in our corner, a mini-kitchen in another, and a round stage with a spotlight.

There were four other children standing around with their moms. They all looked comfortingly anxious too, apart from a beautiful girl with long fair hair in a very short skirt and a sparkly top. She was wearing very high heels.

"She is *so* like Skye," I whispered to Mom.

"Maybe she'll trip in her heels and fall over and show her underpants," Mom whispered back.

The fair girl looked positively ordinary compared to Miranda. She was simply dressed in jeans and a little T-shirt and sneakers but she looked stunning, her long ultra-curly black hair flying everywhere, her honey-colored skin shining, her dark eyes huge and luminous. She smiled at everyone, asking our names, chatting away. Simon was very friendly too, bounding about pulling funny faces and tweaking the nose of the very little boy who was the magician.

I smiled shyly at Miranda and Simon but I felt paralyzed with fear. I didn't know what I was going to do. I knew how to make cookies—but what was I supposed to *say* when I was mixing and baking? I asked Jules in panic.

"It's OK, Miranda and Simon will ask you stuff and you just say whatever you want. We're not going to go through it word by word just now. We find it makes things much fresher when we start recording," said Jules.

I had to stand in the kitchen and pretend to make cookies, while Miranda and Simon bobbed about. I felt so shy I barely said a word. Then a tall red-haired girl called Megan did an acrobatic dance, a tiny kid called Tina sang a song in a surprisingly deep strong voice, the little boy Darren did his magic tricks, and then the blonde girl in the short skirt and high heels, Nancy-Jo, sang and danced. She was depressingly good at it too.

"Then we'll come back to you, Beauty, and we'll look at the cookies and you'll draw the bunny and then . . . well, we'll just chat for a couple of minutes and that's the end of the show," said Jules. "OK, let's take you back to your dressing room. I'll come and fetch you for Makeup in a tick, Beauty."

"Should Beauty change into her best dress now?" Mom asked.

"Well, we think Beauty looks great for the show just the way she is," said Jules.

"Oh yes, wear your jeans. I'm wearing mine," said Miranda.

"And we all love your red boots," said Simon.

"*Sooo* much more sensible than some of the others," Jules muttered in my ear, raising an eyebrow at Nancy-Jo.

So I didn't change after all. I think Mom was a

bit disappointed and worried people would think I looked scruffy in my jeans.

"Let's hope your dad *doesn't* get wind of this and watch. He'd go bananas," said Mom. "I wonder what they're going to do to you in Makeup? I hope they don't plaster it on you."

The makeup lady was lovely. She just put a little foundation on me so I wouldn't look all shiny, and the palest pink lipstick, and then she combed my hair and said my bob style really suited me.

"There, you look fabulous, pet, if I do say so myself," she said.

I stared at myself in the mirror. I didn't look fabulous—but I looked kind of OK. I gave myself a soppy little grin and the girl in the mirror smiled back at me encouragingly.

Then Jules came to collect me and we went back into the studio ready for the start of the show.

They stood me in the kitchen with all the ingredients in front of me. I suddenly felt so sick and so scared I wondered if I was going to throw up right there and then in my mixing bowl.

"Are you OK, sweetheart?" said Simon, suddenly gentle.

"I'm scared!"

"I know, I know. Don't worry, Miranda and I get scared too before the start of the show. But it'll be fine once the cameras start rolling."

"But what about all those thousands of people who'll be watching us?" I whispered.

"Forget about them. It's just you and me and Miranda and the other kids having fun, OK?"

"OK," I said, swallowing.

"That's the girl. Now listen, I want at least *four* of these famous cookies, OK? I'm a growing lad," he said, patting his big tummy.

Then they started the countdown to the show and Simon whizzed over to the red sofa beside Miranda. I heard the *Watchbox* signature tune and Simon and Miranda started singing it too.

"Hi, everyone!" said Miranda, smiling at the camera.

"Welcome to *Watchbox*," said Simon. "We've got a *g-r-e-a-a-a-t* show for you today. You just wait and see! First of all, we're going to do some baking. Are you any good at cooking, Miranda?"

"No, I'm terrible, but I know a girl who's a *great* cook—and that's Beauty Cookson," said Miranda.

They both walked over to me. That was my cue to start mixing the flour and the sugar and the butter. I started so determinedly that some of the flour flew up all over my T-shirt. I froze.

"Whoops, it's snowing!" said Simon, flicking a tiny bit of flour too.

"Hey hey, stop messing about, you two," said

Miranda. "OK, Beauty, tell us how to make your special bunny cookies. I hear they've become ever so popular where you live, in Rabbit Cove. That's a lovely name!"

"It's a lovely place. It's the seaside and it's so special," I said, suddenly not shy at all. "My mom's great at making all sorts of cookies and I'm her number one helper. Now we specialize in making these bunny cookies with this special cutter."

Simon held it up, making the bunny run up my arm and across my shoulders. It tickled and I couldn't help laughing.

"They've become really popular and we sell tons," I said, still mixing.

"And you've designed the special bunny logo on the packaging?" said Miranda, holding up one of our bags of cookies. "You like rabbits, do you, Beauty?"

"Yes, I love them," I said, slowly adding my eggs and milk to the cookie mixture.

"Can I have a stir, Beauty?" said Simon. "Have you got a favorite rabbit, then?"

"Well . . ." I said, hesitating.

"Come on, tell us," said Miranda, her head close to mine.

"I like Lily. She's Sam's rabbit on the *Rabbit Hutch* show," I said. "I know I'm an awful baby to watch it, but—"

"*I* watch Sam and Lily. I love Lily too," said Simon.

"I love Sam!" said Miranda. "Well, we've got a little surprise for you at the end of the show, Beauty. But now while you're rolling out your cookie dough and popping the cookies in the oven let's meet some of our other guests. Megan is going to do a special acrobatic dance for us."

"And, boy, is she bendy!" said Simon.

The cameras switched to Megan, who did a handstand and then arched over so her feet touched the floor. By the time she'd finished her display I'd rolled out the dough, cut out forty-eight bunny cookies, and put them in the oven.

Simon looked over at me, did a thumbs-up, and rubbed his tummy. I peered into the darkness at the back of the studio and there was Mom, waving wildly and blowing kisses at me. Tiny Tina came on and sang and then did a short duet with Miranda. Darren did his magic tricks and Simon joked around with him.

"You haven't got a top hat with you, have you, Darren? Then you could make a white rabbit appear for Beauty," he said. "How are those cookies getting on, Beauty? They're starting to smell good."

"Another couple of minutes, that's all," I said, peeping in the oven.

Simon helped Darren through a complicated card trick and a funny routine with a "magic" box. Then it was Nancy-Jo's turn.

I took my cookies out of the oven, Jules helping as the cameras weren't on us. We put them out on cooling trays.

"They look wonderful, Beauty. Well done!" she whispered.

Nancy-Jo threw back her head and went for a high note, thrusting out her arms and tapping her high heels. She wobbled precariously. Jules shook her head and I had to bite my cheeks to stop myself giggling.

Miranda and Simon had a chat with Nancy-Jo and then she tottered off while I was gently shoved towards the red sofas, a plate of bunny cookies in either hand.

"Oh wow, Beauty, they look fantastic!" said Miranda. "May I have one?"

"Of course," I said. "They're for everyone. Though Simon has to have lots because he says he's a growing boy."

They both laughed as if it was my joke.

"Now, you're not just a good cook, you're also brilliant at drawing, Beauty. Will you draw a bunny for us?" said Simon, his mouth full of cookies. "Mm, these are delicious."

I started drawing on the pad he gave me—while

to my embarrassment Miranda held up lots of my Sam and Lily pictures to the camera.

"I love the oil paintings, Beauty," she said.

"My special artist friend Mike showed me how to use oils," I said proudly.

"There, that's a lovely rabbit," said Simon, peering at my page. "Now, I've borrowed this magic wand from our friend Darren. If you tap your drawing it *might* just turn into a real rabbit, Beauty."

I stared at Simon.

"Go on, give it a try," he said.

I tapped my drawing, feeling a bit silly. I sensed someone coming up behind me. Then suddenly there in my lap was a huge, soft, oh-so-familiar white rabbit with floppy ears.

"Lily!" I said.

"Hey there, Beauty," said Sam, coming to sit beside me.

It was the *real* Sam, his shiny hair flopping over his forehead, his eyes bright, his face one big smile. I still wondered if I was dreaming—but Lily felt so warm and heavy cuddled up on my lap I knew I had to be wide awake.

"We're so pleased you like our show, Beauty. Lily's particularly thrilled that she inspired your special cookies. They are *so* good," said Sam, biting one in half. "And I love all your artwork!"

"I drew them all for you," I whispered. "I never dared send any because I was scared you'd think me a silly baby."

"Maybe you'd like to give Sam and Lily one of your paintings now?" said Miranda.

"Oh yes! What about the oil painting of you and Lily? You're meant to be on vacation in Rabbit Cove," I said, shyly handing it to Sam.

"We'll have to go there some day. It looks just our sort of place," said Sam. "We'll hang your picture in pride of place in the Rabbit Hutch, won't we, Lily?"

Lily snuffled sleepily, taking up an awful lot of my lap.

"Lily's almost as fat as me," said Simon, leaning over to stroke her.

"Yes, she's always been a big girl but she's even bigger now," said Sam. "I think she's got a sweetheart at rabbit school, because our Lily's going to have baby bunnies soon."

"Oh, how wonderful!" I said, stroking her too. "Congratulations, Lily."

I had a little nibble of a cookie myself, just to check they were OK.

"Tell you what, Beauty. You've given us a very special present so maybe we can give you one in return. Lily won't be able to keep all her babies. Would *you* like one of the baby rabbits?"

I choked on my cookie. *"Really?"* I spluttered.

"Yes, really," said Sam.

"Aah!" said Simon. "Isn't that sweet?"

"Time to go now, folks," said Miranda, waving.

Simon and Miranda and Sam and Megan and Lucy and Darren and Nancy-Jo all waved. I couldn't wave because Lily was fidgeting and I had to hang onto her, so I gave a great grin to the camera.

"You were so great, Beauty," said Miranda.

"You're a little natural," said Simon. "A total little beauty!"

"Well done, babes!" Mom shouted.

But I hardly heard them. I stroked Lily and looked at Sam—and he smiled especially for me.

Go Fish!

GOFISH

JACQUELINE WILSON

What did you want to be when you grew up?
I've always wanted to be a writer ever since I was six years old. I loved books, even before I could read, and played many imaginary games that I turned into stories as soon as I could write a few words.

What's your first childhood memory?
Well, in my childhood autobiography, *Jacky Daydream*, I talk vividly about the day I was born—but I don't think my memory is quite that brilliant!

As a young person, who did you look up to most?
I didn't really look up to anybody as a small child, but when I read *The Diary of Anne Frank* when I was about eleven, I totally hero-worshipped her.

What was your worst subject in school?
I was useless at math and pretty hopeless at all kinds of

sports. I did always like swimming though, and still swim nearly every day.

What was your best subject in school?
I liked English best, especially writing stories. I also liked art.

What was your first job?
I was a trainee journalist on a women's magazine in Scotland when I was seventeen.

How did you celebrate publishing your first book?
I can't really remember now—but I do know I skipped the length of the street when the editor first told me they were going to publish it.

Where do you write your books?
I'm lucky, I can write anywhere. Sometimes I write in a notebook in bed, sometimes I write in cars or on trains, sometimes I even scribble a few lines waiting in a long queue.

Where do you find inspiration for your writing?
I truly don't know, it's just incredibly exciting when a new idea pops into my mind.

Which of your characters is most like you?
None of my characters are really like me, though I am rather greedy like Gemma, and I fuss about my clothes like Alice.

When you finish a book, who reads it first?
I send it straight to my agent and then my editor. I don't let any friends or family read it at that stage. I like to keep the story to myself; it's as if it's my own private world.

Are you a morning person or a night owl?
I think I'm both!

What's your idea of the best meal ever?
Cauliflower cheese, with lots of vegetables—and then fresh fruit. I eat very healthily—but I do have a weakness for English chips (big versions of your french fries).

Which do you like better, cats or dogs?
I like both. I'd particularly like a little poodle as a pet.

What do you value most in your friends?
I love it when my friends make me laugh and show they really care about me.

Where do you go for peace and quiet?
There's a big park near my house where you can walk for miles and see herds of wild deer. It's my favorite place.

Who is your favorite fictional character?
I love Jo March in *Little Women*.

What are you most afraid of?
I hate it when things need to be repaired in my house. I'm useless at getting workmen to do a job properly.

What time of year do you like best?
I like the summer, when I can lie out in the garden to sunbathe and read.

What's your favorite TV show?
Do you get *Doctor Who* in America? That's my all-time favorite show. I used to love *ER* too—it's such a shame it's finished now.

If you were stranded on a desert island, who would you want for company?
That's easy. I'd want my daughter, Emma, and my best friend, Trish.

If you could travel in time, where would you go?
I'd whizz back to late Victorian England. I've just written a book called *Hetty Feather*, set in the 1880s, and it would be great to see if I've got my facts right.

What's the best advice you've ever received about writing?
I've read several books by famous writers where they give advice which I found most interesting but not necessarily helpful. I think every writer has their own individual way of working.
You just have to sort out what works best for you.

What would you do if you ever stopped writing?
Maybe I'd start up my own secondhand bookshop. I've got 15,000 books crammed into my house—but perhaps I couldn't really part with them!

What do you like best about yourself?
I try to be kind to people—and I think up good ideas.

What is your worst habit?
I worry too much.

What do you consider to be your greatest accomplishment?
Bringing up my lovely daughter. Work-wise, it was becoming the British Children's Laureate.

Where in the world do you feel most at home?
I'm a city girl so I love London—but I adore Boston in the U.S., and try to have a trip there most years. The people are very friendly, the museums are beautiful, there are great bookstores and fantastic ice cream parlors!

What do you wish you could do better?
I wish I could sing in tune. I hear the song inside my head perfectly, but it sounds awful the moment I open my mouth and get going.

What would your readers be most surprised to learn about you?
I can't drive a car—I can't even ride a bike! It's just as well—I'm very good at walking.

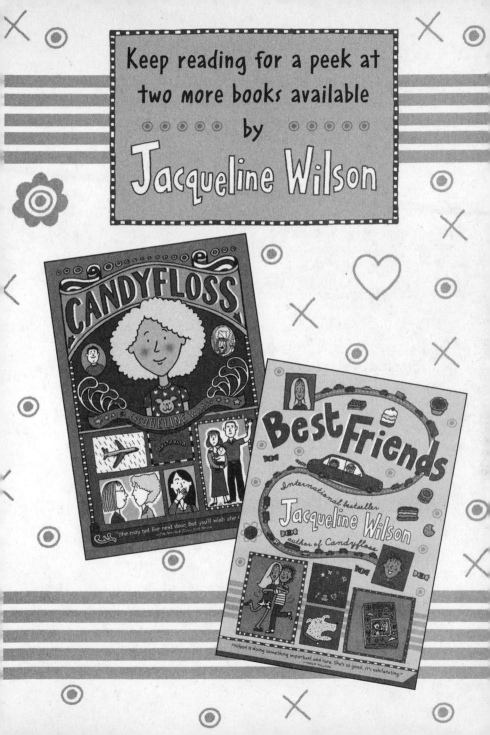

Candyfloss

I had two birthdays in one week.

My first birthday was on Friday. Mom and Steve woke me up singing *"Happy Birthday to you."* They'd stuck candles in a big fat croissant and put a little paper umbrella and a toothpick of cherries in my orange juice.

My little half brother, Tiger, came crawling into my bedroom too. He's too tiny to sing but he made a loud *he-he-he* noise, sitting up on his padded bottom and clapping his hands. He's really called Tim, but Tiger suits him better.

I blew out all my candles. Tiger cried when the flames went out, so we had to light them all again for him to huff and puff at.

I had my birthday breakfast in bed. Mom and Steve perched at the end, drinking coffee. Tiger went exploring under my bed and came out all fluffy, clutching one of my long-forgotten socks. He held it over his nose like a cuddle blanket, while Mom and Steve cooed at his cuteness.

Then I got to open my presents. They were wrapped up in shiny silver paper with big pink bows. I thought they looked so pretty I just wanted to hold them for a moment, smoothing the silver paper and fingering the bows, trying to guess what might be inside. But Tiger started ripping them himself, tearing all the paper and tangling the ribbon.

"Tiger, stop it! They're *my* presents, not yours," I said, trying to snatch them out of the way.

"He's just trying to help you unwrap them, Flossie," said Steve.

"You need to get a bit of a move on, darling, or you'll be late for school," said Mom.

Tiger said *He-he-he*. Or it *could* have been *Ha-ha-ha*, meaning *Ya boo sucks to be you*.

So I lost my chance of savoring my five shiny silver presents. I opened them there and then. I'll list them. (I *like* making lists!)

1. A pair of blue jeans with lots of little pockets fastened with pink heart-shaped buttons. They matched a pink heart-patterned T-shirt with a cute koala motif across the chest.
2. A pink shoebox containing a pair of sneakers, blue with pink laces.

3. A little package of gel pens with a stationery set and stickers.
4. A pink pull-along trolley suitcase.

I left number 5 till last because it was big but soft and squashy, and I hoped it *might* be a cuddly animal (any kind, but not a tiger). He had torn off half the paper already, exposing two big brown ears and a long pointy nose. I delved inside and found two *tiny* brown ears and a weeny pointy nose. It was a mother kangaroo with a baby kangaroo in her pouch.

Tiger held out his hands, trying to snatch the baby out of the pouch.

"No, Tiger, he wants to stay tucked in his mommy's pocket," I said, holding them out of his reach.

Tiger roared.

"Just let him play with the baby kanga a minute. He won't do him any harm," said Steve, going off to the bathroom.

Steve talks a lot of nonsense sometimes. Tiger grabbed the baby kangaroo and shoved him straight in his mouth, first the ears, then the snout, and then his entire *head*.

"Mom, Tiger's *eating* him!" I protested.

"Don't be silly, Floss. Hang on!" Mom hooked her finger into Tiger's bulging mouth and rescued the poor little baby kangaroo.

"He's all covered in Tiger's slobber!" I said.

"Just wipe it on the comforter. Don't be such a baby, Birthday Girl," said Mom, giving me a little poke. "Do you like your presents, Floss?"

"Yes, I love them," I said, gathering them all up in my arms away from Tiger.

I supposed I loved my little half brother, but I wished we could keep him in a cage like a real tiger.

"There's actually another extra present," said Mom. Her eyes were shining as brightly as my birthday candles. She raised her voice, shouting to Steve in the bathroom. "Shall I tell Floss now, Steve?"

"OK, yeah, why not?" he said, coming back into my bedroom, shaving cream all over his face.

He put a little blob of shaving cream on the tip of Tiger's chin and pretended to shave him. Tiger screamed delightedly, rolling away from his dad. He wiped shaving cream all over my special cherry-patterned comforter. I rubbed at the slimy mark, sighing heavily.

"So, OK, what's my extra present?" I asked warily.

I very much hoped Mom wasn't going to announce she was going to have another baby. One Tiger was bad enough. Two would be truly terrible.

"It's a present for all of us. The best present ever, and it's all due to Steve," said Mom. She was looking at him as if he were a Super Rock Star/Professional Soccer Player/Total God, instead of a perfectly ordinary actually quite boring guy who picks his nose and scratches himself in rude places.

Steve smirked and flexed his muscles, striking a silly pose.

"Steve got a promotion at his work, Floss," said Mom. "He's being made a manager—isn't that incredible? There's a sister company newly starting in Sydney and Steve's been asked to set things up there. Isn't that *great*?"

"Yeah, I suppose. Well done, Steve," I said politely, not really taking it in at all. The stain on my comforter wasn't budging.

"*Sydney!*" Mom said.

I blinked at her. I didn't quite get the significance. Sydney was just an old-fashioned guy's name.

"She doesn't have a clue where it is," said Steve, laughing. "Don't they teach kids geography nowadays?"

Then I got it. "Sydney in Australia?"

Steve clapped and he made Tiger clap his little pink fists too. Mom gave me a big, big hug. "Isn't it exciting, Floss! Think of all the sunshine! You just step out of the city and there you are, on a fabulous beach. Imagine!"

I *was* imagining. I saw us on a huge white beach, with kangaroos hopping across the sand and koalas climbing palm trees and lots of beautiful skinny ladies like Kylie Minogue swimming in the turquoise sea. I saw Mom and me paddling, hand in hand. I sent Steve way, way out to sea on a surfboard. I stuck Tiger in a kangaroo's pouch and sent them hopping far off into the bush.

"It's going to be so wonderful," said Mom, lying back on the bed, arms and legs outstretched, as if she were already sunbathing.

"Yeah, wonderful," I echoed. "Wait till I tell Rhiannon and everyone at school!" Then I paused. "What *about* school?"

"Well, Steve reckons we'll be in Sydney a good six months, though we're not permanently emigrating. You'll go to a lovely new Australian school while we're out there, darling," said Mom. "It'll be a fantastic experience for you."

My heart started thumping. "But I won't know anyone," I said.

"You'll soon make lots of new friends," said Mom.

"I like my *old* friends," I said.

"I'm going to pop in the bathroom after Steve. Keep an eye on Tiger for me," said Mom, giving me a kiss.

Then my heart thumped harder I ran to the bathroom. "Mom! Mom!" I yelled.

"What?" Mom was joking around with Steve, splashing him like a little kid.

"Mom, what about Dad?" I said.

Mom peered at me. "I expect your dad will phone

you tonight, Floss. And you'll be seeing him on Saturday, same as always."

"Yes, I know. But what's going to happen when we're in Australia? I can still see him, can't I?"

Mom's brow wrinkled. "Oh, come on, Flossie, don't be stupid. You can't pop back from Australia every weekend, obviously."

"But I can go sometimes? Every month?"

"I'm doing very nicely, thank you, but we're not made of money, kiddo," said Steve. "It costs hundreds and hundreds of pounds for a flight."

"But what am I going to *do*?"

"You can write to your dad," said Mom.

"I *knew* that's why you got me that stationery set. I don't want to write to him!"

"Well, if he'd only join the modern world and get a cell phone and a computer, you could text and e-mail him too," said Mom.

"I want to be able to *see* him like I do now," I said.

"Well, we're not going to be in Australia *forever*," said Mom. "Those six months will whiz past and then we'll be back. Unless of course it's so wonderful out there that we decide to stay! Still, if we *did* decide to stay for good we'd come back on a visit."

"Your dad could maybe come out to Sydney to see you," said Steve.

He said it nicely enough but there was a little smirk on his face. He knew perfectly well my dad was having major money problems. He had barely enough for the bus fare into town. If flights to Australia cost hundreds of pounds, there was no hope whatsoever.

"You're mean, Steve," I said, glaring at him.

"Oh, Floss, how can you say that? Steve's the most generous guy in the whole world," said Mom, deliberately misunderstanding. "He's planned for us to go to TGI Friday's as a special birthday treat for you tonight."

"I'd sooner have a birthday meal at home. A little party, just Rhiannon and me."

"I haven't got the time, Floss. I've got one million and one things to get organized. Come on, you know you love TGI Friday's. Don't spoil your birthday making a fuss about nothing."

I stomped back to my bedroom.

My dad wasn't *nothing*! I loved him so much. I missed him every week when I was at Mom and Steve's.

I'd forgotten I'd left Tiger in my bedroom. He'd gotten at my new gel pens. He'd decided to decorate my walls.

"You are a *menace*," I hissed at him. "I wish you'd never been born. I wish my mom had never met your dad. I wish my mom was still with *my* dad."

Tiger just laughed at me, baring his small, sharp teeth.

Best Friends

Alice and I are best friends. I've known her all my life. That is absolutely true. Our moms were in the hospital at the same time when they were having us. I got born first, at six o'clock in the morning on July 3. Alice took ages and didn't arrive until four in the afternoon. We both had a long cuddle with our moms, and at nighttime we were tucked up next to each other in little weeny cots.

I expect Alice was a bit frightened. She'd have cried. She's actually still a bit of a crybaby now, but I try not to tease her about it. I always do my best to comfort her.

I bet that first day I called to her in baby-coo language. I'd have said, "Hi, I'm Gemma. Being born is a bit weird, isn't it? Are you OK?"

And Alice would say, "I'm not sure. I'm Alice. I don't think I like it here. I want my mom."

"We'll see our moms again soon. We'll get fed. I'm *starving*." I'd have started crying too, in case there was a chance of being fed straight away.

I suppose I'm still a bit greedy, if I'm absolutely honest. Not quite as greedy as Biscuits though. Well, his real name is Billy McVitie, but everyone calls him Biscuits, even the teachers. He's this boy in our class at school and his appetite is astonishing. He can eat an entire packet of chocolate biscuits, or cookies, *munch-crunch, munch-crunch*, in two minutes flat.

We had this Grand Biscuit Challenge at playtime. I managed only three quarters of a packet. I probably could have managed a whole packet too, but a crumb went down the wrong way and I choked. I ended up with chocolate drool all down the front of my white school blouse. But that's nothing new. I always seem to get a bit messy and scruffy and scuffed. Alice stays neat and sweet.

When we were babies, *one* of us crawled right into the trash can and played mud wrestling in the garden and fell in the pond when we fed the ducks. The *other* one of us sat up prettily in her stroller cuddling Golden Syrup (her yellow teddy bear) and giggled at her naughty friend.

When we went to nursery school *one* of us played Fireman in the water tank and Moles in the sandbox, and she didn't stop at finger painting, she did *entire body* painting. The *other* one of us sat demurely at the dinky table and made clay necklaces (one for each of us) and sang "Itsy Bitsy Spider" with all the cute hand gestures.

When we went to kindergarten, *one* of us pretended to be a Wild Thing and roared such terrible roars in class, she got sent out of the room. She also got into a fight with a big boy who snatched her best friend's chocolate, and *made his nose bleed*! The *other* one of us read *Milly-Molly-Mandy* and wrote stories about a little thatched cottage in the country in her very neat printing.

Now that we're in elementary school, *one* of us ran right into the boys' bathroom for a dare. She did, really, and they all yelled at her. She also climbed half-way up the drainpipe in the playground to get her ball back—only the drainpipe came away from the wall. They both went *crash, clonk*. Mr. Beaton, the principal, was NOT pleased. The *other* one of us got made an attendance monitor and wore her silver sparkly top (with matching silver glitter on her eyelids) to the school party, and all the boys wanted to dance with her, but *guess what*! She danced with her bad best friend all evening instead.

We're best friends but we're not one bit alike. I suppose that goes without saying. Though I seem to have said it a lot. My mom says it too. Also a lot.

"For heaven's sake, Gemma, why can't you stop being so rough and silly and boisterous? *Boy* being the operative bit! To think I was so thrilled when I had my baby girl. But now it's just like I've got three boys—and you're the biggest troublemaker of them all!"

There's my big brother Callum, who's seventeen. Callum and I used to be friends. He taught me to skateboard and showed me how to do cannon balls in the swimming pool. Every Sunday I'd balance on the back of his bike and we'd wobble over to Granddad's. But now Callum's got this girlfriend, Ayesha, and all they do is look into each other's eyes and go kissy-kissy-kiss. Yuck.

Alice and I played spies and followed them to the park once because we wanted to see if they did any-thing even yuckier, but Callum caught us and he turned me upside down and shook me until I felt sick.

There's my other brother, Jack, but he's nowhere near as much fun as Callum. Jack is totally brainy, such a nerd that he always gets the top grade in every exam. Jack hasn't got a girlfriend. He doesn't get out enough to meet any. He just holes up in his room, hunched over his homework. He *does* take our dog, Barking Mad, out for a walk very late at night. And he likes to wear black. And doesn't like garlic bread. Maybe Jack is turning into Jacula? I'll have to check to see if his teeth aren't getting alarmingly pointy.

It's annoying having Jack as my brother. Sometimes the teachers hope I'm going to be brainy too and get ten out of ten all the time. As if!

I can do *some* things. Mr. Beaton says I can talk the hind leg off a donkey—and its front leg and its ears and its tail. He says I *act* like a donkey too. I think donkeys kick if you're not careful. I *often* feel like kicking Mr. Beaton.

I get lots of ideas and work things out as quick as quick in my head, but it's soooo boring writing it all down, so I often don't bother. Or I try to get Alice to write it all out for me. Alice gets much better grades than me in all classes. Apart from soccer. I don't want to boast, but I'm on the school soccer team even though I'm the youngest and the littlest and the only girl.

Alice doesn't like sports at all. We have different hobbies. She likes to draw lines of little girls in party frocks and she writes in her diary with her gel pens and she paints her nails all different colors and plays with her jewelry. Alice is into jewelry in a big way. She keeps it in a special box that used to be her grandma's. It's blue velvet, and if you wind it up and open the lid, a little ballet dancer twirls around and around. Alice has got a little gold heart on a chain and a tiny gold bangle she wore when she was a baby and a jade bangle from an uncle in Hong Kong and a silver locket and a Scottie dog sparkly brooch and a charm bracelet with ten jingly charms. My favorite charm is the little silver Noah's Ark. You can open it up and see absolutely minute giraffes and elephants and tigers inside.

Alice also has heaps of rings—a real Russian gold ring, a Victorian garnet, and lots of pretendy ones out of Cracker Jacks. She gave me a big bright silver-and-blue one as a friendship ring. I loved it and called it my sapphire—only I forgot to take it off when I went swimming and the silver went black and the sapphire fell out.

"Typical," said Mom, sighing.

I think Mom sometimes wishes she'd swapped the cribs around when we were born. I'm sure she'd much rather have Alice as a daughter. She doesn't say so, but I'm not dumb. *I'd* sooner have Alice as my daughter.

"I wouldn't," said my dad, and he ruffled my hair so it stood up on end. Well, it was probably standing up anyway. I've got the sort of hair that looks like I'm permanently plugged into the electric outlet. Mom made me grow it long but I kept losing my silly bows and bobbles. Then it got a bit sticky when I went in for this giant bubble-blowing contest with Biscuits and the other boys and *hurray, hurray* my hair had to be chopped off. Mom cried but I didn't mind one bit.

Sometimes I think *everyone* annoys my mom. Everyone except Alice. Mom works in the makeup department of Joseph Pilbeam, the big store, and she gives Alice all these dinky samples of skincare products and little lipsticks and bottles of scent. Once when she was in a really good mood, she sat Alice down at her dressing table and gave her a full grown-up lady's makeup. My mom made me up too, though she told me off for fidgeting (well, it was tickly) and then my eyes itched and I rubbed them and got that black mascara stuff all over the place, so I looked like a panda.

Alice's makeup stayed prettily in place all day long. She didn't even smudge her pink lipstick when she had her dinner. It was pizza, but she cut hers up into tiny bite-size pieces instead of shoving a lovely big slice in her mouth.

If Alice wasn't my very best friend, she might just get on my nerves sometimes. Especially when Mom makes a big fuss of her and then looks at me and sighs.

Still, it's great that Mom *does* like Alice because she never minds if she comes for a sleepover at our house. My mom has banned big birthday sleepovers forever. Callum doesn't care as the only person he'd like to sleep over is Ayesha. Jack doesn't care either. He's got a few nerdy friends at school, but they don't communicate face-to-face, they just e-mail and text each other.

I've got heaps of ordinary friends as well as my best friend, Alice. Last birthday, I invited three boys and three girls for a sleepover party. Alice was top of the list, of course. We were supposed to play out in the garden but it rained, so we all had a crazy game of soccer with a cushion in the living room (well, not quite *all*—Alice wouldn't play and Biscuits is terrible at games). Someone broke my mom's wedding present Lladró lady *and* burst the cushion. My mom was so mad she wouldn't let any of them sleep over and sent them all home. Except for Alice.

I'm still allowed one-special-friend sleepovers so long as that special friend is Alice. So that's great, great, great because as I've probably said before, Alice is my very best friend.

I don't know what I'd do without her.

JOIN IN THE FUN AND READ ALL THE
PIPER REED BOOKS
AVAILABLE FROM SQUARE FISH

A hilarious series about one spunky heroine with lots of spirit
trying to find her place in the world as the middle sister . . .

Kimberly Willis Holt
Illustrated by Christine Davenier
978-0-312-38020-5
$6.99 US / $8.99 Can.

Kimberly Willis Holt
Illustrated by Christine Davenier
978-0-312-56136-9
$6.99 US / $8.99 Can.

Kimberly Willis Holt
Illustrated by Christine Davenier
978-0-312-60881-1
$6.99 US / $8.50 Can.

Meet Piper Reed, a spunky
nine-year-old who has moved
more times than she can count.
From Texas to Guam, wherever
Piper goes, adventure follows.

**"Piper's foray sets sail
with verve, fun and spunk."**
—*Kirkus Reviews*

Piper's dad might be gone again,
but she's got plenty to keep her
busy at home: new neighbors,
a spaceship beach house, a trip
to New Orleans, and most
important, the upcoming
Gypsy Club pet show!

Piper Reed and her fellow
Gypsy Club members are
in need of a clubhouse.
Raising money to buy one isn't
going to be easy. Fortunately for
Piper, her friends and family
come to her rescue!

**"A good addition to the
series . . . a natural for fans of
Clementine or Judy Moody."**
—*Kirkus Reviews*

Join the
Piper Reed
Club at
www.piperreed.com

SQUARE FISH